UNWRAPPING A CHRISTMAS KISS

Amber laughed as Shadow fought to get out from the tangle of ribbons wrapping him up like a steer at a rodeo. "Be still, and I'll help you." She reached for the red ribbon and the cat.

"He's making more of a mess than helping." Ian took the roll of green ribbon away from Light and scowled playfully at the other cat. "You're not helping either, young lady."

Amber shook her head at the disaster the cats were making out of the room. Ian and she hadn't helped matters. Rolls of wrapping paper, ribbons, tags, and tissue paper were everywhere. Shadow had attacked the crinkly tissue paper as if it were a live animal. Shreds of the white paper were still floating around the room. Only half of the gifts were wrapped and they had been at it for two hours already.

"Remind me to thank you properly when we're done," she said.

"Will this thank you be in the same form in which you thanked me for helping you decorate the tree the other night?"

She grinned. "Might be."

Ian yanked his sweatshirt over his head and started to crawl toward her on his hands and knees. He was pushing paper and scissors out of his way and clearing a path. When he reached her, Amber cupped his jaw and brought his mouth up to hers. She needed to taste him. She needed him to hold her like he was never going to let her go.

Ian's mouth teased the corner of her lips and Amber wrapped his arms around her neck, bringing his mouth down to hers . . .

Books by Marcia Evanick

CATCH OF THE DAY

CHRISTMAS ON CONRAD STREET

BLUEBERRY HILL

A BERRY MERRY CHRISTMAS

Published by Zebra Books

A
Berry Merry
Christmas

Marcia Evanick

ZEBRA BOOKS
KENSINGTON PUBLISHING CORP.
http://www.kensingtonbooks.com

ZEBRA BOOKS are pubished by

Kensington Publishing Corp.
850 Third Avenue
New York, NY 10022

All Kensington titles, imprints and distributed lines are available at special quantity discounts for bulk purchases for sales promotion, premiums, fund-raising, educational or institutional use.

Special book excerpts or customized printings can also be created to fit specific needs. For details, write or phone the office of the Kensington Special Sales Manager: Kensington Publishing Corp., 850 Third Avenue, New York, NY 10022. Attn. Special Sales Department. Phone: 1-800-221-2647.

Zebra and the Z logo Reg. U.S. Pat. & TM Off.

First Printing: October 2004
10 9 8 7 6 5 4 3 2 1

Printed in the United States of America

To Glenna: Comrade in arms.
May the dragons of the world
shudder at our battle cry.

Chapter 1

Amber McAllister had her cup halfway to her mouth before she noticed the blue Styrofoam packing peanut bobbing on the surface of the coffee. The headache that had started with her aunt's phone call this morning, telling her she wouldn't be coming to work today because JCPenney was having a sale on all their dresses, had grown into a full-blown pounding. The two aspirins she had just popped into her mouth were now dissolving on her tongue.

They tasted like bug spray.

She plucked the soggy peanut from her drink and tossed it into the oversize waste container in the corner of the workroom of her aunt's shop. With a grimace and a shudder, she washed the now fuzzy pills down her throat with the lukewarm coffee and wondered what kind of damage she was doing to her stomach.

Styrofoam poisoning wouldn't help the ulcer that she was positive was starting to develop. Lately she had been chomping antacids more than aspirins. The cherry antacids tasted the best.

Who would have thought that dragging what had been essentially a "mom and pop" jam business into the techno-savvy twenty-first century would be so consuming?

The jam and jelly business she could handle—if all the other aspects of her life were under control. For the past month, control was an illusion. A wavy, vaporous illusion. One she couldn't seem to grasp, no matter how hard she tried or how far she reached. It felt like David Copperfield was managing her life.

Her aunt, Grace Berry, was the sole proprietor of the jam company, appropriately called It's the Berries Jam Company. For the past month, Grace had been spending more time at the malls in Bangor, and either out on a date or recuperating from one, than she did in her own shop. Having her fifty-four-year-old aunt going out on dates wasn't the problem; after all, Uncle Howard had passed away two years ago and Grace deserved to have some fun. What the problem was, was that Grace's identical twin sister, Gladys, happened to be her own mother.

Mom wasn't real happy that her sister was out nearly every night painting their childhood hometown of Misty Harbor red. When Gladys was unhappy she called her daughter, Amber, to fix the situation. Currently, Gladys was unhappy about three times a day.

How anyone could get in trouble in the small fishing village, nestled on the coast of Maine, was beyond Amber's imagination. Short of bellying up to the bar at the One-Eyed Squid on a Saturday night with one of the local lobster fishermen, there wasn't much action around town.

Amber ought to know. Lately, she had been discreetly looking around at some of the single male population in her own age category. So far no one in particular caught her eye or interested her enough to lower whatever barriers she had erected around her heart.

By the time tourist season ended in late September, she had been ready to get on with her life. She had made a couple of friends since moving to Misty Harbor over a year ago, but she was still lonely. Family and friends didn't keep you warm on cold winter nights, and in Maine, those winter nights were extremely frigid.

Before she could do more than give a casual glance around town, the Internet sales part of the jam business had taken off. The Web site she had set up last spring was getting more hits than a third rank boxer. Orders for the approaching holiday season were coming in faster than she could handle. With the help of her aunt, and the part-time high school student they had hired last month, they should have been able to keep up with the orders and still run the small shop in town.

Should've, would've, and could'ves weren't any way to run a business. Tiffany Moyer, their part-time help, was a very smart, cute, and popular girl. Too popular, and definitely too cute. Tiffany's job was to run the register out in the shop, handle customers, and when she had a few moments, help restock shelves and dust.

It's the Berries wasn't a big shop to anyone's thinking. The small storefront was a beehive of pine shelving stocked with jam, jellies, pie filling, syrup, and just about anything else you could do with berries that were grown in Maine. The gift section consisted of fancy wooden gift boxes filled with a selected assortment of jams, small wooden lobster pots were packed with jams or jelly, and expensive hand-woven baskets were overflowing with an assortment of their best products, all tied off with a gorgeous bow. All the gift selections were tastefully done, and tastefully delicious.

One of the first jobs she did, after Grace had given her free rein of the business, was to redo the interior of the shop. Grace had kept the shop immaculate and well stocked, but it was the same shop as it had been twenty years ago. Nothing had been changed since Amber was a little girl and had spent weeks every summer with her aunt and uncle on the coast of Maine. An update had been way overdue.

She had spent days texture painting the walls in various shades of blues and commissioned a local carpenter to duplicate the pine shelving that her Uncle Howard had made a quarter of a century ago. Then she had doubled the amount of products they sold, and more than tripled the gift section. New labels were designed for the new shaped jars. It's the Berries had gotten a total face-lift. She had even added one product they didn't produce themselves. Berry-scented candles were made and supplied by a woman who lived about a half hour away. The candles were a great complementary addition to the merchandise and were selling extremely well.

By May she had been confident enough to start up the Web site and a toll-free number for orders. During her first year at the helm of the business she had increased sales and the company was actually pulling in a profit. She was pleasantly surprised. Aunt Grace was ecstatic. Once the holiday rush was over, she was going to see what other berry related items she could bring into the business. As a long range goal, it was a great one. Now all she needed to do was find the time to achieve it.

The firm she employed to take the 800 number orders faxed them to her every day. The last week of orders was still sitting in the fax tray, because she hadn't found the time to fill them yet. She couldn't even keep up with the Web site orders, and she had been putting in sixteen-hour days for the past two weeks.

The large spacious workroom, which took up the entire back of the shop, was a disaster area. Packing peanuts, shipping boxes, baskets, and empty lobster pots were everywhere. Boxes of jam, jelly, and syrup were piled nearly to the ceiling. Candles where scattered throughout and the clear plastic shrink-wrap was tangled up with the mailing tape. Ribbons and bows were everywhere. Posting inventory on the computer was three days behind, and she had no idea what she had on hand besides a now-empty aspirin container and an economy size bottle of Tums.

All the cherry flavored antacids were gone.

The business was a disaster waiting to happen, and her personal life was so nonexistent that her most intimate relationship was with the UPS man.

There were a lot of people she could blame for her current predicament. First being herself, for expanding the business way too fast. But who would have guessed that the world would suddenly fall in love with blueberry jam?

Second could be her Aunt Grace, for missing work more than she showed up.

She really shouldn't blame her aunt, though. Grace had married young and had turned her love of cooking into a business. In the beginning Howard had worked a full-time job, and helped Grace out with the shop. Grace and Howard never had children of their own, but they had always made room in their home and hearts for their nieces and nephews.

Amber had been on the receiving end of their love all her life. Grace, even while working six days a week at the shop and spending countless hours over a hot stove, always put everyone else first. Now, for the first time in her life, Grace was putting herself first, and having fun doing it. There was no way Amber could deny her aunt that freedom.

The other person she could blame for the chaos in her life was Ian McNeal. It was incredibly unreasonable, and she knew it, but it was totally safe to lay all the responsibility for her lack of sleep and fun on his doorstep. Ian had been her late husband's business partner in an ad agency they owned back in Boston. When James had died in a pileup on the expressway, she had lost a husband, lover, and best friend. Ian had lost his business partner, former college roommate, and friend. While Ian had been trying to figure out how to dissolve the partnership and still keep the agency open, she had packed her bags and moved to Maine.

Boston had become too big and held too many memories for her. Boston had been James's kind of town, while she preferred a more relaxing, slower pace. She had needed a quiet place to grieve and then heal. The small fishing village of Misty Harbor, nestled on the rocky coast of Maine and holding nothing but wonderful memories of her childhood, was the perfect place.

When she needed an ad campaign for the berry business, she contacted the best, Ian. James's friend had been more than willing to help her out, and had created a wonderful slogan for the upcoming holiday season: "Have a Berry Merry Christmas." The photo shots of the gift baskets were great, and a dozen billboards from New York to Bangor enticed motorists to call the toll-free number or log on to her Web site.

Problem was, Ian had made it look too darn good. She had been hoping for a pile or two of orders. Instead she received a mountain's worth, and a glacier of ice was now formed over her head. Any day now an avalanche was going to come crashing down, wiping out her, the business, and Aunt Grace's retirement years.

Amber sat down on the stool and glanced around the room. Cold coffee was churning in her stomach and the aspirin hadn't kicked in yet. It was nearly lunchtime and there were only two dozen boxes neatly piled up waiting for the UPS man to come in and pick up this afternoon. Six dozen packages wouldn't have been enough. She'd realized two days ago that she was spending more time looking for the correct items than she did on the actual packing.

The spiral of chaos was continuing and she was getting farther and farther behind.

The deep treble of male voices coming from the front of the shop interrupted her depressing thoughts. Tiffany's young and carefree laughter joined in the medley. It sounded like Miss Popularity was holding court once again. She didn't care if Tiffany was charming every male in the county between the ages of sixteen and sixty. She just didn't want the enticing going on in the store and on It's the Berries very slim dime.

Customers usually bypassed the shop once they saw the entire high school football team crammed in the aisles and vying for Tiffany's attention. A few local girls might squeeze and flirt their way into the shop, but they weren't big jam buyers. Tiffany was lucky to ring up the sales for a couple of candles.

Amber hated to break up the fun, but she had a business to run, and Tiffany had a job to do. With a weary sigh, she stood up and headed for the curtained doorway that separated the back room from the shop.

Quiet descended as soon as she stepped into the store. A blush swept its way up Tiffany's cheeks. Amber couldn't tell if it was because the girl was embarrassed by her friends once again invading the shop, or if the six-foot hunk leaning against the counter and crowding Tiffany's space had anything to do with it. Either way, she knew two things immediately. The boys knew they shouldn't have been there, and that football season had ended.

It now appeared that the entire basketball team had overrun the shop. "Hi, guys."

"Hi, Amber. We're just leaving," said Ryan Albert. Ryan was eighteen years old, and had lived his entire life next door to Aunt Grace. Amber had been his babysitter a couple of times one summer when she had been sixteen. At four years old, Ryan had been a handful. By the cocky grin and the blond cheerleader hanging on his arm, he didn't seem to have changed very much over the years. The little four-year-old Ryan, who hadn't been able to ride a two-wheeler yet, was all grown up and one short step away from being a man. And to think she used to sneak him candy all the time.

When in the hell did I get so old?

"Good to know, Ryan." Amber glanced around at his teammates. "You guys had practice this morning?" Being the day after Thanksgiving, the schools were closed, but it looked like basketball didn't follow the same schedule.

"Yeah, the coach made us come in at eight this morning." Ryan flashed a grin that was destined to cause trouble and a few gray hairs for the parents of every female high school student at Hancock County High. "Coach Beamer said we need all the practice we can get."

"You're that bad?" She eyed the group of boys. Every one of them was taller than her own five-foot-seven height. Most of the players hit the six foot mark and beyond. Every one of them looked like they knew what to do with a basketball and the cheerleaders that seemed to be glued to many of their sides. She recognized most of the guys and girls from the football season.

"Nope, coach always says we need the practice." Ryan seemed to give it some thought. "I think it's his way of motivating us."

"Does it work?" She didn't think negative reinforcement would work, but what she knew about teenagers and basketball could be written on one of the blueberry syrup labels with a really thick Magic Marker.

"Nah," Ryan added with a grin, "but nobody likes to be told they stink."

"True." She could well remember the feeling when her mother told her she was crazy for leaving Boston, and a very high paying job, to move to Misty Harbor and help Grace with the jam business. She had silently vowed then and there that Aunt Grace's jam business was going to be the best darn jam business in North America. Maybe there was something to negative reinforcement after all.

"Heard we might get some snow by Sunday." Ryan smiled at the prospect.

"If you're hinting at a job, I already told you last winter the job was yours." Ryan's used and battered pickup truck, with a massive plow attached to its front bumper, had been kept busy last winter clearing Grace's and her own driveway. Everyone in town knew that Ryan's parents were having a hard time of it financially. Every dime that Ryan made was squirreled away for his college education. He had been doing odd jobs around town since he was fourteen.

Gracie and Howard had bought out her brothers' and sister's share of their parents' home on Spruce Street when they all inherited the house years ago. The old stately house was in the older and more influential section of town and generations ago had been filled with antiques from France and England. Today it was filled with mostly mismatched comfortable furniture, empty bedrooms waiting for family to visit, and clanky old radiators. It also needed a coat of paint about five years ago and three of the five chimneys no longer worked.

The carriage house out back had been converted into a massive kitchen where all the jams, jellies, and other products that they sold were made. Grace no longer actually made the jams and jelly, but it was her recipes that made every batch. Grace employed two local women to work the kitchen while she handled the shop.

The upstairs of the carriage house had been modified into an apartment about twenty years ago. Howard Berry's brother had rented the apartment until about five years ago when he decided to move to Florida and take up plaid polyester pants and the game of golf. It had taken Amber over a month of scrubbing, painting, and calling in a plumber to make the apartment livable again.

The apartment allowed her the privacy she had needed while still being close to her aunt and the business. It was the perfect solution for them both. The driveway of the old family home was long and massive. One she definitely wouldn't want to shovel every time it snowed. Keeping the outside stairs leading to her apartment clear of snow and ice was a full-time job in itself. Ryan could do all the plowing he wanted.

"I'll plow as soon as it stops snowing, okay?"

"It doesn't matter to me when you get to it. If it snows more than an inch or two, I usually walk to the shop, and Grace hates to drive in the stuff." She knew Ryan sometimes had a difficult time of balancing the odd jobs, schooling, and all the team sports he played. He was a gifted athlete who was praying for a scholarship. "Just make sure you give me the bill, not Gracie."

Ryan winked as he started to hustle the team toward the front door. "Got ya. Same arrangement as we had for when I cut the grass and raked the leaves."

"Don't forget chopping enough firewood to see us through the winter, cutting down those two dead trees and planting new ones, painting Gracie's kitchen, and fixing the loose boards on the front porch." She had kept Ryan busy most of the summer, when he wasn't hauling in lobsters with one of the local fishermen, hadn't been away at different sports camps, or driving some poor parents gray while dating their daughter.

Most of the players had managed to find their way

out of the store before Ryan asked, "Are you sure you're not inventing jobs for me to do?"

"Believe me, there are a couple hundred more jobs for you to do around Gracie's house. If I can convince her to take down that horrible wallpaper in the living room, you'll be painting it before spring." She still had nightmares if she spent more than ten minutes in that room. She had never seen such large, ghastly pink cabbage roses before in her life. They actually looked evil.

Ryan shuddered. "Heck, I'll volunteer to rip down that wallpaper for free. When I was a kid I used to have nightmares about those nasty, ugly roses trying to eat me. Just tell me when you want me to start on it."

Amber laughed as Ryan and the giggling cheerleader left the shop leaving nothing behind but a whip of cold wind and quiet. Quiet was good. Customers would have been better. Paying customers who plucked a gift basket or two right off the shelves and took them home with them would have been heavenly. No packing, no shipping, and no more Styrofoam peanuts floating in her coffee.

"I'm sorry, Amber," Tiffany said quietly. "I didn't know they were going to stop by."

Tiffany looked so apologetic there was no way Amber could issue a reprimand without feeling like more of a Scrooge. Even Tiffany's baby blue eyes held a sheen of tears. It was probably the same look she gave her parents when she missed her curfew by an hour or wanted the car to drive all her friends into Franklin to go catch the latest movie. It was the look that wrapped her daddy right around her little finger, and it worked like a charm.

"No problem," she lied as the pounding in her headache increased in tempo. "Did you get all the mulberry candles displayed?" She had given Tiffany a box filled with the deep burgundy candles this morning. Karin Warner, the woman who made them, had dropped six boxes of candles off late Wednesday night, just as the shop was closing.

"Not quite." Tiffany picked up crumbled candy wrappers from the counter and tossed them into the trash can that was beneath. Obviously the basketball players were once again hitting the complimentary candy dish next to the cash register. "I was busy taking down all the fall decorations, like you asked."

Amber glanced at the window display area and did a quick inventory of the shop. Silk fall foliage was still everywhere she looked. A box overflowing with fake pumpkins and stuffed turkeys was sitting behind the counter. The way Tiffany was working, it was going to be Valentine's Day before the Christmas decorations were up. She really couldn't blame Tiffany. Being able to morph into Martha Stewart wasn't in her job description. The girl was only supposed to ring up sales and dust.

Grace or she usually did all the decorating.

"I'll go get you another box." The boxes for the fall decorations were on the top shelf in the storage room. Right next to the half dozen boxes of Christmas decorations that Ryan had put away for her last year. She should have had Ryan get the boxes back down for her while he had been in the store.

"It's almost lunchtime." Tiffany anxiously looked out the front window as she twirled a lock of her blond hair around a finger sporting burgundy colored nail polish. The polish matched her sweater perfectly, which set off her pale hair. "I'm going to Krup's to grab something to eat. Can I bring you back something?"

Amber followed the young girl's gaze and spotted one of the basketball players leaning against the lamppost in front of Krup's General Store. It was the same six-foot, two-inch hunk who had been crowding the counter and making her sales clerk blush. Krup's had a soda fountain area in the back of the store that served a light lunch daily. They also made the best chocolate shakes in the known universe. Tiffany's lunch break wasn't for another hour, but who was she to fight true love.

She knew Krup's menu by heart. "I'll take their Friday lunch special, the tuna fish sandwich and a bowl of clam chowder." She reached into the front pocket of her worn jeans, and handed Tiffany a five dollar bill. Breakfast had been five hours ago, and had consisted of a banana and a cup of nonfat yogurt.

"Want something to drink with that?" Tiffany grabbed her coat from the back room.

It was on the tip of her tongue to order one of Krup's famous chocolate shakes. The one that was so thick that the inside of your cheeks touched each other and your eyes crossed when you tried sucking it up through a straw. The same shake that had managed to make her gain twenty pounds since moving to Maine eighteen months ago.

Whoever heard of being addicted to chocolate shakes?

Amber watched as Tiffany zipped up her suede coat with its warm fleece lining. The brightly colored scarf wrapped around Tiffany's neck had to be eight feet long. The girl looked like a damn movie star.

If she wore a jacket that thick and bulky she would look like the Michelin tire man wrestling a flock of sheep.

"No, I have a soda in the back refrigerator." The small dorm-size refrigerator held nothing but diet soda and bottled water. Her punishment for becoming a shake addict. Twenty pounds didn't seem like a lot until you only had two pairs of jeans in your closet that barely buttoned or zipped and baggy sweaters and sweatshirts were the norm. "Enjoy your lunch, and thanks."

Tiffany practically sprinted out of the shop and raced across the street with barely a look in either direction. The girl was either going to get run over, or suf-

fer a broken heart. No girl or woman should be that excited to see a boy or man.

She watched the boy straighten up and flash a wide
smile at the sight of Tiffany crossing the street toward
him. As he held the door to Krup's open for Tiffany,
Amber revised her thinking about that future heartbreak. Having some excitement in one's life just might
be a good thing.

Amber swiped a peppermint from the candy bowl, as
her consolation for not ordering that shake, and headed
for the back room.

It seemed like the entire town of Misty Harbor had
gone from pilgrims and pumpkins to lit Christmas
trees, wreaths sporting huge bows, and sleigh bells overnight. While she had been enjoying a slice of pumpkin
pie every shopkeeper must have been employing magical elves to hang their mistletoe, haul in pine trees, and
deck every hall that needed decking.

How was it possible for her to be so far behind? She
had only taken a couple of hours off to enjoy the holiday meal of roast turkey and Grace's famous stuffing.
The rest of the evening was spent downloading orders
and printing out shipping labels.

She had given thanks in the relaxing warmth of her
aunt's kitchen instead of driving four hours to her parents' home. By the two phone calls she had taken from
her mother yesterday, dinner would have been one disas-
trous affair. Her mother would have spent the entire
time picking apart Grace and Amber's lives instead of
the turkey. She hadn't been in the mood to suffer her
mother's unasked-for opinions or the long drive. Grace
had seemed just as thankful to not face her twin's
ridicule of her dating life while passing the giblet gravy.

She just wished that Grace hadn't been lured away
today by her favorite four-letter word: sale. The shop
needed to be decorated, but more importantly, the

back room was in dire need of straightening. She could have really used Grace's help.

Maybe they should hire another part-time helper for the holidays. She glanced at the stack of orders waiting to be filled. Maybe they should blow the profit margin and hire the entire basketball team. Better yet, she should send Ian McNeal a stocking full of coal and week-old lobsters wrapped in seaweed as a Christmas gift.

She positioned the small stepladder and reached for the first box. The more she thought about all the work that needed to be done, the madder she became at Ian and his talent for marketing. It was unreasonable, and in the back of her mind she knew this. She also knew how safe it was to blame Ian. He was the perfect target for her foul mood and lack of sleep. She couldn't very well yell at her aunt and demand that she put in twelve-hour days into the same business she already had put twenty-five years in.

Tiffany was only seventeen and had only one thing on her mind: a gorgeous basketball player with a killer smile. Sniping at Tiffany would smack too close to jealousy.

It wasn't her aunt's or Tiffany's fault they were seeing more action than she was. When she had moved to Misty Harbor eighteen months ago she had definitely put out the *Do Not Approach—Widow Grieving* sign. The men had read the sign, and respectfully allowed her time to heal. It wasn't their fault they hadn't seen that the sign was now put away. She was ready to move on with her life.

James McAllister was gone and no amount of tears or heartbreak would bring him back to life. If they could, James never would have been laid in the ground on that gorgeous spring day. The first few months after his death had been the hardest. The grief and pain had been unbearable. But over time, and with the love of her aunt, her family, and a new career in the jam business to keep her busy, the grief and pain had faded.

James would always hold a special place within her heart, but it was time for her to move on with her life. Even while working sixteen-hour days, living in her aunt's carriage house, and being involved with friends and the community, she realized one thing about herself. She was lonely.

Last Christmas season had been horrible for her. This year wasn't looking any better.

Amber set the empty box down on the worktable and figured she might as well haul down the Christmas decorations while she was at it. What difference would another half a dozen boxes make to this mess? They had to come down either later this afternoon or tomorrow morning anyway.

The first two boxes weren't too heavy. The third strained her arms and back, and it made her knees wobble as she slowly climbed down the three steps and nearly dropped the box onto the table. What in the world was in it, cannonball ornaments to hang on the Christmas tree? She tried to remember what Grace had packed away last year, but came up with nothing heavier than a bunch of glass ornaments and strings of lights.

She glared at the three remaining boxes on the top shelf and silently cursed Ian's soul to advertising hell as the fax machine beeped and another stack of orders started to print. The chimes over the front door rang as she climbed back up the ladder. The forth box was light, but the fifth box felt like lead.

"Hello, anyone here?" A male voice came from out in the shop.

"I'll be right there," she called back. Whoever it was hadn't taken a lot of time to look around and shop. She yanked the box forward and nearly lost her balance when the weight of the entire carton caused her to sway dangerously on top of the ladder. Forget the cannon-balls, this box contained anvils.

She managed two steps down before the box was lifted out of her arms and a familiar voice demanded, "Give me that. What are you trying to do, kill yourself?"

It took her a moment to catch her balance and to realize who was yelling at her. When she did, she yelled right back. "No, I think you and your darn ad campaign are already doing a fine job at that, Ian McNeal."

Chapter 2

Ian placed the heavy box on the floor and stared at the woman before him. He barely recognized her. The Amber McAllister he knew wore designer business suits, sparkling jewelry, and a cloak of cool sophistication. This Amber had on jeans tight enough to accent every curve, a baggy Boston University sweatshirt, and a pair of worn hiking boots.

He did a retake on the boots before his gaze returned to her face. Not a hint of makeup concealed its perfection.

Amber had the face of an Irish angel. Eyes the color of spring grass and an intriguing dusting of freckles high across her cheeks and nose implied at her heritage. Auburn hair, that glistened and gleamed its way past her shoulders confirmed it. McAllister might have been her married surname, but there was no mistaking that there was Irish blood running through her veins.

The famed Irish temper was currently blazing in her eyes and amazingly, it seemed directed at him.

"What's wrong with the ad campaign?" Ian had just spent the entire morning driving up Interstate 95. He had spotted and admired at least three billboards displaying his idea of a holiday ad campaign while heading north from Boston. He had thought the slogan and billboards were festive and eye-catching. The 800 number and the Web site had been easily read while passing by at sixty-five miles per hour. He had been immensely proud of his company's work and couldn't see one thing wrong with it. *Have a Berry Merry Christmas* was not only catchy; it was, in his opinion, brilliant. After all, he had been the one to think of it.

"The problem with the campaign is, it's too darn good." Amber stepped off the ladder and flung her arms to encompass the entire workroom. "Look at this mess, and it's your entire fault."

Ian frowned as he glanced around the room. He couldn't argue the point about the room being a mess. It was a disaster area. How anyone could work in the crammed, disorganized, and chaotic place was beyond him. The part that threw him was, how was he responsible for the mess? He had never stepped foot in Maine before, let alone in Amber's aunt's store, It's the Berries.

He had to be the world's lousiest friend. He should have physically checked up on Amber, his best friend James's widow, before now. Instead he had relied on a few phone calls and E-mails to check in with her once in a while and to make sure she was okay. Obviously Amber was very adept at hiding a few mental problems over the phone.

"Amber, what are you talking about?" He stepped around a case of strawberry jam, and accidentally stepped on a fancy gold bow.

"Your ad campaign." Amber looked at him as if he was the one having a hard time dealing with reality. "You remember it don't you? *Have a Berry Merry Christmas.*"

"Of course I remember it." Ian gave her what he hoped was a reassuring smile. "I wrote it."

"That proves it. You're to blame for this mess."

"How do you figure?" He unstuck the smashed bow from the bottom of his shoe and handed it to Amber.

Amber frowned at the ruined bow before tossing it into the trash can. "Look at these." She waved a couple dozen papers, which had been sitting in the fax machine tray, at him. "And all of these." Amber waved at another stack of paper, which had been buried under a box of candles. "Orders, every sheet of paper is another order."

"You're blaming me for orders?" He didn't see any bottles of liquor lying around, but that didn't mean Amber wasn't hiding one somewhere. Lord help her. It wasn't even lunchtime yet, and she was already three sheets to the wind. "Wasn't getting orders the whole idea behind the ad campaign?"

"Of course I wanted orders." Amber started to straighten up a dozen or so bottles of syrup. She lined them up by size: smaller ones in the front, larger ones in the back. "A nice slow stream of orders would have been great. Instead of a nice holiday trickle, I'm getting flooded. The water is rising, and any day now I'll be going under for the third time."

"Are you blaming me for *too many* orders?" he asked incredibly.

Amber placed her hands on her hips and glared. "I don't see anyone else standing there."

He tried not to grin, but it was hard. "I've never had anyone ever complain before about our campaigns working too well." He bit the inside of his check to keep his lips from twitching. "In fact, I know quite a few businesses that would love to have that problem."

Amber looked around the room and seemed to study the stack of orders for a long minute or two. With a heavy sigh, she asked, "You're laughing at me, aren't you?"

"What gives you that idea?" The anger that had been

blazing in her eyes a moment before had died down and turned to amusement.

"The fact that I'm acting like an idiot and making no sense at all might have something to do with it." The corner of Amber's lips began to twitch. "We won't even get into the part where I didn't even say hi, how are you, and what are you doing in Maine?"

"You're not an idiot. Overwhelmed, definitely, but no one could ever claim you're stupid, Amber." He liked a woman who didn't take herself too seriously. "Where's all your help?"

"Aunt Grace is in Bangor fighting the mob at the mall while looking for that perfect discounted dress to dazzle some unsuspecting man. Our part-time help, Tiffany, is across the street at Krup's eating lunch and flirting with her boyfriend."

"Leaving you to not only handle all those orders, but to hold down the shop?" He was beginning to see the problem and her frustration.

"I'm a big girl. I can handle it." Amber picked up the dark green candle that was sitting in the center of the worktable and placed it on a shelf containing jars of blueberry jam. "So, Ian, what brings you to Maine?"

It was on the tip of his tongue to say *you*, but he didn't think that would be appropriate in this situation. How could he explain the need to drive five hours to see her when he didn't even understand it himself? "I had some free time and I always wanted to see the coast of Maine."

"In November? What are you, nuts?" Amber chuckled as she gathered up a dozen bows lying around the room and put them into a box that was already overflowing with more brightly colored ribbons and bows. "If you waited a couple more days it would be December and then you could really freeze your butt off."

"I brought a pair of long johns." It was good to hear Amber's laughter again. He nodded toward the last box marked *Christmas Decorations* on the top shelf. "Want me to get that down for you?"

"Please."

He climbed up onto the stepladder and lifted the lightweight box down off the shelf. "I think you're the only shop in town not decorated for the season yet." He placed the box down on top of the one he had taken out of Amber's arms when he had seen her nearly losing her balance on the stepladder. He refused to think about the jolt his heart had taken at that unsettling sight.

"Don't remind me." Amber's fingers absently rubbed at her temple. "I swear, the Christmas shopping season comes earlier and earlier every year. I bet you that within the next ten years we'll be putting out the reindeer and the Santas along with the flags and fireworks."

"I won't take that bet. Back in Boston there were Christmas cards and some decorations next to the Thanksgiving decorations."

Amber's laughter faded as the sound of bells drifted in from the front of the shop. "I'll be right back, customers are calling. Make yourself comfortable and pull up a stool. There're some drinks in the refrigerator."

He watched as she maneuvered around a bunch of boxes and then disappeared out into the shop. Seeing Amber with his own eyes quieted his concern for her well-being. She appeared to be in excellent health, and even though she seemed a little frazzled around the edges, he had a feeling Maine agreed with her. Strange, he never figured the cool sophisticated Amber as a small fishing village type of woman.

Then again, this Amber appeared more down-to-earth and comfortable than the one he had known in Boston.

Ian opened the undersize refrigerator door and

studied his choices: diet soda or water. He chose a bottle of water and twisted off its cap before heading for
the opening to the shop. He stood to the side and
watched as Amber helped some elderly woman pick out
gift baskets to be mailed to distant relatives. He tried
not to chuckle as the woman named another relative
and then explained she hadn't even started on her husband's side of the family.

Amber was going to need another set of hands to
handle all the orders.

He glanced around the workroom and sadly shook
his head. What Amber really needed was to get organized. He couldn't imagine how she even found anything in this mess. While he hung up his coat and
finished off the water, he studied the storage shelves
around the room and figured out where the organiza-
tion ended and the chaos began.

After tossing the empty plastic bottle into the recy-
cling bin, he rolled up the sleeves of his flannel shirt
and got to work.

Amber watched Eleanor Ripley leave the shop with a
spring in her step and a smile upon her lips. When
Eleanor had handed Amber her credit card she had
proudly announced that she was now done with her
Christmas shopping. The entire shopping experience
had taken her a grand total of thirty-nine minutes.
Nineteen minutes in Krup's General Store to pick up
the circular saw her husband wanted, and twenty minutes in Amber's store.

She wasn't sure if she should deck the eighty-year-old
woman, or envy her. Amber hadn't even thought about
her own Christmas shopping. She was too worried
about everyone else's.

She now had another eight orders to be added to the
avalanche in the back room. A very crowded back

room. Ian McNeal's six-foot presence seemed to fill the room and penetrate every corner. She hadn't believed him when he said he had always wanted to see Maine. Oh, Maine was a gorgeous state, and anyone in their right mind would want to come to visit for a while. Just not in November. By late October all the snowbirds had flown or driven to their Florida condos. No one came to play tourist on the rocky coast. Maybe up in the mountains at the ski resorts, but not on the icy wind-swept shores.

So why had Ian driven over two hundred miles to hang out in the back room of some jam shop in a village that was nothing more than a speck on the map?

Amber slowly walked to the doorway, where a curtain printed with branches of blueberries was pulled back and tied with a dried grape vine, offering some privacy to the room beyond. She expected to see Ian sitting on one of the stools impatiently twiddling his thumbs. Instead she watched as Ian unpacked a case of ten-ounce strawberry jam and neatly placed the jars on their proper shelf.

Ian had been one very busy man while she had been out front with Eleanor. The six Christmas decoration boxes, along with the empty fall box, were sitting near the doorway. Five empty cases, that had held jam and jelly, were sitting by the back door. The two shelves of assorted syrups were neatly organized and every candle in the room was now on the huge worktable.

"What are you doing?" she asked. She knew what it looked like, but she couldn't think of one reason why Ian was stocking shelves and helping her out.

"What does it look like I'm doing?" Ian piled the now empty box on top of the other ones, and then reached for another case.

"Applying for a stock boy position." She watched the play of muscles across his back bunch and gather beneath his green plaid flannel shirt. Why hadn't she ever noticed how broad Ian's shoulders were before now? "I've got to warn you, the pay is lousy, and the hours are worse."

"My first job, when I was still in high school, was at the local supermarket stocking shelves during the weekends." Ian expertly located the shelf for the twenty-ounce sugar-free blueberry jam and started to unload the case. "My boss claimed I was a natural at it."

"I can see why he would say that." She watched as Ian's thigh muscles bunched and stretched his jeans as he squatted to reach the low shelf. Misty Harbor just got a whole lot more interesting. It was a real shame Ian was just passing through. "Ian, stop that." *Before I embarrass us both by drooling down the front of my sweatshirt.*

"Why?" Ian placed the last jar onto the shelf and stood.

She finally figured out what Ian was doing in Misty Harbor, and she didn't like it one bit. "You're checking up on me, aren't you?" She watched his expression and knew she was right the moment his eyes looked away from her.

Ian neatly placed the now empty box on top of the other ones by the back door. "You're low on the blackberry jam and so far I haven't found any cases of it waiting to be shelved." Without struggling, Ian lifted the top three cases of jelly off the tallest stack. "You shouldn't pile the cases that high, Amber. It's dangerous."

"Ian"—she pointed to the stool closest to him and barked out an order—"sit."

Ian sat and tried to appear innocent. On him, the expression only made him look more handsome, if it was possible. Ian McNeal was one attractive man, and it wasn't the first time she had noticed him or his looks. Back in their college days, she and a bunch of girlfriends had always been hanging out near Ian and James. The two gorgeous college roommates were total opposites from each other. James was blond, blue-eyed, and nearly pretty in his masculinity. Ian, with his dark brown hair and eyes that were nearly black, was more rugged in his appearance. James was the Brad Pitt, while Ian leaned more to Harrison Ford.

Their personalities were as different as their looks. There wasn't a party that didn't have James's name on it. Ian tended to skip the parties. James was the outgoing social butterfly, while Ian was the quiet studious one.

In her senior year of college it had been Ian who had fascinated her, but James had been the one who asked her out. James had been the one she eventually fell in love with and married. Ian had been James's best man at their wedding and a pallbearer at his funeral.

It had been a great and caring friendship that had ended when a drunk got behind the wheel of a car.

James and Ian had been unstoppable in their business together. James had been the sophisticated go-getter. There wasn't a client whom he couldn't get to sign on the dotted line. He had wined and dined them all, and loved every minute of it. James had been the businessman behind the successful M & M Ad Agency. Ian had been the talent. James would have been the first one to tell the clients that it was Ian who performed the magic on the drawing board. Ian had been, and still was, the creative genius.

She had worried more than once about how Ian and the business were surviving without James's vibrancy and aggressiveness. "Maybe it should be I who needs to check up on you, Ian."

"What do you mean?"

"How's the business going?"

Ian seemed to take his time answering. "It's going good. Real good."

She wondered what he wasn't telling her. Something wasn't right, because Ian wouldn't look her in the eye. "So there's plenty of work?"

"Sometimes we suffer the same problem you seem to be going through right now. Too much work, far too few hands to do it all." Ian rolled a thick bayberry candle back and forth over the smooth surface of the table. "I hired on a couple of new people, but the work keeps piling up."

"How are things going out of work?" She never knew Ian to be in a long-term relationship with any one woman. The few social events that he did attend with James and her over the years, he either came alone, or with some woman never to be seen or heard of again.

"If I'm not at work, I'm usually sleeping."

"Doesn't leave much time to enjoy yourself or relax." She was a fine one to talk. When was the last time she took a day off?

"That's why I decided to take some time off now."

"This is your idea of a vacation? Coming to the coast of Maine when today's high will be thirty degrees and a storm is due here by Sunday?" She shuddered at the thought of what tonight's low temperature would be. "May I suggest Sugarloaf Mountain. I hear the skiing there is excellent."

"I didn't bring any of my ski equipment." Ian grinned. "From what I've seen of Misty Harbor, it's just what I thought a small fishing village would look like."

"Frigid, nearly deserted, and worn around the edges?" Compared to the high-rises in the heart of Boston, Misty Harbor was as obsolete as the horse and buggy.

"Boston isn't exactly in the tropics, Amber." Ian started to put the candles into piles, according to their color. "From what I've seen of your town so far, and granted, I haven't seen very much, I find it quaint. There were even quite a few people out and about. I ended up parking down by the docks and having to walk back up to your shop."

"Yeah, we're a booming metropolis." She loved the

town, but she wasn't blind to its faults. In her four and half years of marriage to James, they had visited Misty Harbor together twice. The first time was supposed to have been for a week's vacation. James had been bored within three days, and they had ended up staying in Bar Harbor for the rest of the week. The other visit had been a quick weekend getaway. To Ian, who was born, raised, went to college, and still lived in Boston, the fishing village must seem like the ends of the earth. Heck, Ian probably had more people living on his city block, with its high-rise apartments, than the entire population of Misty Harbor combined.

"Well, does your metropolis have a hotel?" Ian continued sorting the candles. "I did see a sign advertising a motor inn near by."

"That's Wendell Kirby's place." She knew Wendell kept a couple of the rooms ready for winter occupancy, but they weren't what she would consider comfortable lodging. A twelve-by-twelve bedroom with a microscopic bathroom wasn't anyone's idea of luxury. "If you're planning on staying the night, or even a few days, there's a new bed-and-breakfast in town. Olivia Wycliffe is running the place, and you won't get a better breakfast in Misty Harbor."

"Sounds perfect." Ian turned on the stool and studied the shelves behind him. "Where were you planning on stocking the candles? I can't see a designated place for them."

She didn't see how anyone found anything in the room. Designated or not. "Grace piled all the extra baskets and empty gift boxes on the two shelves that I cleared off for them." She only started to unload the two shelves because she was beginning to feel funny watching Ian do all the work. "Stop sorting those candles, Ian."

"Why?" Ian had just about all the candles matched by

color, except those that were still in the boxes Karin
Warner had delivered them in.

"Because you still haven't told me why you're here."
She managed to fit all the wooden gift boxes on the
shelf with the other boxes, but there was no way all the
baskets were going to squeeze on with the other baskets. "I don't believe your vacation story." She wedged
in as many baskets as she could. "I believe you needed a
break from work. Knowing you, you probably haven't
had a vacation all year." If she was a betting woman, her
money would be on Ian not taking any time off since
James passed away. "I just can't see you picking Misty
Harbor as the place to come to unwind and relax. Your
first choice should have been some nice warm Caribbean island where they serve drinks with umbrellas in
them."

Ian must have seen her dilemma with the baskets. He
got up and found her a large empty box. "I'm not the
kind of guy who enjoys lying around on the sand baking
like a Christmas cookie."

"Not even when the view is blue skies, a clear tropical
ocean, and women wearing nothing but string bikinis
and suntan lotion?" James had loved the Caribbean.
They had even had their honeymoon down there.
James once told her that one of his goals in life was to
visit every island in the Caribbean. He never achieved
that goal.

"Is that what I'm missing?" Ian helped her clear off
the rest of the baskets and dumped them into the box.

"Afraid so. In this weather, the women up here wear
long johns, flannel pajamas, and smell like skin soft-
ener and ChapStick. None of the things that are con-
ducive with a man trying to relax and have some fun."
She stood in front of the two now empty shelves, and refused to allow Ian to place the candles in his hand onto
them. "So, why are you here, Ian?"

"Maybe I just wanted to see how you're doing, Amber." Ian stepped closer and placed the bayberry candles onto the shelf as she stepped to one side.

"You could have called me to find that out." She started to organize the candles by size. "Try again."

"Maybe I just wanted to see for myself that you were okay." Ian gently laid a bunch of mulberry candles on the other shelf. "James was my partner and friend. I would like to think that if I were married and passed away, James would look in on my wife and family to make sure they were doing okay."

It didn't escape her notice that Ian hadn't referred to her as a friend. Over the years she was lucky if she saw Ian three times a year. Once at the company's Christmas party, and maybe twice socially—usually while James was wining and dining some big shot client and Ian's presence was required. Ian's friendship with James had turned into more of a business friendship than a personal one. As far as she knew, they had grown to have very little in common beside the ad agency. "I'm sure James would have."

In a way she thought it was sweet of Ian to drive all the way up to Maine just to check on her. But it was also unnecessary. She had family who checked up on her constantly—way too much family, who tended to butt their noses into her business.

She opened up one of the boxes on the table and unpacked the bayberry candles. She shelved them with the ones Ian had found lying around the room.

"It's sweet of you to be concerned, but as you can see, I'm fine, Ian. I have three older brothers who find excuses to call me at least once a week. Every month one of them finds some reason to come to Misty Harbor and check up on me. The last thing I need is another older brother." The scent of the bayberry candles nearly overpowered the blueberry. "Business is booming and no one would claim I'm pining away to nothing." She wondered what a psychologist would say about a widow gaining twenty pounds after her young husband's death. Maybe she was overcompensating for the loneliness with food? Particularly, chocolate shakes.

"I can see that you're fine and I met all your brothers at your wedding." Ian placed all the light green pearberry candles next to the raspberry ones. "I can also see that you're shorthanded here. If I'm not mistaken, you did accuse me of that being my fault." Ian's voice held a touch of laughter.

It went unspoken that Ian had also met all her brothers again, at James's funeral. "It's not your fault that you did too good of a job convincing the public it just wouldn't be Christmas without a blueberry jam gift basket. I'm an ungrateful client, that's all."

"You're a client who is in desperate need of an extra pair of hands." Ian continued to shelve the candles. "I should have warned you about some of the hazards of having a brilliant slogan."

She snorted. "Yeah, like this happens to all your clients."

"Only the ones I do."

"Which reminds me, Ian; why did you take on the It's the Berries account?"

Ian looked at her as if she were nuts. "You asked me to."

"No, I mean why did you personally work on the slogan and everything else? Why didn't you just pass it on to one of your employees to do? It wasn't as if it was a major account, heck, you wouldn't even let me pay for anything but the rental of the billboards." She hadn't known Ian was the one who came up with that catchy slogan, but she should have guessed.

"There was no way I was taking your money, Amber." Ian shook his head as he gathered up the last pile of candles. "Your husband was half owner of that business. If it wasn't for James, M & M Ad Agency would never have gotten off the ground. He was the one who had to convince me it could work. I was all set on taking a job with a firm in New York when I had graduated from college. It's the least I could do for you."

"James just wanted to be his own boss, and he pulled you in for the ride." She had been so proud of James when the ad agency had taken its first floundering steps months before their wedding. By their first wedding anniversary the agency wasn't only walking, it was running. James hadn't been satisfied with just running, he wanted it to climb, and climb it did. By the time the agency had celebrated its fourth anniversary, their letterhead was sporting a prestigious address and they had twenty-some people on their payroll.

"It was some ride, Amber. I couldn't have done it without James."

"He couldn't have done it without you." James might have done all the celebrating, but he had never once taken all the glory. "I guess that's what being partners is all about."

Ian looked sad for a moment. "That brings me to another reason as to why I'm here." Ian reached into the pocket of his coat, which was hanging on a peg by the back door, and pulled out a large envelope. "I could have mailed this, but I wanted to give it to you in person."

"What is it?" She didn't like the way Ian was staring at her.

"It's the final paperwork on dissolving the partnership, and your check for James's share. The lawyers worked it all out and gave their final approval last week. The amount is what had been agreed upon months ago."

She stared at the envelope in Ian's hand, but she didn't reach for it. The amount was way more than what she thought it should have been, considering both James and Ian were putting everything they could back into the business. She knew their office space was being leased, and their biggest assets were the equipment in the office and their talent. James had been the salesmen, Ian the talent. How could you put a dollar figure on talent?

She knew from experience that lawyers could put a dollar figure on anything. Some lawyer, for the drunk who had caused the pileup on the expressway that had taken James's life, had put a dollar on James's life. That check had arrived three months ago by certified mail.

She knew the amount of the check in the envelope Ian was still holding out to her. The lawyer handling James's estate had discussed it with her months ago. While it wouldn't make her independently wealthy, she wouldn't have to worry about milk money for a very, very long time. Seeing that envelope, and knowing what it contained, made her feel like she was profiting from James's death. Ian and James had worked so hard to build that agency, and now she was the one getting a hefty check. It didn't seem right that Ian had to be the one paying her.

She understood the need to dissolve the partnership and to compensate James's estate. The agency had to move forward, and Ian was left with the task of settling the past before that was possible. Logically she understood that, but it still felt as if the check inside that envelope was blood money. James's life insurance checks had been a surprise. She hadn't realized that he had taken out a second policy through work. Then there was the settlement from the accident. Now this check. In all, it was one overwhelming generous amount.

She would give every cent of it, and more, just to have James alive again.

"I would like to reinvest that check back into the agency, Ian." She didn't know why she hadn't thought of that idea before. "James believed in the company, and so do I. I think he would like to see his share put to good use; to grow M & M Ad Agency into the biggest and the best ad agency on the East Coast. He always wanted to give those boys in New York a run for their money."

"I can't take your money, Amber. The agency is now privately owned by me. I've already got three separate people willing to buy out James's share of the company and go into a partnership with me. The company isn't short on cash, and as I explained before, business is great." Ian placed the envelope onto the table. "But, I thank you for the offer."

"I don't need the money, Ian. I can support myself quite nicely." Of course the way she was dressed today might cause Ian to doubt that statement, or if he ever saw her paychecks from the jam company he would have her committed. She had given up a high paying job in the business sector to work for a salary barely above minimum wage. Funny thing was, she still could afford everything she wanted or needed.

"It isn't about need, Amber. It's about what's right." He pushed the envelope toward her. "Take it, Amber, James would want you to have it. The business must have put one hell of a strain on your marriage. How many late business meetings did he attend? How many dinners did he miss because he was out with clients? How many overnight trips did he have to take? I know it doesn't compensate for all the lost time, Amber, but it's the only thing I can do."

She felt the tears pool in her eyes as she looked down at the envelope. Money would never make up for all those lost hours, or the nights James had been away from home. She knew she wasn't making this easy for Ian. She could hear the strain in his voice.

"There"—she picked up the envelope and tossed it onto the desk behind her—"I took it." At that moment she was upset at Ian for forcing her to once again accept the fact that James was gone and that someone, somehow, had placed a dollar sign on all he had done in life.

Before Ian could respond, the ringing of the bells above the front door filled the shop.

Tiffany, with her jacket undone and her scarf dragging on the floor, came flying into the workroom while saying, "Here's your lunch, Amber. Sorry I'm so late." Tiffany's feet skidded to a halt when she spotted Ian leaning against the worktable.

Amber almost chuckled at the surprised look on Tiffany's face. One would have thought the girl never saw a man before. "Thanks for picking up my lunch." She was tempted to tell her employee that her mouth was hanging open, in a very unladylike way. "Tiffany, this is Ian McNeal."

She wondered how she was supposed to introduce him to the people of Misty Harbor. *An old college friend* sounded lame, and there was no way she was introducing him as James's business partner. She glanced at Ian who was staring back at her with something akin to hurt in his gaze. She wasn't sure if he was hurt because of the way she had snapped at him when she took the check, or for the hesitation in the introduction. One thing she did know, deep down inside. "He's a very good friend of mine."

Chapter 3

Ian released the breath he hadn't realized he had been holding. For a moment there he had thought Amber was going to introduce him as her late husband's business partner. He didn't want to think about why that would have upset him, because it was true.

"Ian, this is Tiffany Moyer, our part-time employee." Amber took the paper bag containing her lunch out of Tiffany's hands.

"It's nice to meet you, Tiffany." He could see the girl's bewildered look and wondered if finding Amber with a man was such a rare occurrence. A year and a half was a long time to grieve for someone. Especially when you were as young as Amber, and had your entire life still ahead of you.

"Nice to meet you, too, Ian." Tiffany glanced between Amber and him and seemed to pick up on the tension in the room. "I didn't know Amber was expecting company, or I would have picked you up something, too."

Amber reached into the front pocket of her jeans and pulled out another bill. "Tiffany, could you do me a big favor and run across to Krup's and pick up another Friday's lunch special?"

"Sure, no problem." Tiffany snatched the money and headed for the door.

By the quickness of Tiffany's departure, Ian had a feeling that boyfriend Amber claimed she had been flirting with earlier was still around somewhere. "You don't have to buy my lunch, Amber." He reached into his back pocket for his wallet.

"Put that away." Amber nodded toward the wallet. "It's the least I could do for all your help. I still might not be able to walk in here, but now I can find the right candles."

Ian put away the wallet, but he was old-fashioned enough not to be comfortable with a woman paying for his meals. His father, who was still on the police force back in Boston, would probably smack him in the back of the head and give him a lecture if he found out that James's widow had paid for his son's lunch.

"By closing time you'll be able to dance in here." He had no intention of abandoning Amber to that impressive stack of orders. "After I get everything stocked, you're going to have to teach me how to fill some of those orders." He reached for the next case of jam to unpack.

"Ian?"

"What?" He frowned at another dozen ten-ounce jars of blueberry jam. Where in the world was the blackberry jam?

"You're not responsible for all the orders." Amber put her lunch on the table.

He flashed a big grin. "I know that, Amber. But I really do want to help."

"Why?"

"Because, that's what friends do for each other. Help them out when they need it."

"Doesn't sound like much of a vacation to me." Amber glanced around the room and then at the stack of orders.

He could tell she was tempted to take him up on the offer. "I'll tell you what. I'll straighten up in here today, and tomorrow I start helping you pack up some orders. Sunday we'll both take the day off and you can show me around the area."

"And if I say no?"

"Then I'll meet you here Sunday morning and we'll pack up some more orders."

Amber was still considering it. "It's supposed to snow on Sunday."

"Then we can shovel walks, build a snowman, and drink cups of hot chocolate." He couldn't remember the last time he had built a snowman. He had to have been back in elementary school.

"With marshmallows floating on top?" Amber's green eyes sparkled with laughter.

"If that's how you like it." He made a mental note to find a bag of marshmallows.

Amber nibbled on her lower lip for a moment. "I shouldn't take you up on the offer, but I am."

He watched her white even teeth tease her plump lower lip and quickly looked away. Desire tightened his body. What in the hell was he doing? Amber was James's wife. It didn't matter if James was no longer among the living. Amber would always belong to James. He had to clear his throat before he finally grated out, "Great."

Amber stood by the table for a moment before saying, "I'll go call Olivia and see if she has an available room for you."

Ian watched as she hurried from the room. A couple minutes later he heard her talking to someone on the phone. There must have been an extension out near the cash register. His gaze swung to the phone sitting on the desk on the other side of the room. The desk held a computer, copier/fax machine, a telephone, lots of papers, and the envelope he had brought with him from Boston.

He had to wonder why she hadn't used that phone to call the bed-and-breakfast.

Grace Berry was exhausted and there was a blister on her little toe from mistakenly wearing a new pair of sneakers shopping. She had gotten up before six so she could make it to all the stores that were opening early and having great after Thanksgiving Day sales. She had made it to about half of the stores, which, taking into account her age and the viciousness of the other shoppers out there today, she considered that an amazing feat worthy of at least one glass of wine with an extra slice of pumpkin pie after dinner tonight.

For being fifty-four years old and a good thirty pounds overweight, she did all right for herself. She had found not one, but two really nice holiday dresses at bargain basement prices. She almost had a sequined purse, shaped and decorated like a Christmas tree, for only fourteen ninety-nine. Some nimble little thirty-year-old housewife had snatched it up first. If it wasn't for the fear of aggravating her bursitis, she would have beaten the woman to the purse. As it was, she would have to make do with the penguin purse for Saturday night's date with Clyde. Black was always slimming.

The best part of the day was the knowledge that she had put a dent into her Christmas shopping list. The worst part of the day was knowing that her list was exceedingly long and varied. Almost all of her nieces and nephews were married with children of their own now. All those wonderfully endearing children needed a present to open from Auntie Grace. What would Christmas be without stacks of presents and piles of ripped wrapping paper and mountains of bows?

Christmas was the one time during the year that made the pain of never being able to have children of her own flare up once again. She loved all her nieces and nephews as if they had been her own. She loved all of their children. But there was still this dull ache, deep within her heart, that questioned and resented the fact that her own body had not only failed her, but her husband, Howard, as well.

Thankfully Howard had never once blamed her for their lack of children. He used to hold her in his arms as she cried as another month went by and another menstrual cycle began. Howard had been a firm believer in that old Doris Day song, "Que Sera, Sera," whatever will be, will be. He used to tell her as long as they had each other, all was right in the world.

Two years ago, the world had gone wrong. Horribly wrong. Howard had left one morning for work, kissing her for all he was worth, and promising he would pick up where he left off, once he got home that night. If she closed her eyes, she could still see the devil dancing in Howard's gray eyes and the way the morning sun had reflected off his lunch container as he had tossed it onto the front seat of his truck.

Fifty-four-year-old men weren't supposed to have heart attacks and die while working in a machine shop. Fifty-two-year-old women weren't supposed to be widows. She had married Howard three weeks after graduating from high school. They had both been virgins on their wedding night, and she could still remember the awkwardness. It had taken a week's stay, in some little rundown cottage on the shore, on the outskirts of Bar Harbor, to dispel any shyness. They had made it to the grocery store once, and never did get into town to sightsee.

Her never getting pregnant and not having any children wasn't from lack of trying on Howard's part. She'd give the old coot that.

Grace chuckled as she pulled into her driveway thinking of Howard and all the fun they had shared. Her foot, the one with the aching toe, stepped off the gas and onto the brake as she studied her home. Her laughter slowly faded. She had never lived anywhere else but in this home, and couldn't imagine doing so. The old clapboard house, with its peeling white paint and dark green shutters, looked as if it had seen better days. It was a perfect match to her. They were both too old, too worn, and way too big. What in the world was she doing with a house that had five bedrooms and three working fireplaces?

Because Howard had insisted they buy out her brothers' and sister's shares once her mother passed away. She and Howard had lived with her mother after their wedding. It had been her mother who had insisted on it, since Grace was the baby of the family, by six minutes. It had been Grace who had nursed her mother the last six months of her life.

Howard had known how much she had loved the house, and he had been confident thirty years ago that it was only a matter of time before they would fill up a bedroom or two with little ones. She never regretted buying the house. The clanging of the cranky old radiators lulled her to sleep every night in the winter, and the cry of the gulls woke her every summer's morn.

In the weak light of the fading afternoon, the house seemed lonely and sad. The front porch was tilting downward on the left. A shutter on one of the spare bedroom windows was crooked, and two others were missing totally. One of the many chimneys was in dire need of a few bricks and a good mason. Even the lawn, with its bare trees and brownish grass, seemed forlorn. Two pumpkins, guarding the front door, were the only splash of color.

There should have been tricycles and wagons on the porch and a tire swing dangling from the huge oak tree.

Maybe some of those orange Halloween lights that everyone seemed to put up nowadays should have been wrapped around the porch railings, waiting to be exchanged for the Christmas garland and bows.

Who was she kidding? Grace blinked away the burning of unshed tears. Even if she and Howard had had a couple of kids, they would be grown up by now and living their own lives. She would still be coming home to an empty house.

There was no sense crying over spilled milk—especially milk that had been spilled a quarter of a century before.

Grace released the brake and drove her car around to the back of the house. The house might be empty, but she wasn't alone anymore. She had her niece, Amber, living right out back above the carriage house. The driveway was empty, and the carriage house locked up tight. Carol Orwig and Paulette Newman, the two women she employed to do most of the cooking, hadn't worked today, because the kids had off from school. Her niece was handling the shop in town.

Amber had been handling everything for the past year and It's the Berries was having a banner year. In fact, it was the best year, financially, since its conception twenty-five years ago. She had Amber to thank for that. She had Amber to thank for a lot of things.

When Amber had moved to Maine eighteen months ago, she had been grieving deeply for the loss of her husband. Grace hadn't been too much of a help to the young widow, since Howard had passed away six months before and she was having a hard time accepting that fact. In the beginning, they had made one sorry, weepy-eyed pair. Over time it had been Amber who had helped Grace get on with her life, and the business had helped her niece.

Strange, Grace always figured it should have been

the other way around. The business should have been a comfort to her, since she had started it with nothing more than a couple cases of mason jars and what seemed like a million blueberries piled all around her kitchen. Instead it was Amber who stepped right in and picked up the reins Grace had freely handed her.

Grace laughed at herself as she retrieved her purchases from the trunk of her car. She hadn't handed Amber anything, she had forced the girl to take them. Her heart hadn't been in the jam business any longer. Everything was, as the younger generation says, going down the tubes. Amber had saved the business. And how did she repay her niece? By going shopping all day instead of helping out in the shop.

She should be ashamed of herself. She knew what that back room of the shop looked like. She had seen the pile of orders. She knew Tiffany was probably flirting with some boy or talking on her cell phone to one of her girlfriends. Yet, even knowing all that, she had driven to Bangor before the sun had lightened the skies to hunt for dresses and sales.

She was the world's worst aunt. It was only last night, during Thanksgiving dinner, that she had silently given thanks for Amber. Not only for sharing her meal and taking care of the business, but for encouraging an old woman to start to live again. If it hadn't been for her niece's support, there would have been no way she would have accepted Joe Clayton's invitation to the movies months ago and officially entered the dating game.

Since that first date on that hot summer night, she had gone to plays in Bangor with Clyde Davenport, fishing with Lenny Holmes, and on long scenic drives with Mac Pierce. She had joined a singles group in Franklin that played pinochle every Wednesday night and she flirted shamelessly with the firemen during Friday night bingo games. If it hadn't been for Amber she wouldn't have discovered the joys of dating or the realization she really didn't want to spend the rest of her life alone in her sad-looking house.

Howard had been her first true love, and there was no way he would ever be replaced in her heart. What they had shared had been special and rare. But as Amber explained, she hadn't died with Howard. She was the one who had to go on living, and that there was nothing wrong with finding friendship, compatibility, or possibly even love, with another man. The love would never be the same love as she had shared with Howard, but it didn't mean she couldn't have a fulfilling life.

Over the past month she had discovered that finding that special partner to share that fulfilling life with was one tiring experience. Dating, at over fifty, should be classified as an extreme sport. She was ready to accept the first marriage proposal that came her way, just so she wouldn't have to wear a girdle anymore.

Grace dropped all her bags on the kitchen table and glanced at the clock. It was only four in the afternoon. There was plenty of time to get to the shop and kick Amber out for the rest of the day. Between Grace and Tiffany they could handle the customers and hopefully straighten up some of that back room. Usually Amber and Tiffany worked Friday night, until they closed at eight, while she was at the firehouse playing bingo and flirting with all the single volunteer firemen. Tonight's bingo was cancelled, because of the holiday. There wasn't a reason in the world why she shouldn't be at the shop.

The only thing preventing her from walking right back out her kitchen door was the fact that her toe was killing her. She'd leave just as soon as she put a bandage on the blister and changed into more comfortable shoes.

* * *

Amber tried to ignore Ian as he bustled around the room like a man possessed. During the past four hours, Ian had whipped the room into shape like a five star general commanding his troops of preserves. Every case had either been unpacked or neatly piled in the appropriate area. The empty boxes were now out in her SUV, parked behind the shop, ready to be returned to the carriage house kitchen. The three cases of blackberry jam that she had brought in with her this morning were now unpacked and neatly lined up on the shelves. All the fall decorations were packed away and the boxes were once again on the top shelf. Bows and ribbon had been plucked from the huge corrugated box filled with Styrofoam peanuts. Tangled packing tape had been cut away from the clear wrap used to wrap gift baskets. Even the garbage barrel had been emptied into the Dumpster out back.

Any minute now she had a feeling Ian was going to stand at attention while she did the white glove inspection routine.

She could hear Ian's soft whistling while he swept the floor and was tempted to join in if she could have placed the tune. Ian was a lousy whistler.

For the past four hours she had been sitting in front of the computer doing inventory, printing mailing labels, and downloading more orders. She had also called Karin Warner and ordered more candles, and had left a message on Fern's answering machine telling her she needed more baskets and wooden gift boxes. America was taking the fact that blueberries were the number one antioxidant fruit to heart.

Amber watched Ian empty his dustpan, filled with a few smashed and dirty peanuts, into the barrel. "Your room at the bed-and-breakfast should be ready by now."

Ian glanced at his watch. "Four o'clock, right?"

"Olivia said any time between four and six would be fine with her." Her friend and fellow computer geek had been awfully interested in meeting Amber's friend Ian. Olivia Wycliffe had been champing at the bit waiting for Amber to be ready to get on with her life and start dating again. Olivia had a list of single of men she was dying to fix Amber up with. Olivia was newly married, and was still of the opinion that everyone should be as gloriously in love as she and her husband were.

Newlyweds were as bad as reformed smokers when it came to their preaching ways.

Amber purposely had not told Olivia she was ready to follow in Aunt Grace's footsteps and start dating anybody who wore pants and smelled like Old Spice cologne. Misty Harbor had an above average population of single males and she wasn't blind. At twenty-nine she knew what to look for in a prospective date.

So far no one in particular stood out and made her hormones scream, but there were a couple of possibilities. Ned Porter and his brother Matthew definitely stood out in her mind, but both were a little too "out-doorsy" for her taste in men. She wanted someone to sweep her off her feet, not take her camping.

"I'm almost done in here." Ian frowned at the baskets overflowing the shelf and then turned his gaze toward her desk.

She quickly spread her arms over the different piles of papers scattered across the desk. "Don't, and I repeat, don't even think about straightening this desk." She knew the area looked hopelessly disorganized, but she had a system. "I know exactly where everything is."

Ian raised a brow in disbelief. "If you say so."

"I say so." She shuddered at the thought of anyone touching one piece of paper, let alone the stacks upon stacks that were scattered about the desk. Aunt Grace and Tiffany already knew the number one rule of the workshop: don't touch the desk!

The back door opened, and with a strong winter's

breeze Aunt Grace, in all her glory, came barreling into the workroom announcing the obvious, "I'm here."

"So we see." She studied Ian's face to see what he thought of her aunt. Ian's reaction was priceless. Total bewilderment mixed with shock. To say her aunt loved to wear color would be the understatement of the year.

Today's outfit was a bright purple sweatshirt proclaiming Shop Till You Drop! in honor of Black Friday. Bold colored shopping bags had been appliquéd on the front of the shirt. Black stretch pants and a pair of black ankle boots with Dalmatian print fur trim completed the, for Grace, anyway, tame outfit. Her aunt's love of color did not stop at her clothes. Grace changed her hair color the way some women changed their nail polish.

Her aunt tended to go blond during the summer months, but by late September she started in on the darker shades. Last week Grace had pitch-black hair, until Tiffany told her that she looked "Totally Goth." The next day Grace had shown up at work with what she called "Festive Auburn" for the approaching holiday season. There was no two ways about it: Grace's short and shaggy hair was red.

A pair of huge poinsettia earrings swung from Grace's ears and nearly touched her shoulders. The flowers perfectly matched her hair and lipstick.

"Ian McNeal, what are you doing here?" Grace smiled with pleasure as she hung up her leopard print coat and oversize zebra purse.

Sometimes Amber thought her aunt had watched one too many Disney films or had an obsession with Cruella DeVil. "Ian, you remember my aunt, Grace Berry."

"How could I forget?" Ian made it sound like a compliment as he reached for Grace's hand.

Her aunt ignored the hand and planted a kiss on Ian's cheek. "Tell me some lucky woman hasn't taken you off the market yet."

Ian flashed a grin that probably melted the lycra in Grace's girdle. "I'm still looking. Have anyone particular in mind?"

Grace pretended to blush as she fanned her face. "If I was twenty years younger, I'd take you up on whatever you're offering."

Amber wasn't fooled. She had seen the sideward glance her aunt had shot her way. "Grace, if you were twenty years younger, the men of Misty Harbor would lynch Ian before they would let him, an outsider, take you away."

Her aunt beamed at Ian. "But think of all the fun we could have together before they caught us."

Amber shook her head and chuckled at her mischievous aunt. "This is why my mother has gray hair."

"Gladys has gray hair because she not only worries about stupid things, she refuses to go to the hairdresser and do something about it." Grace wrinkled her nose. "My twin sister thinks a woman should be proud to show her age."

Ian smiled. "There's nothing wrong with age."

Grace snorted. "Only two things improve with age, Ian, cheese and wine, and I'm not either."

She chuckled along with Ian. "Stop teasing, Grace, and tell me, what are you doing here? Aren't you supposed to be shopping?"

"I'm all shopped out"—Grace winked at Ian—"for the day." Her aunt pulled up a stool and sat. "I came to help clean up this room, but by the looks of things, I'm too late."

"Ian did all the work, while I kept out of his way."

"Hmmm . . ." Grace wrinkled her nose at the computer. "I didn't know you were planning on hiring a stock boy, but I do applaud your choice."

"Pay's great. So far I got a free lunch out of it," Ian said, not helping the situation out one bit.

"Really, Amber, you've got to give the man more than one meal for the wonderful job he did in here."

"He's not here to eat, Grace." She could see the wheels turning in her aunt's romantic brain. Grace was putting two and two together and coming up with a wedding. "He came to Misty Harbor to relax and to check up on me." There wasn't anything romantic sounding in that.

Grace looked surprised and then concerned. "Why do you need checking up on?"

"I don't." Amber shot Ian a look that she hoped conveyed her displeasure at him. "When he showed up, I was in one of my frazzled moods and I inadvertently yelled at him for making the billboards and the rest of the ad campaign look so good that we were being flooded with orders."

"I see." Grace looked from her to Ian, and then back again.

"He's feeling guilty, so he's pitching in to help me get caught up with the orders. I, in turn, will show him the sights, so his vacation isn't a total bust."

"Sounds like a boring compromise," Grace said.

"What do you mean?"

"I mean, packing up jam all day is boring, Amber. Then to compensate Ian for a job well done you're going to show him the sights of Misty Harbor? May I ask what sights? You can drive from one end of Main Street to the other in less than four minutes, and that's if you're speeding."

"There's plenty to see and do in town."

"Name three things," Grace challenged.

"Ice-skating on Sara's Pond." She knew everyone in town flocked to Sara's Pond, once it had frozen over, to skate. Some of the local men even had their own ice hockey teams and they played against each other every Saturday morning and Sunday afternoon. Most of the town turned out to cheer them on.

"Sara's Pond is a couple miles out of town, but I'll give you that one."

"Ethan Wycliffe's art gallery is having a holiday open house this weekend." Olivia, Ethan's wife, had been bugging her for weeks about attending it Saturday night. She had halfheartedly promised that she would be there.

"That's two."

"The choir from the Methodist church will be singing out at the lighthouse Sunday night to kick off the holiday season. The Women's Guild will be selling hot chocolate and baked goods. All the proceeds will be going to the upkeep of the lighthouse." Aunt Grace was vice president of the Women's Guild and had been telling her about the fund-raiser for weeks. She had just repeated her aunt's sales pitch back to her.

"Okay, so Misty Harbor isn't a boring town. But Ian, did you pack your ice skates, really warm clothes and a suit? Spending an hour or so up on the cliffs at the lighthouse can be daunting. The wind can cut right through you."

"Check on the warm clothes and suit, but I was in the market for a new pair of skates anyway."

Too late Amber realized what her aunt had been up to. She had virtually just set herself up for three dates with Ian. It was one thing to show him around town, and point out a spot or two of interest. It was something else entirely if she brought him to the gallery's open house or the choir's fund-raiser. Those events seemed more personal. More intimate. Aunt Grace was playing matchmaker, and Amber had fallen right into her trap.

She didn't like being played. "I don't think . . ."

"It's okay, Amber, you don't have to show me any of those places." Ian looked uncomfortable.

"Amber, really, you're embarrassing Ian." Grace stood up, flashed a satisfied smile, and headed for the front of the shop. "Didn't you just say you'd be showing him around? What's the big deal?"

She watched as her aunt disappeared into the other room. She could hear Tiffany and her aunt talking. Hopefully between the two of them they could figure out what to do with the six boxes of Christmas decorations now sitting in the corner of the shop. For all of Grace's vivid and often horrible fashion sense, her aunt always managed to decorate the shop with an understated classy sophistication.

The shop was in great hands and it was one less thing she had to worry about.

She turned to Ian and wondered how to apologize for her aunt's heavy-handedness. "She means well."

"Don't apologize, Amber. If you got within ten feet of my mother she'd be throwing me at your feet and begging you to make her a grandmother." Ian leaned against the worktable and chuckled. "I knew what your aunt was up to, and she did mean well."

"Are you sure about that?" She chuckled at the thought of Ian's mother having to throw women at him. The man was handsome enough to be tripping over them as it was.

"Positive. You don't have to take me to any of those places. I'm a big boy. I can amuse myself."

"It's not that." How could she explain to him, that once she went out in public with him, the entire town would know she was ready to start dating again? From what she heard from Olivia and some of the other women in town, the single men of Misty Harbor looked at dating as a competitive Olympic sport. In this case, instead of a gold medal, it was a gold ring that mattered. No silver. No bronze. Only a gold ring and a preacher declared the winner.

She wasn't looking that far ahead. She needed to get her toes wet, and test the dating waters, before plunging in headfirst. But she was awfully sick of her own company.

"Ian?"

"Yes?"

She took a deep breath, and did something that she had never done in her life. She asked a man out. "Would you like to go to an art gallery open house with me tomorrow night?"

Ian's smile flashed in his dark brown eyes. "It would be my pleasure."

Chapter 4

Ian pulled up in front of the carriage house and stared at the lit windows on the second floor. *What in the hell am I doing here?* There was no way he should be taking Amber out to dinner and then to the gallery's open house. A holiday affair, even if the entire town had been invited to it, still smacked too close to being a date.

Being shown around town, shoveling walks, or even building snowmen wasn't a date. Working side by side all day long, while packing up a small mountain of jams and jellies, wasn't a date. Calling the best restaurant in town and making dinner reservations for two was a date. Getting dressed in a suit and tie, and shaving before picking up a woman, was a date. He had even shined up his shoes and splashed on some cologne.

There was no way around it. He was going out on a date. He was taking James's wife out on a date and there was probably a special place reserved for him in hell.

He got out of his car and headed for the wooden stairs running up the side of the building. Amber had told him that her apartment was the entire second floor and to head up the steps. The downstairs of the aged, yet still graceful and architecturally unique, carriage

house had been converted into the kitchen that pro-
duced all the jams, syrups, and jellies. It was the heart of
It's the Berries Jam Company.

It didn't surprise him that Amber had chosen to live
above the kitchen. What did surprise him was that she
wasn't in that kitchen cooking up the jam herself, and
taste-testing every batch. From what he had seen in the
past two days, Amber had taken the reins of the business and was calling every shot.

Her aunt didn't seem to mind one bit; in fact, Grace
was encouraging Amber all the way. Grace appeared
content to do her own thing. Between last night and all
day today, the shop had been elegantly decorated for
the upcoming holiday season. If he hadn't seen Grace
do most of the decorating herself, he wouldn't have believed it.

Grace Berry's wardrobe would give Ralph Lauren indigestion, yet his meticulous mother wouldn't be able
to find one thing wrong with the way Grace had decorated the shop. She had called him away from filling
some orders with Amber to assist her in setting up the
tree in the front of the shop. A local boy had delivered
the seven-foot Douglas fir around ten that morning.
While he had struggled, strained, and silently cursed
the fir into an antique cast-iron stand that weighed
more than a Civil War canon, Grace had talked his ear
off.

Grace had told him she and her sister, Gladys, Amber's
mother, were mirror twins. Grace was left-handed, Gladys
right. Grace, who had been wearing a red sweater with
Rudolph's face knitted onto the front and a pair of red
and black plaid stretch pants, swore she had inherited
all the fashion sense, while Gladys couldn't decorate a
Christmas cookie. The pair of felt antlers that Grace
had been wearing at time bounced and bobbed with
her every word, making the bells sewn onto them jingle
and sway. Per Grace, Gladys's idea of decorating a

Christmas tree was to throw on a dozen strings of lights, hang every ornament in the box, and enough garland to wrap the state of Vermont. Twice. Then Gladys would cover the entire mess with at least five boxes of silver tinsel, put on a Bing Crosby CD, and call it Christmas.

Ian had no way of knowing if this was true, but it did propose an interesting question. Had Amber been raised by a woman who dressed in Armani and decorated her home like a Jerry Springer holiday special?

He frowned at the wooden steps as he made his way up them. Snow and ice would make them treacherous. A plastic can with a lid, containing rock salt, sat on the top landing waiting for the next ice storm. Seeing the deicer didn't relieve his fears that Amber was going to break her neck if she wasn't careful. A metal snow shovel was propped against the house and a welcome mat, depicting fall leaves and a scarecrow, was beneath his feet.

Thankfully, not a tacky Christmas decoration was in sight.

He knocked on the door and shifted his weight as he glanced around the big yard that was in dire need of an excellent landscaper. The tightening in his gut told him this evening meant more to him than he first thought. More than he wanted it to. Maybe he should just tell Amber how uncomfortable he was feeling about this evening. She would understand. After all, wasn't she the one to claim they were friends?

All thoughts of ending the evening early vanished the moment Amber opened the door. "You're right on time, Ian." Amber turned around and walked away from the door. "Come on in while I get my coat."

His only thought was: it had better be a very heavy coat. The dark green dress Amber was wearing offered her very little warmth and him way too much of it. Amber would be suffering frostbite, of some very sensitive body parts, if she wasn't careful outside. If Jack

Frost was a smart boy, he would be nipping at something besides her nose. He stepped into her apartment and closed the door against the frigid November night air.

Good Lord, Amber didn't play fair. They were supposed to be friends. How was he supposed to act like a platonic friend when she looked so darn delectable? Green was definitely her color. The knee-length, long-sleeve dress clung in all the right places and was cut low in the front, offering him and anyone else who cared to look, a view of her pale throat and impressive cleavage. The back of the dress had dipped lower and there was no way she could be wearing a bra. Amber had swept her hair up in some complicated twist that showed her neck to perfection and the tiny silver teardrop earrings. The earrings matched her necklace.

By today's standards, the dress was modest and totally appropriate for dinner and a gallery's open house. He just wished she had chosen something different—something warmer and with a lot more material. Wool slacks and a thick, baggy, cable-knit sweater would have been his first preference.

He could smell the seductive scent of her perfume and wondered how Amber afforded to keep the thermostat turned up so high. It was getting uncomfortably warm.

He unbuttoned his winter coat as he glanced around the place. Thankfully, Amber hadn't inherited Grace's fashion sense. "Your place looks"—he saw Amber's curious glance as he slowly finished the comment—"comfortable." He had been trying to think of a more complimentary word, but he couldn't, so he had settled for the truth.

He had been in Amber and James's home back in Boston. While he couldn't remember all the details, he did remember it being mostly white and spaciously furnished. The word glamorous came to mind when he thought about the occasional parties James and Amber had thrown.

Amber's apartment was one big area, divided into three sections by some bearing walls. From the small eat-in kitchen, where he was standing, he could see everything in the living room, from the thick-cushioned couch to a comfortable-looking, overstuffed reading chair. A stone fireplace took up the space between the television and an armoire holding Amber's computer equipment. The fireplace was unlit, but he could tell it had been used recently. A soft-looking afghan had slipped off the couch and was pooled onto the thick sage colored carpet. Magazines and a few books were scattered across the coffee table and her work space surrounding the computer was on the messy side. There were a few dishes in the sink and a bunch of overripe bananas were sitting on the counter.

The place looked lived in.

A ten foot opening led directly into the bedroom. He could see Amber's queen-size bed with its white iron headboard, a half a dozen pillows, and patchwork quilt. He spotted two doors that opened into the bedroom. He figured one was the bathroom, the other a closet. There wasn't enough room for anything bigger. The entire place was done in various shades of green, giving it a warm, relaxed feeling. There wasn't any doubt that a woman had decorated the place, but a man would feel comfortable and right at home in it. There wasn't a ruffle, bow, or smothering yards of frilly lace in sight.

Amber smiled. "Great, that was the look I was going for." Amber finished transferring a set of keys and a tube of lipstick into a tiny, gold beaded purse.

He spotted a white and gray striped cat curled up on the back of the couch. "I didn't know you had a cat."

"I have two, or should I say they have me." Amber walked over and scratched the cat behind its ears. "This is Light, and she's a sweetheart. Her brother, Shadow, is probably buried in the pillows on the bed. That's his favorite place to nap."

He glanced at the bed, but couldn't see any sign of a cat. "Shadow and Light?" He smiled as Light rolled onto her back, almost fell off the couch, regained her balanced, and stretched.

"They were strays, and I'm pretty sure they were from the same litter. I made the mistake of feeding them once, and the next thing I knew, they were moving in and hogging the pillows at night."

He didn't want to think about feeding Amber, and then having her hog his pillows. He thought cats were supposed to be curious creatures by nature. Weren't they supposed to at least come out and check out who Amber was talking to? Didn't they care who was invading their domain? "They don't seem to make very good watch cats."

Amber raised an eyebrow at that comment, and gave Light one last belly scratch. "You never owned a cat, right?"

"I had a goldfish when I was about eight. I won him at the fair and my dad promised I could keep him. I named him Killer, and he lived for about two weeks." He could still remember how he had to hide his tears from his older brother Sean when he flushed Killer down the toilet. "My mom wasn't big on the animal kingdom, especially if they wanted to live in her house."

"I grew up surrounded by dogs, cats, and the occasional snake. My mother should have been a vet."

"What about your Aunt Grace, does she like animals?"

"She claims she can't stand them, but every time I turn around she's buying some treats or catnip toys for them." Amber brushed at the cat hair clinging to the sleeve of her dress. "Would you like a drink or something before we go? I think I only have some white wine, though."

He glanced at his watch. "We better not. The reservations are for six-thirty, and if you want to make it to the gallery before eight, we better not be late."

"I'll never hear the end of it from Olivia if we don't get there before eight."

"She seemed quite excited about the whole thing." He had met Olivia Wycliffe last night when he finally went and settled in at the bed-and-breakfast. "She's quite supportive of her husband and was filling me in on some of the local artists whose talents will be on display tonight."

Olivia also had been trying to find out everything she could as to why he was in town and how long he had known Amber. She had been dying of curiosity as to how he persuaded Amber to invite him along to the open house. Olivia acted as if Amber didn't get out much. It was the second time he had gotten the impression that Amber didn't date much, or at all. Ian also didn't think Amber would appreciate him getting the third degree from her friend.

"Ethan loves to find new talent, especially local talent." Amber pulled a full-length, black wool coat off a peg by the front door. "Ethan only had a small opening for the gallery back in June when he opened the doors for business. A lot of the renovations weren't done then, but he needed to open then, or he would have missed the tourist season." Ian helped Amber on with her coat. "From what I understand almost all the renovations are now complete, and the gallery looks stunning."

"The gallery is down by the water, isn't it?" He thought he had seen it yesterday when he had driven through town looking for Amber's store. "It looks like an old marine building, but with a lot more windows? If I remember correctly, it's a deep crimson color with white trim?"

"That's the place. It's only a short walking distance

from the restaurant, so we can either park there and walk to dinner, or we can walk to the gallery after we eat." Amber finished buttoning her coat, picked up her purse, and headed for the door. "Ready?"

"As ready as I ever will be." He watched as Amber locked the door behind them and frowned at her high heels. "Be careful on these steps, Amber, they don't look safe."

Amber chuckled as she headed on down the steep stairs. "They're fine, Ian. I'm used to them."

Amber glanced around the crowded room and couldn't believe the changes Ethan had made to the place since June. She really needed to get out more. She knew Ethan's wife, Olivia, had computerized the business, but it had been Ethan who had personally overseen the renovations. Ethan was a tad of a perfectionist when it came to his gallery, and it showed. She couldn't decide what impressed her more, the actual building with its wide plank flooring and massive windows that overlooked the harbor or the artwork itself.

Ethan had embraced the building's heritage and brought many aspects of the sea into his gallery. The stairs leading to the second floor were made from wooden planks, and thick braided rope was used for railings and banisters. Some of the original wooden walls had been saved and used to partition off certain spaces throughout, adding a rustic charm that offset the stark white walls. Discreet lighting was everywhere, highlighting one piece of art, casting intriguing shadows on another. The building itself was a piece of art.

The works of art being displayed were either breathtaking or expertly crafted. The pottery on the second floor was wonderful, and she had already told Ethan that she'd be in on Monday to purchase the large bowl with the hand-painted pinecones and branches. The bowl would look right at home sitting on her coffee table, and it was big enough that she wouldn't have to worry about the cats knocking it off.

For a species known for their grace and agility, Shadow and Light had managed to knock over or break quite a few things since they moved in and took over her apartment. She hadn't pinpointed which one was the klutz yet, but she had a sneaky suspicion it was Shadow. Something about his golden eyes and the way they seemed to laugh at her while she was cleaning up the latest misfortune told her he wasn't sorry to see that particular item go into the trash.

Amber took another sip of wine and studied the painting before her. Dark angry skies and powerfully churning surf crashing onto a rocky shore dominated the oil painting. The scene was way too dark for her taste, but there was no denying the talent of the artist. A discreet card listed the title of the painting as *Balmy Eve*, which was an eye-opener, but the price listed below made her gasp.

She wondered what Ian had thought of the picture. She had seen him studying it when she had been upstairs getting cornered by Wendell Kirby. She had known that as soon as she was seen with Ian, the word would get around town that she was over her grieving and moving on with her life. She just hadn't expected Wendell, the president of the Chamber of Commerce and the owner of Misty Harbor Motor Inn, to ask her out while she was already on a date.

She blamed that on Ian, who had practically deserted her once they started to mingle in the gallery. She hadn't expected him to stay glued to her side, but the man seemed to be going out of his way to avoid her, and she hadn't the faintest clue as to why. Dinner at Catch of the Day had been delicious and relaxing. Ian had acted like the perfect date, friendly, interested in what she had to say, and charming. He had complimented her on her looks and dress, but he hadn't been overly flirtatious. Ian McNeal hadn't acted like a man who thought he was going to *get lucky* at the end of the evening. Which was fine by her.

Amber took another sip of wine and revised her opinion on the stormy seascape. It wasn't too dark after all. She still couldn't picture it above her mantel, but for some reason it was hitting the right tone with her.

"Intense." Karl James had silently joined her in the study of the painting.

She gave Karl, a local artist whom she had met before, a startled glance before looking back at the turbulent painting. She hadn't realized anyone had joined her. "Powerful."

"Commanding."

"Dark." She hid her smile by taking another sip of wine. She was as qualified to debate art with Karl as he was to compare jam recipes with her. It didn't matter if she was unqualified to list the merits of a particular piece of art, Karl didn't seem to mind. She liked the laid-back artist with his long gray hair that he always wore back in a ponytail, and his full, bushy beard. Karl reminded her of Jerry Garcia, from the Grateful Dead. Usually Karl was seen around town riding his Harley and dressed in Hawaiian print shirts and ratty jeans. Tonight, in honor of the occasion, Karl had on an expensive gray suit and tie. The tie boasted a dozen pink flamingos, each wearing a Santa hat and sunglasses.

"Brilliant," Karl said as he squinted at the signature.

"Violent." She had studied the signature before Karl had joined her. The closest she could make it out to be was, C.J. That was it. Just a set of initials for a very talented artist who had three paintings on display this evening. All three were of the sea in some way. All were powerful, dark, and violent.

"Tempestuous."

"Angry."

Karl lifted his wineglass, smiled, and said, "Touché. You hit that one right on the head: short, blunt, and to the point. You can almost see the hostility in every brush stroke."

She laughed back at him and hoped she hadn't offended one of his friends. The only thing she would be able to tell from a brush stroke was the color of the paint the artist had been using. "Do you know the artist?"

"No, but I've seen his paintings in here before." Karl glanced across the room to where another of the artist's work hung.

The picture hanging on one of the depressed walls was of Misty Harbor's lighthouse. It had taken Amber ten minutes to realize it was the same charming and quaint lighthouse of her youth. The same lighthouse where the Methodist church choir was singing tomorrow night hoping to raise enough funds for some much needed work. Time, and the constant battering of the winds, were taking their toll on the historic landmark. Whoever C.J. was, the man, as the saying went, had issues. Misty Harbor's lighthouse appeared to be perched on the edge of hell, drawing in ships to their doom.

It was the only painting in the gallery where she had questioned Ethan's taste, until she had seen the discreet price tag with the red sold sticker attached. Ethan's commission alone would force him into a higher tax bracket. No one could dispute the artist's talent, only his mental mindset. The artist had titled the painting, *False Promises.*

"What makes you think it's a man? C.J. could be a woman." She didn't know why she had said that. There was nothing either soft or feminine in any of the paintings.

Karl turned back to the seascape. "You think C.J. is a woman?" Karl sounded as if he had never considered the intriguing possibility.

"I don't know. Why don't you ask Ethan? I'm sure he knows." She glanced about ten feet to her right, to where Ethan and Ian were either discussing the massive wooden sculpture before them, or football. With men, it was always hard to tell. Ian turned to her and smiled and she immediately forgave him for deserting her earlier.

"I asked Ethan a couple times, but every time he cited me the confidentially clause."

"What's that?"

"It means that if an artist prefers to stay anonymous, I see that it stays that way," Ethan said as he and Ian joined them. "I don't give out artists' phone numbers or home addresses either, right Karl?"

"True, and it's an excellent policy." Karl shook his head. "You'd be amazed at how many people think it would be okay just to stop in at my studio and watch me work."

She cringed. "Ouch."

"It's not the locals. They couldn't care less what I do, or how I do it. It's the tourists who are always trying to get Ethan to hand out my address." Karl looked at Ian and asked, "So what did you think of Madison?"

"The mermaid?" Ian glanced back over his shoulder at the nearly life-size mermaid carved out of some massive tree trunk. "She's exquisite."

"Yes, she is." Karl's chest seemed to expand. "I named her in honor of that Tom Hanks film."

"*Splash?*"

"That's the one." Karl put his half empty wineglass on a passing waiter's tray. "I spent over a month getting all those scales on her tail just right."

Amber glanced at Madison's tail and tried not to roll her eyes as all three men nodded their head gravely at the importance of that particular undertaking. Karl had spent a month playing with fish woman's ass. She was thankful that Madison's flowing seaweed-shaped hair covered her obviously bare chest or the mermaid might never have made it out of Karl's studio. "Did you use a live model, Karl?"

She had no idea how Karl took massive stumps and trunks of trees and carved some of the most breathtaking sculptures she had ever seen. If he had used a model, the young woman had to have been beautiful beyond belief. Madison had the face of an angel, the grace of a ballerina, and the body of a siren.

"I never use models. They would distract me from the vision."

"What vision?" Ian asked.

"When I look at a piece of wood, I see the wonders beneath. It's the wood that dictates to me what to carve. I only follow the vision." Karl chuckled at Ian's bewildered look. "I don't see the visions all the time, and some pieces of wood take a long time to tell me what it is. I've got this eight-foot-tall trunk that's got a circumference of about five feet sitting in my studio for over a year now. After all that time, I still haven't got a clue as to what it wants to be."

"Karl, may I introduce you to Ian McNeal, Amber's friend from Boston." Ethan slipped into his host role. "Ian, this is Karl James, Misty Harbor's resident sculptor."

"I take it you did the sea horse and the dolphin that's out on the back deck?" Ian shook Karl's hand. "They're magnificent."

"Thank you." Karl nodded toward the stairs. "There's also an old sea captain upstairs."

"Karl's pieces are one of the main reasons I had to get this place. I needed the room, but as it is, I still can't display them all." Ethan glanced across the room, to where his wife, Olivia, was signaling him. "Now, if you would excuse me, I believe the 'little woman' is calling." Ethan winked at Amber.

Amber shook her head at Ethan's teasing. "I'm

telling her you said that. Olivia will hurt you for that one."

Ethan was still chuckling as he walked away.

Karl shook his head. "So, Ian, friend of Amber's from Boston, what do you think of *Balmy Eve*?" Karl nodded toward the painting directly in front of them.

"Honestly?"

"They are the only opinions that matter." Karl glanced between Ian and the oil painting. "I certainly didn't do it, and I don't even know the artist, so you wouldn't be hurting anyone's feelings here."

"I like it." Ian's head tilted slightly. "It shows courage, fortitude, and an unbending strength. My parents' fortieth wedding anniversary is coming up in March, and my brother and I are throwing this big party for them. When I first saw it, I seriously considered purchasing the painting for them. My father loves the sea and has this thing for storms. He's also an ex-military man who would appreciate the strength and the beauty of such a painting."

Amber stared at the painting and wondered what kind of drugs Ian was on. Beauty? What beauty? "What about your mother?"

Ian chuckled. "She'll run screaming from the room and probably disown me."

Karl joined in Ian's laughter. "So, honestly again, who do you think painted it, a man or a woman?"

"A man. Definitely a man." Ian didn't even hesitate.

Karl nodded and looked at her. She shook her head in disagreement. There was something about the painting that was almost haunting in its pain.

"There you are, Amber, we've been looking all over for you." Aunt Grace's voice echoed off the high ceilings. No one noticed. There were just too many people milling around and mingling.

Everyone in town seemed to be in the crowded gallery. Either they came for the free refreshments, or

Misty Harbor was turning into the "cultural center" of the state. Her money would be on the free wine and tiny wieners.

Amber hoped Ethan made enough sales tonight to cover the cost of the wine and hors d'oeuvres that had been circling the entire evening. "Hello, Grace, Clyde." She smiled at the stately man beside her aunt. Clyde Davenport was a worldly gentleman who obviously was smitten, if not dazed, by her flamboyant aunt. She couldn't say what her aunt's feelings were toward Clyde, or any other man she was dating. Grace Berry seemed to be having a blast playing the field, but somehow she didn't think her aunt's heart was in any jeopardy of being broken.

"Hello, Amber, and may I say you look quite lovely this evening." Clyde lightly pressed his lips to the back of one of her hands.

Ian raised a brow at the hand kissing and took a step closer to her. She hid her smile behind a sip of wine. It was the same glass of white wine she had accepted when they had first entered the gallery over an hour ago. The party was winding down, and Grace and her date were just getting here. One had to wonder what they had been up to since Clyde had picked her up four hours ago.

Amber was curious, but she would cut out her own tongue before she would ask. Questioning her aunt would not only signal distrust, but she would suspiciously sound like her mother. The last person she wanted to become was her mother. Her aunt was fifty-four, old enough to make all her own decisions.

She had to give Ian and Karl credit for not blinking an eye at Grace's outfit. The long black skirt, see-through black lace, long-sleeve shirt that was left unbuttoned, and an emerald green sleeveless top were wonderful and perfect for the occasion. She could even forgive the sequined penguin clutch bag her aunt was carrying. The earrings were another matter. Grace had two big green Christmas balls, hooks and all, hanging from her ears. As if that wasn't bad enough, they actually were lit.

Amber stared at her aunt's ears, and asked the obvious question. "Aren't the batteries heavy?"

Grace chuckled and lightly flicked at the balls with a fingertip. "They're solar powered." The balls swung drunkenly back and forth. "No batteries required. I just put them on the windowsill, and presto! They'll stay lit all night."

Clyde, bless his soul, smiled sweetly and patted Grace's hand. "Isn't she remarkable?"

Amber flipped up the collar of her coat, and shrugged. The thick black wool helped block the wind from her ears. She always hated getting her ears cold, and leave it to her to forget a scarf on the coldest night of the year, so far. It didn't matter if Sara's Pond was already frozen over; technically winter hadn't even officially begun. It was going to get a lot colder before they would ring in the new year.

"I did offer to bring the car around so you wouldn't have to be out in this cold." Ian moved to her other side, gently cupped her elbow, and stepped up onto the sidewalk.

"I know you did, but it's only a short walk, and the air will do us good." She moved closer to him and shamelessly used his body as a wind block. "It feels like a cold front is moving in."

"Moving in? Hate to disappoint you, but it's already here." Ian hurried them along.

A moment later she was bundled into his car and waiting for the heater to warm up. She buried her hands deep into the pockets of her coat and studied Ian's handsome profile in the shadowy light. His face was the finest work of art she had seen all night. Ian's broad shoulders and lean, athletic body were the ideal podium to display such perfection. Underneath his expensive suit and polite smile there was a hidden depth. Ian had a sensual depth that women naturally picked up on and of which he seemed totally unaware.

Not for the first time that evening Amber wondered what it would be like to tap into that depth. If only for a moment. If only for a night. Ian McNeal looked like a man who knew how to satisfy a woman.

"Did I grow a second nose or something?" Ian rubbed at his face.

"I was staring, wasn't I. I'm sorry, that was rude of me." She was thankful for the deep shadows within the car, or Ian would surely see her blush.

"Why were you staring?"

"I was trying to figure out what you thought of Misty Harbor and some of its residents," she lied.

Ian flicked the heater switch and lukewarm air blew into the car. "From what I've seen so far, I like both the town and its residents." Ian put the car into gear and pulled out onto the street. "You sure you don't mind if I play hockey tomorrow afternoon?"

"It will be fun to watch. I only saw one game last year, but from what I remember the guys play like they mean it." She felt obligated to warn Ian. "The game was more like a free-for-all than a controlled regulation game. Bodies littered the ice everywhere."

"Great, if you don't play like you mean it, why play?"

"Okay, but it's your body that's going to take the abuse, not mine. I'll be sitting with the rest of the town, watching the game, grilling up food, and drinking hot chocolate." The town really got into the games and there was a slight rivalry between the opposing teams. As far as she knew, while bloodshed occasionally spilled on the ice, it never had been spilled off.

Ian pulled into her driveway, and drove around to

the bottom of the stairs. He turned off the car and un-fastened his seat belt. "I had a great time tonight; thanks for inviting me."

"You're welcome." She didn't remind him that the open house was for anyone. You didn't need a special invitation to get in. She had already thanked him three times tonight for all the help he had been around the shop. While the orders were nowhere near caught up, they had put one big dent into the pile of orders today.

Ian opened his door. "Come on, I'll walk you up."

"You don't have to."

Ian ignored her, walked around to her side of the car, and opened her door. They silently walked up the stairs.

She wasn't looking forward to this part of the date. The awkward good night part. When she had been younger, she never knew how to handle the next few moments. Now that she was older, and hopefully wiser, she figured she'd manage. After all, this was Ian stand-ing on her doorstep, not some stranger.

She dug into her purse. "Would you like to come in?" It was a little after ten—way too early to end a Saturday night date. "I could make some coffee." She slipped the key into the lock. Coffee sounded like a good idea. Maybe they could even build a fire.

"Thanks for the offer, but I really should be going." Ian jammed his hands deeper into his pockets as her door swung open.

No boogey men were waiting for her within. "Oh, okay." She should be thankful that Ian was acting like the perfect gentlemen. Right? "Do you want me to pick you up tomorrow afternoon?" The first game started at one. After a brief rest, there was usually a second game. If the players hadn't been beaten and injured too badly.

"No, I'll pick you up. Say, noon?"

"That works for me." It would also give her a couple of hours at the shop, packing up more orders.

"Great, see you then." Ian turned and hurried down the steps.

Amber stood at the top of the stairs, ignoring the stinging of her frozen ears, and watched as he drove away. Ian acted as if he couldn't get away fast enough.

For the first date, or any other interaction with the opposite sex in eighteen months, it sucked.

Chapter 5

Olivia Wycliffe gently blew across the top of her steaming hot chocolate and said, "He sure does look good out there."

Amber followed her friend's gaze through the lightly falling snow. It was hard to tell who "he" was, but she had a feeling it had to be Olivia's husband, Ethan. The men of the two opposing hockey teams were either clumped together or moving fast. Only the goalies seemed to stay in their position in front of the nets. The rest of the men were skating around the pond either trying to kill each other, or score a goal. From this angle it was hard to tell which.

She cringed as Gunnar Olsen slammed into his twin brother Erik, and both of the married Norwegian hunks went down and slid across the ice. Their booming laughter filled the crisp cold air, along with some cheers and jeers from the sidelines.

"Yes, Olivia"—she tried not to roll her eyes—"Ethan looks great. He's the perfect male specimen." Lovesick newlyweds could wear on one's nerves. Olivia was still in that stage where everything Ethan did was amazing.

"I wasn't referring to Ethan, but he does look exceptionally great this afternoon, if I do say so myself." Olivia's gaze lovingly followed her husband as he sped across the pond and stole the puck from Ned Porter. Olivia let out a cheer. "You go, Ethan!"

This time, Amber did roll her eyes.

Ned, who was the bigger of the two men, didn't take it well. He skated after Ethan with a vengeance. A moment later four men went down in a heap of flailing legs, sharp skates, and groaned curses. Hockey sticks went sliding in every direction. Thankfully, because of the distance, no one could understand what was being muttered and groaned in that pile, but she could hazard a guess. There were a lot of young ears on the sidelines cheering on the melee.

It seemed as if the entire town had turned out for today's match.

She heard Olivia gasp to see her husband go down, but Amber felt her heart actually skip a beat knowing that Ian was somewhere at the bottom of that pile of overly abundant testosterone, razor-sharp skates, and sticks. One minute Ian had been kicking up the freshly fallen snow with his skates, the next he was gone.

Paul Newman, the mayor of Misty Harbor—and the referee of this first game—blew his whistle. Paul might have the famous actor's name, but not his looks. Misty Harbor's mayor looked more like Fred Flintstone than Paul Newman. He also wasn't a very good skater.

Erik Olsen skated over and pulled his brother Gunnar up off the pile. Ned Porter was the next to stand. Ethan slowly got his feet under himself and stood. Ethan flashed his wife a reassuring smile before turning to the only man still down on the ice: Ian. Amber felt nauseated. Ethan and Ned reached down and pulled a grinning Ian to his feet.

She had this sudden urge to whack Ian on the side of his head with his borrowed hockey stick. The man had to have a death wish. Protective gear or not, there was still plenty that could, and usually did, go wrong out on the ice. Why would anyone want to play such a dangerous game?

Ian flashed a smile in her direction before quickly skating back to his position. The mayor dropped the puck between Ethan and Ned. Ethan connected with the puck first, and won the face-off. The game continued as if the latest melee never happened and her heart settled back into its normal rhythm. Ian appeared to be still in one piece.

"Who were you talking about, then?" Amber tried to pick up the conversation with Olivia. She was curious to see who her friend thought was "looking good" this snowy winter day. So far the fresh fallen snow was only about a half an inch deep. In Maine, that didn't even rank as a nuisance. The heavy stuff wasn't due until after midnight.

"Your friend from Boston is doing all right for himself out there." Olivia cradled her hot chocolate between red knitted mittens and continued to watch the game. "He's played hockey before."

"He's from Boston, Olivia. Almost every kid in Boston has played hockey at least once or twice in his life." She felt funny discussing Ian with Olivia. She noticed how everyone on the sidelines just assumed she and Ian were an "item." Nothing could be farther from the truth.

"Ian looks like he played it more than a couple of times." Olivia cringed as Ethan got bodychecked from Erik, but amazingly he didn't lose control of the puck. "Did he play in school?"

"I have no idea." There was a lot about Ian she didn't

know. She had just found out last night that he had an older brother and preferred steak over lobster. Ian also wouldn't eat clams, no matter how they were served.

"I thought you two were friends?" Olivia brushed the light dusting of snow from her lap blanket.

"I knew him in college."

"He didn't play on the college team?"

"Not that I know." She squirmed in her folding canvas chair and stomped her feet a few times to get the blood moving again. Just sitting in the elements, watching the game, was a sure way to freeze to death. She had on two pairs of socks under her boots, and her toes were still going numb.

"Doesn't sound like you two had a very close relationship back then." Olivia polished off the rest of the chocolate.

"We didn't." Maybe Olivia could figure out why she was so attracted to Ian, when he obviously didn't return those feelings. "Ian was James's roommate."

Olivia stopped watching the game and turned toward her. Not even the sound of bodies slamming into each other distracted her attention. "Continue."

"Ian was also the best man at our wedding, and had been James's business partner in the advertising agency I told you about. Ian McNeal was the other M, in the M & M Ad Agency."

"Whoa boy." Olivia first looked stunned, then confused. "So why is he here?"

"Business." She brushed at the snow accumulating on her coat and blanket. "He wanted to deliver the check for James's share of the business to me personally."

"Again, the same question; why is he here?"

"I just told you, to deliver a check." Olivia's brain must be frozen. The goofy purple knit hat her friend was wearing hadn't kept out the cold.

"He delivered it, right?"

"Yeah, on Friday, right after he got into town. He found the shop and me buried under a mountain of orders and suffering from a severe case of bitchiness. The greeting I gave him wasn't what you would consider heartwarming."

"He's still here, Amber." Olivia glanced across the pond to where Ian was sitting on a wooden bench, waiting for someone out on the ice to signal they needed relief. "There's got to be a reason."

"He says he needed to relax. He's taking a vacation."

Olivia snorted. "On the coast of Maine, in November?" Olivia snorted again for good measure. "The man doesn't look insane."

"He's not." Amber watched as Ian skated back out onto the ice at full speed and bodiedchecked Ned Porter. Maybe she should revise that statement. No one sane would try bodychecking Ned when he had that look on his face. "I think he's checking up on me. You know, making sure the little old widow isn't eating cat food and thinking about finding a bridge to jump off."

Olivia's laugh caused a few heads to turn in their direction. "Is that honestly what you think?" Olivia gave her a look that said if Amber admitted to being abducted by aliens, she wouldn't have been more surprised.

"I just told you that it was." Great, she was being laughed at now.

"Who invited him to the gallery's open house last night?"

"I did."

"And he accepted, right?"

"He was there, wasn't he?" A cheer went up as Erik Olsen scored his second goal so far in the game. Ian's team was now down by two. "It wasn't a date. I agreed to show him around the town while he's here. He agreed to help me pack up orders. It's a trade-off, nothing more."

"When did you become so blind that you can't see what's in front of you?" Olivia shook her head.

"Now what are you talking about?"

"I'm talking about the way Ian was looking at you last night."

"Explain?" So far as she knew, Ian hadn't been looking at her in any particular way.

"He watched you the entire night, Amber. I'm not an expert on the male species, but I do know when a man wants a woman, and Ian wanted you last night."

Amber rolled that one around in her mind for a moment and still came up with zero. "You're mistaken. You're confusing Ian with how your husband looks at you. After Ian drove me home, and walked me to the door, I invited him in for coffee. He said thanks but no thanks, and then he left. That doesn't sound like a man who wanted me."

The ref blew his whistle and the game ended. Ian and Ethan's team had lost. The men gathered up their gear from the bench and started skating over to where their family and friends waited.

Olivia stood up and shook out her blanket. "I still think you're wrong."

"And I think those honeymoon stars, which are still in your eyes, are blinding you to reality."

"A person doesn't box up jam all day, or let his body get creamed on the ice, and claim he's relaxing. Ian McNeal isn't here to take a vacation. He's here for one reason, and one reason only, and that reason is you. Hell, I bet you ten to one that he didn't have to hand deliver that check. There is a thing called the U.S. Postal Service, you know."

Amber watched as Ethan and Ian skated across the ice and headed directly for them. For just losing the game, both men looked incredibly happy and were grinning from ear to ear. Maybe their brains had been scrambled during the last skirmish that had erupted minutes before the ref ended the game. She still thought Olivia was wrong, but she'd give it some thought later on, when Ian wasn't two yards away and looking so dangerously adorable all rumpled and disheveled.

There was a certain gleam in Ian's eye, but she couldn't tell if it was because he smelled the pot of chili bubbling away over an open fire nearby, the hamburgers sizzling on a grill someone had brought, or her charming imitation of an overstuffed couch. She had on so many layers of clothes that she could barely get to her feet.

Then again, the sheen in his eye could be due to the effects of someone kneeing him in the face. A red mark was already swelling on his right cheekbone.

Ian was lying in front of the roaring fire with Light, the feline purring machine, perched on his chest. One of Amber's cats seemed to like him, while the other one, Shadow, had disappeared under the bed as soon as he and Amber had entered her apartment. Then again, Light just might like to bask in the heat of the dancing flames, and his chest made a very fine pillow.

He glanced over his shoulder at Amber, who was standing at the kitchen counter shredding cheese. "Are you sure I can't help?" He felt like a slug lying there. A warm, toasty, and contented slug. His feet were finally starting to defrost but every bone in his body still ached. He wasn't looking forward to getting out of bed tomorrow morning. Damn, he was getting old if a couple hours out on the ice did this to his body.

"You did help." Amber bustled about some more. "You got the fire going, and carried up how many loads of firewood?" A jar of something was dumped into a pot, and the burner turned on low. "When it's time, you can set the table."

He had made seven trips up the stairs with his arms loaded with wood. It had taken two trips to restock Amber's wood box next to the fireplace. The other five loads were neatly stacked out on the landing, so Amber wouldn't have to carry the logs up the stairs. "I brought up enough wood to last you a couple of days." He stretched his feet out closer to the fire. "It wasn't as if I had to chop it."

"Ryan Albert, the kid next door, was the one who did that for us." Amber slid a casserole dish into the oven. "We pay him to do odd jobs around the place. All that chopped and neatly stacked wood out there was from two huge trees we lost last winter during an ice storm. One of the trees missed Aunt Grace's house by mere inches. We were two of the lucky ones in town. A lot of people had structural damage, plus the inconvenience of losing electricity for days. We only lost it for one night."

He rolled onto his side, so he could see Amber better. There was something seductively enticing about the way her blue jeans fit. Light, who had tumbled off his chest, strutted away with her tail in the air. "Did you spend the night here, or at your aunt's?"

"I gathered up Light and Shadow and we had a sleepover at my aunt's. Grace's house has five fireplaces, but only three are safe to use." Amber poured hot coffee into two mugs and carried them into the living room. She added sugar and cream to hers, but left his black, just the way he took it.

He tried not to groan as he sat up.

Amber handed him one of the cups, and sat down on the floor, using the armoire that held her computer and all her business papers as a backrest. "Since Grace's dining room and living room open up into the rest of the house, we bunked down in the back den, which has double pocket doors, so the heat stayed in the room." Amber stretched her toes toward the warmth of the flames. "It was one cold and scary night. I never heard the wind howl like that before in my life. For a while there I thought the whole house was going to come crashing down on top of us. Grace was stretched out on the davenport, snoring up a storm, while I kept investigating every noise. When the first tree came down, I nearly had heart failure."

"I can imagine." He took a sip of coffee and felt the warmth of the drink pool in his stomach. The first game of hockey had been great and exciting. Even the outdoor picnic had been fun, along with filling. Halfway through the second game he felt as if he had been beat into the ground, and the cold had finally taken its toll.

Of course it hadn't helped that when he hadn't been playing, he had been sitting on the bench with an ice pack slapped onto his eye. At least the swelling hadn't gotten worse. "Did anyone check up on you two?" He didn't want to think about two women alone on a night like that.

"A couple of the neighbors came over when the trees went down." Amber cupped her coffee between her hands and stared into the fire. "By daylight we had a swarm of men in the yard with buzzing chain saws."

"Sounds like everyone in town looks out for everyone else." He noticed how friendly everyone seemed to be, even Erik Olsen, who every time he knocked Ian onto his ass during the hockey game, always shouted an apology as he skated away with the puck. He wasn't sure if he should hate the Norwegian, or award him a Mr. Congeniality award.

"When a nor'easter hits, everyone pulls together to make sure no one goes without. Neighbors help neighbors. It's the way of life here."

He couldn't even tell her who lived across the hall from him in his apartment building. Sometimes he saw a middle-aged man with a bulging briefcase. Occasionally he spotted a tired-looking woman who usually had grocery bags and a scowl upon her face. They might have been a married couple, but he had never once seen them together. So much for his neighbors helping each other. They didn't even know each other.

"So you like living in Maine? You don't miss Boston?" All these months he had been worrying about Amber, and how well she had been adjusting to the coast of Maine. He wouldn't classify Misty Harbor as some backward town, but he also couldn't see it as a thriving cultural center either or in the same league as a major city. James had once told him that Amber was a social butterfly who loved flittering from one party to the next as much as James had, and that was what had made their marriage so strong. Common interests. Common goals. James had once declared that he and Amber had the perfect marriage. Ian never saw anything to dispute that statement. Now he was having a hard time relating this jean wearing, jam packing Amber to the one James had always bragged about back in Boston. Amber's thick and colorful socks, which had puffins printed all over them, were throwing him for a loop.

"I don't miss the town as much as some of the shops." Amber reached down and scratched Shadow, who had come out of hiding and climbed up onto her lap, behind the ears. "There're a lot of people back there who I miss, and wouldn't mind seeing again."

"Ever think about moving back, especially now that you got your aunt's jam company up and running again?"

"Not even for a moment." Amber chuckled as Shadow stretched up and rubbed the top of his head under her chin. "Misty Harbor fits me. I'm comfortable here."

The computer armoire had its doors wide open and was twice as messy as it had been yesterday when he'd come in to pick Amber up for the gallery open house. Today the bed hadn't been made, and there were clothes draped over a small chair near the bed. A magazine was lying facedown by the overstuffed chair, and an empty coffee cup was sitting on the coffee table. Amber obviously didn't obsess over her housekeeping.

Seeing her sprawled near the fire, with her baggy gold sweater and silly puffin socks, he had to admit she did look comfortable. Steam drifted up from her cup, and her cheeks were still flushed from the cold. When she had yanked off her hat earlier, she had run her fingers through her hair, but never once looked into a mirror. He liked that about her. He especially liked the freckles that were scattered across her nose and cheeks.

"So what's for dinner?" He could smell something cooking, but had a hard time placing it. When Amber had asked him to dinner, he hadn't really thought about what she would make. Now that his stomach was rumbling, he was curious.

"Macaroni and cheese and stewed tomatoes." Amber gave him a stern look over the rim of her cup. "You aren't one of those men who has to have meat at every meal, are you?"

"I think the two hamburgers and the bowl of chili I had between games boosted my cholesterol sufficiently for one day." He tried not to laugh at her stern look. Amber looked as threatening as a pixie. A gorgeous green-eyed pixie.

"I'd say." Amber chuckled as Light climbed into Ian's lap. "I think you made a friend there."

His fingers automatically started to scratch the top of Light's head. "She just likes the attention."

Before she could respond, the phone rang. Amber groaned and got to her feet. "Excuse me for a moment."

Ian continued to drink his coffee and pet Light. Shadow sat in the spot Amber had dumped him and stared after her in disgust. He couldn't blame the cat. If he had been sitting in Amber's lap getting scratched, he'd be upset too, having the phone interrupt them.

"Hi, Mom," Amber said as she picked up the phone and glanced at the Caller ID box.

He could hear the weary sigh in Amber's voice, and wondered if her mother had picked it up, too. Amber didn't seem too pleased to be talking to dear old Mom.

"No, I have no idea where Aunt Grace is. I told you before, I'm not her keeper." Amber stirred the pot on the rear burner.

"No, I haven't seen her since last night at the open house at the gallery." Amber's voice lightened considerably when she added, "She was with Clyde Davenport and seemed to be enjoying herself immensely."

Whatever Amber's mother said to that had Amber slamming down the lid to the pot a little too loudly.

"I'm cooking dinner, and yes, I enjoyed myself last night." Amber glanced over to him and gave him a fleeting guilty smile. Amber started to load dishes into the sink and turned the water on full blast as her mother talked on.

"Priscilla Patterson must have been one very busy lady." Amber's voice lowered, but he could still hear her over the sound of rushing water. "How old am I, Mother?"

Amber was silent for a moment.

"And how old is Grace?" After another pause Amber asked, "Don't you think we're old enough to make our own decisions?"

He thought he heard the word vulnerable, but he wasn't sure. Short of cupping his hands over his ears, there wasn't a whole bunch he could do not to hear this conversation.

"Do you want me to tell Grace to call you?" Amber positioned the phone between her ear and shoulder and started to scrub the cups in the sink. "You could try leaving her a message on her answering machine."

A moment later Amber left the sink, and with bubbles clinging to her hands walked across the kitchen to where the phone was connected to the wall. "Yeah, you're right. There are messages there." Amber rolled her eyes and marched back to the sink. "Of course I didn't check. If I would have known they were from you, I would have called you back."

Amber's mother must have been mollified. "No, Grace won't be home tonight. The Methodist church choir is singing up at the lighthouse. Grace is scheduled to work either the bake sale table, or the greens table. I forget which."

Amber chuckled. "No, Mom, they haven't let her join the choir yet. They keep giving her all these other jobs to do, so she won't have time to practice singing with them." Amber rinsed the dishes and stacked them in the rack, next to the sink. "You know Reverend Winslow would never tell her that."

Amber wiped her hands on a towel. "When I see her tonight I'll tell her to call you first thing in the morning." Amber looked slightly embarrassed. "Yes, Mom, I will wear my hat and gloves. I've got to run now; I'll talk to you later." Amber walked back over to the wall mount, and softly said, "Yes, Mom, I love you, too," before hanging up the phone.

He gave her a big grin. "I take it that was your mom?"

"Yeah, doing her triple daily checking up on us call." Amber reached over and hit the play button of her answering machine. The first message was from Amber's mother: "Amber, are you there? Pick up if you're there. Where are you? It's only nine o'clock on a Sunday morning. I know the shop isn't open. Call me."

The second message was also from Amber's mother, but this time she sounded anxious. "Amber, where are you? Pick up. Priscilla just called me, and she said you were out on a date last night? Is this true? Who is he? Priscilla said she's never seen him before. Call me."

Amber glanced over at him. "This is the time where sane men go running from the apartment, never to be seen with the daughter of a meddling mother ever again."

He laughed as he got to his feet. "Have you thought about an unlisted phone number?"

"More than once." She hit the button one more time, to hear the last message.

Her mother's voice came in loud and clear. "A hockey player! You're dating one of the hockey players? Hockey's a rough and dangerous sport—that means it's played by rough and dangerous men. What are you thinking? You never should have left Boston. Boston has . . ." Amber hit the delete button, and Gladys Donovan's voice stopped in mid-screech.

"Well, that was embarrassing." Amber handed him two plates and some silverware.

He thought it was sweet the way her mother still worried about her. He imagined that once he had children, he would continue to worry about them long after they were old enough to make their own decisions. Long after they wanted him to butt out of their lives. He took the plates to the small table and started to set the table. "I don't know, Amber. I kind of like being thought of as a 'rough and dangerous' man."

Amber snorted. "That sounds like something James would have said."

He froze in horror, with a fork in one hand, a knife in the other. "Oh, God, Amber, I'm sorry."

She watched as Ian's face paled. "For what?" The two cans of soda she had just gotten from the refrigerator were cold in her hands.

"For bringing up James." Ian slowly placed the silverware on the table.

"You didn't bring him up, I did." She didn't see what the big deal was about.

"I know, it's just"—Ian seemed to search for the right word, but came up empty—"awkward I guess."

"Why?" She put the soda on the table and got down two glasses. "James was my husband, and your business partner, along with being your friend. It would seem strange if his name didn't come up once in a while."

"I guess." Ian still looked distinctly uncomfortable with the subject.

She poured the hot stewed tomatoes into a bowl and set it on the table along with a loaf of Italian bread and some butter. She wondered if Ian thought she would start crying and wailing into the night if they talked about James. She carried the hot casserole dish to the center of the table. "Dinner's ready."

She settled into her chair and shook her head at Ian. The man looked guilty. "Relax, Ian, I'm not going to cry."

"Cry?" Ian's expression went from guilty to horror in a flash.

She chuckled. "I said I'm *not* going to cry." She served herself some of the macaroni and cheese and then passed Ian the spoon. "James had been a very big part of my life. I thought it might be good to talk about him with someone who had known him, like I did." *Who had loved him as much as I had.*

The look of horror remained on Ian's face as gooey

strings of cheese followed the spoon. "You want to talk about James?"

By Ian's expression she guessed she just had committed a faux pas in the male-female relationship process. Rule number one: no talking about past husbands. "Not really." She gave Ian a rueful smile and passed him the stewed tomatoes. "I'm more interested in how the business is doing. You said you hired a couple of new employees, right?"

"Actually I hired six new employees this year. Business has grown by over thirty percent, and we were starting to fall behind." Ian dug into his dinner, and into the new topic of conversation. "We landed a huge stock broker account and a really big seafood account just last month."

She relaxed and started in on her own meal. Talking advertising she not only understood, but could hold up her end of the conversation without really trying. It had been James's life.

The discussion flowed easily and comfortably while they ate. She noticed that while Ian talked about the business and the employees, he very seldom mentioned his own accomplishments. Ian was too busy praising everyone else, from the simplest task to landing a huge account.

It was Ian who changed the subject by declaring, "This is delicious, Amber," while helping himself to another serving of the macaroni and cheese.

"What? You didn't think I knew how to cook?" She chuckled as she polished off the last of her meal. She would have loved to go back for a second helping, but two things were stopping her. There was that bake sale up at the lighthouse tonight and she knew from experience just how tempting that was going to be. The Methodist Women's Guild consisted of the best bakers in town. Every bake sale they tried to outdo each other in both quality and quantity. A plate of brownies had been known to weigh as much as five pounds.

Also, those twenty pounds she had gained since she had last seen Ian, were playing heavily on her mind, as well as her butt. No more seconds until she could zip up a couple more pair of jeans hanging in her closet, and definitely no more chocolate shakes from Krup's.

"So, Ian, where did you learn to play hockey like that?" Ian might not have been the best player out there today on the ice, but he had managed to hold his own. In Misty Harbor, that was saying something. From the way the men were bantering with him during the break between games, she knew he had earned their respect with his skills on the ice.

"I learned from my older brother, Sean, but I didn't join a team until I was in high school."

"Did you play in college?" She didn't think he had, but since she hadn't met him till his senior year, there was always that possibility. There was so much she didn't know about Ian.

"No, I wanted to concentrate on my studies, so I stayed away from sports." Ian twirled a string of cheese around his fork, and then popped it into his mouth. "What's with the two Viking gods, Erik and Gunnar?"

"What do you mean?" There was no getting around it. Erik and Gunnar did look like a pair of Viking gods from old.

"Why aren't they playing for the Boston Bruins or at least the U.S.A. Olympic team? They were both great out there. I never saw anything like that, let alone try to skate against one of them. If both of them were on the same team, no one would be able to beat them."

She had to laugh. "You might have noticed that they weren't allowed on the same team. The men of Misty Harbor had put an end to that one, just after the first game they played together. Whipped the seasoned veterans twelve to zip, and they hadn't even been trying hard."

"Ouch."

"I'd say. A lot of pride took a pounding that day, but now Erik and Gunnar mostly go after each other out there on the ice."

Ian's hand went to the seat of his pants and rubbed at a very tender spot where he had connected with the ice more than once this afternoon. "I'm guessing 'mostly' is the key word there."

Chapter 6

Grace Berry knew when she was being snubbed, and she was being snubbed royally by the three women at the other end of the greens tent. Priscilla, Norma, and Ruth were trying their best to ignore her. She should be the better woman, and ignore them back, but some perverse little demon sitting on her shoulder wouldn't allow them the satisfaction.

The white canvas tent that the church had erected was protecting her and Connie Franklin, the other helper, from the wind, but not from the cold. Thankfully the heavy snow was holding off until later tonight. The two inches or so of snow that was already lying on the ground wouldn't deter anyone who wanted to come to the holiday fund-raiser from coming. Down Easterners were made of stronger stuff than that.

Kreider's Christmas Tree Farm had really outdone itself this year. While there weren't any trees to purchase tonight, Kreider's had donated, at their cost, plenty of fresh pine wreaths, swags, and garland. The Women's Guild had spent the last week adding some decorative touches to a lot of merchandise. She, herself, had spent three afternoons and two evenings down at the church decorating many of them. She had spent this morning, after church services, and all of this afternoon helping to set up the displays so everything was shown to the best advantage.

In all modesty, her wreaths and bows were the best of the bunch. Even Reverend Winslow had told her so. Of course that had been said confidentially, so she couldn't go bragging, but anyone who wasn't legally blind could see the difference between her wreaths and, say, Priscilla's. It didn't matter that she had gotten to the church by seven o'clock this morning to doctor up some of the wreaths, before they were to be boxed up for the ride up to the lighthouse grounds. She had pulled a couple of them back from the brink of death, but some had been hopeless.

Grace winked at Connie, who was helping Olivia Wycliffe pick out some garland for her mantel and banisters, and walked over to where Priscilla, Norma, and Ruth were standing. Connie, who had witnessed the snubbing and knew how ridiculous the whole situation was, chuckled.

"See how I used birds as a theme on this one?" Norma proudly pointed out one of her wreaths.

Grace held back a laugh by sheer will. So far the women hadn't notice she was standing directly behind them. Norma's wreath had been one of the ones she had saved. Of course, Norma hadn't noticed the changes. Norma's version of a bird theme was the same as Alfred Hitchcock's. The more birds the scarier. Norma had wired a flock of feathered friends, six yards of ribbon, one fake nest, and a birdhouse the size of shoebox to the poor pine wreath. The wreath had been beyond scary. Alfred would have been proud.

Grace had spent a large portion of her time untwisting wire and deflocking the wreath.

"I love how you put the nest right in the center of the

bow, Norma," Priscilla said. "And that birdhouse is just adorable. The perfect touch."

Norma, a bird-like woman with a sharp nose and tiny eyes, stared at the wreath. "Funny, I thought the house had been bigger. You know, something the birds could fit into."

Grace rolled her eyes, but didn't comment. Norma always got on her nerves for the simple fact the woman barely weighed a hundred pounds, yet she ate like a horse. If she ate the amount of food that Norma devoured, Lawrence Blake would be able to use her as an anchor on his whale watching boat. Hell, she'd be one of the whales the tour boat went looking for.

"I like the one I did in the red and gold the best," Ruth said, not to be outdone by Norma. "It would look wonderful on my front door." Ruth stared at the wreath she had made days before, as if trying to figure out what was different about it.

Grace could tell her that the string of gold beads hadn't been on her original version. Neither had the holly branches with the pretty red berries. Of course a couple of the red and gold ornaments that had been wired on were now gone, and the bow had been redone. On the whole it hadn't been too bad of a wreath; it had just needed a little tweaking.

"Are you going to buy it?" Priscilla asked as she studied some of the other wreaths hanging on the PegBoards positioned around the tent.

"I believe I am." Ruth took the wreath off the hook and smiled. "I'm also going to get two of those swags with the matching bows."

Grace was about to be noticed, so she jumped in on their conversation. "Glad to hear it, Ruth." She held out her hand for the wreath. "Let me hold that for you, while you go chose the swags."

"Oh, I didn't see you standing there, Grace." Ruth looked guilty about something.

She widened her smile and poured on the charm. "I'm the graceful one in the family." She winked at Ruth. "That's why they call me Grace."

Ruth shyly smiled as she handed over the wreath. "Thank you, Grace. How's business so far?"

"Doing a booming job. The cold hasn't kept anyone home that I know about." She nodded to Norma's bird wreath. "If you want that one, Norma, you better snatch it up now. The mayor was here earlier, and he seemed taken to it, but he wanted his wife's opinion first." She wasn't telling a lie. The mayor had liked the bird wreath, along with four other ones. "I love what you did with the birds, Norma. I must say it was very creative."

"Why, thank you, Grace." Norma's thin lips curved into a small smile. "I don't know. Would it seem selfish of me to buy my own wreath, knowing how much the mayor loved it?"

"Absolutely not. It's first come, first served." She purposely glanced at some of the other wreaths. "There're plenty of others for him and his wife to choose from." Which was the truth. She wasn't looking forward to boxing up all the unsold greens, and then trying to sell them at next week's Christmas bazaar. The reverend had put her in charge of the greens portion of the fund-raiser, and she was determined to sell every last pine needle.

"Grace is right, Norma. Buy your wreath," Pricilla said as she straightened out one of the wreaths that had been knocked crooked. "Look, both of mine are still here. The mayor could buy one of them."

All four women stared at the two wreaths hanging at the far end of the Peg-Board. Grace felt a twinge of guilt for hanging them in the shadows, but there hadn't been anything she could have done to save the poor things. "I love that color combination you used Priscilla. Blue and silver is one of my favorites."

It was the truth, and Priscilla had used them on one

of the wreaths. Priscilla had hot-glued blue ornaments all over the poor wreath and then she had used silver glitter spray, and sprayed every inch of the thing. Grace couldn't touch the wreath without leaving behind huge patches of green pine. She had redone Priscilla's huge silver and blue bow, but all that had managed to do was draw more attention to the poor thing. It looked like a kindergartener had decorated the wreath.

"Really?" Priscilla's ample chest seemed to expand to an alarming proportion. "I think I prefer the green on green theme of the other one, myself."

Green ribbon, green bows, green ornaments, green stars, and green beads covered every square inch of the pine wreath. If the lack of oxygen didn't wither and kill the pine before Christmas day, the amount of hot glue Priscilla had used to hold the whole thing together would. "The green has its charm, too." She'd be hard-pressed to name it, but she'd think of something if asked.

Norma and Ruth both looked like they wanted to ask.

"You know what," Priscilla said and she took the green on green wreath off the board, "I think I'll take this one. It matches the green on my front door."

It was on the tip of her tongue to tell Priscilla to buy the silver and blue one, and ship it to her best friend and current phone buddy, Gladys. Priscilla was calling her sister a couple of times every day, and telling her everything that went on in town. From who Grace was going out with to whom said what to whom. Grace had been putting up with Gladys's long-distance advice, concerns, and rude behavior for one simple reason. She truly believed Gladys did love her, and was only doing what any older sister would do: try to protect her little sister.

Today, for the first time, she not only started to

doubt Gladys's love, but her sanity. When she had run home late this afternoon, to grab a quick bite to eat and to get into some warmer clothes, Gladys had called. That conversation hadn't been about Grace's love life, or the embarrassment Gladys was feeling, thinking her baby sister, at the ripe old age of fifty-four, was painting their hometown red and dating any man who happened to be wearing pants. Gladys had jumped right in on a more serious topic—Amber.

Priscilla had called Gladys and told her about Amber being seen at the gallery's open house last night, and today's hockey game, with the same man. Gladys had wanted all the details about her daughter's life. For the first time that she could remember, Grace had told her to butt out, and slammed down the phone.

The sad truth was, if it wasn't Priscilla feeding Gladys all the information, someone else would. Gladys had a lot of childhood friends in town. Currently Grace was on the short end of the stick when it came to female friends. The men were coming out of the woodwork but most of the women, even the married ones, were feeling threatened. It was as if someone had taken out a full page ad in the local paper saying: "Caution, Single Female On the Loose, Lock Up Your Husbands, Ladies."

As if there weren't enough single men in Misty Harbor to fill every seat on Lawrence Blake's whale watching boat, and then some.

Priscilla, Norma, and Ruth were some of the women who took the threat seriously. Each and every one of them had already celebrated their silver anniversary years ago. None of their husbands would win the Sean Connery look-alike contest, or even place in the Bill Gates wallet test. None of the swinging trio of grouchy old fishermen had a romantic bone in their body.

In other words, she couldn't think of a single reason why anyone would try to steal their precious scrawny husbands. Priscilla, Ruth, and Norma were a bunch of insecure housewives who obviously had nothing better to worry about.

Let them try kissing their husbands good-bye one morning, and then the next time you see him, he's lying in some darn coffin wearing his best Sunday suit and the tie you had bought him for Christmas one year, that he had never worn.

"Grace, are you all right?" asked Ruth, who was staring at her funny.

She blinked back the sudden desire to cry and mustered up a small smile. "I'm fine. Just mind wandering for a moment." She put Ruth's wreath in her left hand, and took Norma's and Priscilla's in her right. "Let me go put these up front on the table while you ladies go look at the swags and garland. We have plenty to choose from."

She hurried away before she could make a complete fool of herself and give Priscilla a reason to rush home and call Gladys again. She would hate to see Priscilla's phone bill. After placing the wreaths on the table, she stepped outside of the tent and walked toward the cliff. She looked up at the black sky and its shining stars. *Oh, Howard, you must think I'm a silly old fool.*

Way out over the ocean a star seemed to twinkle back. She knew she was imagining it, because scientists would tell you that stars couldn't twinkle, blink, or even flicker. Her heart told her that Howard was listening.

She had to believe that Howard was still around, watching over her. That he understood how lonely she was without him. That he would approve of her dating, and even possibly finding someone to spend the rest of her life with. It wasn't as if she would be replacing him, because he wasn't around to be replaced. She just didn't want to go through the rest of her alone. *You understand, don't you, sweetheart?*

Another star winked. Or maybe it was the tears in her eyes.

"Hey, Gracie, you okay?" A deep rusty-sounding voice pulled her from her musing.

She turned and stared at the man beside her. Abraham Martin was looking at her as if she had been talking to herself, or possibly a ghost. She was pretty sure her one-sided conversations with Howard were in her head, but who knew for sure. Crazy people were always the last ones to know that they're crazy.

"I'm fine, Abe. Yourself?" She had known Abraham Martin her whole life. He had been two years ahead of her at school, and in a town the size of Misty Harbor, you might as well had said you were classmates. Abe was a crusty old bachelor who had never married and still lived at home with his mother. He was a lobster fisherman who loved his boat and the sea more than anything on land. Abe never once bowed to public opinions, and she always admired that in him. He was hardworking, honest, and kind to his mother.

The years hadn't been kind to Abe, but then again, she didn't know too many people they had been kind to. She surely didn't look like her high school graduation picture.

Tonight Abe was wearing a thick red and black plaid coat, which had probably been around since the depression, or at least the year he had purchased his truck. Abe's ancient pickup truck had been classed as a hazardous waste site by the EPA back in ninety-two. A black knitted hat covered his growing bald spot.

"Can't complain." Abraham glanced at the tent and the group of women standing there staring at them. Abraham shuffled his booted feet and jammed his hands deeper into the pockets of his coat. "Mom sent me up here to buy a wreath for the front door. She comes every year, but she's not feeling herself tonight."

She walked beside Abe, back to the tent, and was relieved to get out of the wind. "What's wrong? Has she seen Doctor Sydney?" Abe's mother was into her eighties and one of those sweet old ladies who was nice to everyone. Mamie Martin never had a bad word to say about anyone.

"It's just a cough, but she didn't want it to turn into anything else, so she's staying nice and warm by the fire at home." Abraham looked at the Peg-Boards full of decorated wreaths. "She said to make sure I got one of yours, because she loved the one you did last year. She also said to make sure it has red in it. Red's her favorite color."

"You're in luck." She waved her mitten-covered hand in the direction of the displays. "You came early, and we have plenty left to choose from." Her purple mittens had a big brown moose knitted onto the back. They matched her hat and scarf. "Do you think she would like something simple and more on the country side or something frilly, with lots of beads and a fancier bow?"

"Country, definitely." Abraham walked up and down the makeshift aisles and looked each wreath over, paying special attention to any one that had a lot of red on it. "What about this one? Did you make this one?"

She had to smile at the wreath Abe was looking at. "Yes, I made that one." It also happened to be her favorite one of the bunch. It really wasn't what anyone would consider country style, but it wasn't one of the frillier Victorian ones, either. The gold and red decorations, which she had wired onto the wreath, were at the minimal. It was the gorgeous and quite elaborate bow that made the wreath. She had used five different ribbons and even some gold beads to make that bow. "You have excellent taste, Abe."

"I do?" Abraham seemed quite pleased with the compliment.

"This happens to be my favorite one." She carefully

took the wreath off the board and laid it into a box for him to carry. "Mamie is going to love it." She tried to ignore the trio of women staring at her and Abe.

Priscilla, Ruth, and Norma's mouths fell open when Abraham pulled out his wallet and paid her for the wreath. Abe had the reputation of being a tightwad with his money. Seeing Abe pay for something as inessential as a Christmas wreath was on the same level as Ebenezer Scrooge buying that Christmas goose for Tiny Tim's family.

Abraham picked up the box. "Thank you, Gracie." Abraham knew the trio of old biddies was listening to his every word. A spark of mischief gleamed in his eyes when he added, "Mom always said that you have the best taste in town."

"That's awful sweet of Mamie." Grace tried not to chuckle, but it was hard. "Since she's feeling a bit under the weather, why don't you stop at the bake sale table, and pick her up something sweet to nibble on. I know your mother has a sweet tooth." She had a hard time picturing Abe cooking a nice hot meal for his mother. Mamie would be the queen of her kitchen, and Abe was probably only allowed in it to eat. "They're also selling some homemade soup over in the coffee tent. I hear the clam chowder is especially good. Nothing will pick your mother up faster than a bowl of nice warm soup on a night like this."

"That's a great idea, Gracie." Abe nodded to the trio. "Ladies."

All three women watched Abraham as he walked away, and then they turned to her. "My, *Gracie*," said Priscilla, "I didn't realize that you knew Abraham so well."

"No better than you, Pris." She smiled charmingly, knowing that Priscilla hated having her name shortened. "You, after all, were in all his classes at school. You graduated the same time he did, that was two years be-

fore my class, right?" She gave herself two extra points
for the added age slam.

It was a shame. Three women who had nothing better to do with their time or brain matter. To think, if all
three had dedicated their time, energy, and intelli-
gence to something productive, they might have discovered the cure for the common cold, or at least how to
get stubborn blueberry stains out of carpets.

"So ladies, did you find everything you wanted?"
asked Connie Franklin. "How about I ring you up,
Norma? I think the choir is starting to gather, and I'm
sure they wouldn't want to do without your beautiful
voice."

Norma started to flutter about, like a bird. "Oh, my,
I've got to hurry." For an amazing bird-like tiny woman,
Norma had a powerfully wonderful voice.

Grace added up Ruth's purchases and neatly placed
them in a large box. Connie handled Priscilla's things.
Not to be outdone by each other, all three purchased
one of their own wreaths, and two swags. All three
women hurried out into the night clutching their boxes
against the wind.

Connie chuckled as the women blended in with another group of people. "I hear Priscilla's still reporting
in to your sister every day."

"Does the whole town know?" So much for airing the
family's dirty underwear in public. She might as well
strip naked and go running up Main Street. That would
give the town something really big to talk about.

"Afraid so." Connie started to reposition some of the
wreaths so there weren't any empty spaces on the display boards. "Gordon Hanley, over at the Pen and Ink,
is even taking odds on who and when you'll kill first,
your sister or Priscilla."

She had to chuckle. Gordon took odds on anything.
The man should have been a bookie in Las Vegas. "You
place any money?"

"Maybe a five fell out of my pocket the last time I was in his shop." Connie appeared very casual about the fact she was gambling illegally.

"On?"

"You taking Gladys out, before Priscilla." Connie hung up a couple more swags while she draped an eight-foot-long piece of garland over the back of one of the boards. "Everyone knows that Priscilla is just looking for acceptance from anyone who would give it to her. Gladys played on that need, and is using her."

She couldn't argue that point. Priscilla wasn't worth going to jail for. Her sister was another matter entirely. "So when am I supposed to do the deed?" Maybe she'd make Connie a rich woman.

"My money's riding on December eighteenth."

"Why the eighteenth?" She straightened out a bunch of bows. Some gusts of wind were making their way into the shelter of the tent and playing havoc with the bows.

"The week before Christmas is always the worst. Everyone is rushing around trying to finish their shopping, the wrapping, and the baking. There are parties to go to, hairdresser appointments, and a thousand little details that need to be handled. I figured the stress alone will push you over the edge."

She chuckled along with Connie. "I can't fault your reasoning."

Her amusement slowly faded as she spotted her niece, Amber, and Ian making their way toward the tent. Even bundled up against the elements, they made a striking couple together. By the envious glances being cast in their direction, she wasn't the only one who thought so.

Ian was protectively close to Amber, but not quite touching, just blocking the worst of the wind. She liked that quality about Ian. The more time she spent with him, the more she liked him. She wasn't blind or stupid. She noticed that spark of friction whenever Ian and Amber were in the same room. She saw the way he looked at her, when he thought no one was noticing. It was an interesting development, considering Ian's relationship with Amber's late husband.

The truly amazing part was, if she wasn't mistaken, Amber was looking back. Hallelujah, her niece was returning to the land of the living.

When Amber first came to live with her, she was like some wounded animal in her grief. Amber had hid from everyone and buried herself in the job of saving her aunt's jam business. They had made one sad-looking pair, the two grieving widows of Spruce Street. Over time, Amber started to get out more, got involved with the community, and made some friends. But her niece never once showed any signs of being interested in a man.

At first she had been worried about the amount of time Amber spent either in front of the computer, or down at the shop. She slowly came to realize, while she had lost interest in the business as a way to handle her own grief and distance herself from some memories of Howard, her niece embraced the challenge.

When she had been ready to test the dating waters, it had been Amber who encouraged her, while Gladys had been appalled by the very thought. Her niece hadn't been ready to test those same waters, and she hadn't pushed her.

Amber had been all business, until Ian McNeal showed up in town. For the first time since losing her husband, Amber was having some fun. She was getting out, and causing a stir in little boring Misty Harbor.

Bless her soul; Amber was just like her dear old Aunt Grace.

Grace chuckled as Amber and Ian entered the tent. Gladys must be having a stroke down there in Rhode Island.

"What's so funny, Grace?" Amber gave her a funny look.

"Nothing, just thinking." She smiled at the man standing next to her niece. "Hello, Ian. I heard you did pretty well out there on the ice today." There was a slight red mark high on his cheekbone, but beyond that, he didn't appear to have any broken bones.

"I didn't let the Vikings kill me, if that counts for anything," Ian said.

"Careful there," Connie said, "that's my son-in-law you're talking about."

"Ian," Amber said, "this is Connie Franklin. Her daughter Maggie is married to Gunnar." Amber moved to the side to allow room for more browsers to enter the tent. "Connie, this is Ian McNeal, a friend of mine from Boston."

Grace noticed that the browsers seemed more interested in what Amber was saying than looking at the wreaths. Lord help them all if there was a weak link in the small town gossip chain.

"Nice to meet you, Ian. Gunnar said he'd take you on his team any day." Connie gave him a wink. "Now if you will excuse me, I'll go see if I can help Janet and Sandi find anything to their liking."

Grace watched as Connie expertly maneuvered Janet and Sandi to the other side of the tent and started in on a sales pitch guaranteed to have both women walking out of the tent carrying boxes. Grace turned her attention back to Amber and Ian. "I was wondering when you two would show up." She'd been wondering a lot about these two, but once again she was trying to be the better woman. "Did you guys have dinner yet? I hear the clam chowder over in the refreshment tent is excellent."

"We just ate, Grace. I made my specialty, macaroni and cheese." Amber looked around at all the greens with interest. "Show me what you have in the way of garland."

"What are you planning on doing with it?" Garland she could handle.

"Laying it across the mantel on my fireplace. It's four feet across." Amber walked farther into the tent. Ian followed slowly, his gaze taking in everything.

"I also need a wreath for the door."

"Those we have plenty of." Grace was happy to see Amber get into the spirit of the holiday a little more. Last year, Amber had still been using her guest room, and had only halfheartedly helped decorate the house and the tree. Grace hadn't blamed her, but she still wanted the house to look festive for the holidays. Two more people entered the tent. "The garland is hanging by size"—she waved a hand toward the back of the tent—"and all the wreaths we have are on display. Just take down the one you want."

"What about for your house?" Amber looked at a particularly beautiful wreath. "How about if I pick up your greens while I'm here? Ian can help me carry it all back to the car."

"Normally, I would say great, but I'm going to wait and see what's left over. I'll take what's left." She lowered her voice and whispered, "It's not like I can't redo it." She stared at Priscilla's blue and silver monstrosity. "Well, then again."

Her niece followed her gaze, but couldn't manage to conceal her chuckle. "Let me know if you change your mind. I was picturing something a little less, glittery."

Grace didn't want to think about having Priscilla's wreath hanging on her front door. Someone had to buy it, and knowing Priscilla, she would be driving around town until she spotted it on someone's door. Grace just didn't want it to be her door.

Connie was finishing up with Sandi and Janet when Abraham Martin walked back into the tent. He was carrying a box filled with assorted Styrofoam cups. Abe nodded to the women, but kept on walking until he stopped directly in front of her. "Gracie."

"Abe?" She was fifty-four years old, and he was still calling her by the name she went by in elementary school: Gracie. "Did you forget something?"

"Nope." Abraham shifted the box to one hand, and pulled out a cup with the other. He handed her that cup, and then reached for another.

Bewildered, she took that cup, too, when he handed it to her. "What's this?"

"Something to keep you warm while you work." He passed her a plastic spoon. "One's that clam chowder that you said was so good, the other is hot chocolate." Abraham nodded to everyone, turned, and walked right back out of the tent.

Grace felt everyone turn and stare at her in open shock. She couldn't blame them. Abraham Martin had just bought her dinner. It was the sweetest, most unexpected thing he had ever done for her. She hadn't even gotten the chance to thank him.

She hurried to the opening of the tent and caught sight of Abraham making his way toward the parking lot. She yelled at the top of her lungs, "Hey, Abe!"

Abraham stopped and turned, but he didn't yell back.

She had the attention of half an acre of people, and all of the Methodist choir, including the reverend. Living in a fish bowl was playing havoc with her dating life. "Thanks!"

Abraham nodded his head once, and if she wasn't mistaken, he might have smiled before he turned and continued on his way.

Chapter 7

Ian looked all the way down to the bottom of the steep hill and then back at the woman standing beside him. "I don't know who's crazier, me for agreeing to this, or you for suggesting it."

Amber laughed. "What? You've never been sledding before?"

"Not down a slope called *Suicide Hill*." A string of bare light bulbs was strung through the trees edging the course. The distant hum of a generator, that supplied the lights, could be faintly heard above all the shouting and noise. Off to the side was a much smaller hill, designed for little children and rational adults. It was virtually deserted at this hour. Eight o'clock must be bedtime for toddlers and the sane residents of Misty Harbor.

He glanced down to the bottom of the snow-packed hill again. Some enterprising soul had piled up hay bales at the bottom of the run, just in case one couldn't stop the sled before reaching the freezing cold water of Sunset Cove. "Who named it that, anyway?" Whoever had named it was either one sick individual, or had a twisted sense of humor.

"Got me. It's always been called that. Even when I was a little girl, and we visited Aunt Grace and Uncle Howard." Amber didn't seem too worried about the wickedly steep hill. In fact, the crazy woman looked eager for their turn at challenging death.

He watched as a group of teenagers piled on a toboggan. Two guys and two girls went flying down the hill, only to wipe out halfway to the bottom, where a gentle curve changed the direction of the run. He could hear the screams of the girls and the laughter of the guys as they went bouncing, rolling, and sliding across the icy snow, only to end up in the snowbank that protected the sledders from the trees and what surely would be a broken neck or two. He watched in amazement as all four got to their feet, laughing and having a good time, and then started to make their way back to the top of the hill, dragging their toboggan behind them. The idiots were going to try it again.

"Come on, we're next." Amber tugged at his hand as the next sled full of people started its run.

Ian put their shorter toboggan down at the beginning of the run, and silently questioned his own sanity. Grace had had a startling selection of sleds to choose from out in her garage. Amber had picked this one, claiming the eight-footers were just too big for the two of them. The longer toboggans were used for when Grace's family descended on Misty Harbor, and then Amber claimed there were never enough sleds to go around.

Needing some reassurance, he asked, "If I break a leg, are you going to take care of me?" He sat at the back of the sled and waited for Amber to join him. He refused to see if the sled before them made it to the bottom in one piece, but he was comforted by the fact he hadn't heard any bloodcurdling screams.

"Suck it up, Ian. This is supposed to be fun." Amber

sat down in front of him and snuggled up against his front. "Now remember, you're the one steering."

His arms instinctively went around Amber's waist as the guy standing behind them shoved his back. Amber in his arms short circuited his brain process for a vital second. As they went flying down the hill, in a blur of white and flashing trees off to their left, he shouted into the wind, "What do you mean I'm steering?"

The turn was before them, and all he saw was the trunks of huge trees and a pitifully low snowbank. He distinctly remembered hearing Amber shouting, "Lean, lean, lean!" as she threw her weight to the right. He threw all of his weight to the right, and they both went rolling off the speeding toboggan.

His arms clamped protectively around Amber as they slid their way into the snowbank. Amber's body cushioned his impact with the three-foot-high wall of snow. He landed with Amber squeezed between him and the snowbank. One end of Amber's scarf covered his face. In the momentary darkness, while his brain was still bouncing off the walls of his skull, he tried to take stock of the situation. Amazingly, he didn't feel any pain, only the warmth of Amber, still in his arms, and the ice below him.

A muffled, "Ian!" had him rolling to the side and pushing Amber's scarf out of his eyes.

Amber slowly lifted her face out of the snow, and turned to look at him. Snowflakes clung to her eyelashes, and in the swaying light from the overhead bulbs swinging wildly in the wind, he could see that her red cheeks were damp. Her knit cap had been knocked crooked, and her hair was now tangled around her face. Amber slowly spit out a mouthful of snow, and said, "Let me guess, you don't know how to steer a toboggan, do you?"

In the dim lighting, he couldn't tell if she was angry or not. There was something to the tone of her voice, but he couldn't quite place it. "I'm better at sleds." He put his hands up and mimicked the crossbar of a sled. "You know, a steering mechanism and all that."

Amber squinted and her lower lip started to quiver. For one horrifying moment he thought she was going to start crying. Then Amber did the most amazing thing; she started to laugh. It wasn't a giggle or a chuckle. It was a full-blown, throw-back-her-head, laugh.

It was the most beautiful, carefree sound he had ever heard. Amber's merriment tugged at his gut and squeezed his heart. He sat there in snow, with the freezing cold seeping into his jeans, and realized that not only was Amber certifiable, but he was falling in love with her.

Feeling attracted to Amber he knew and understood. After all, he had first been attracted to her back in college. Before he could ask her out, his roommate, and friend, James had. The rest, as they say, was history. Over the years he had conditioned himself to ignore Amber's appeal.

What he was now feeling wasn't just attraction. There was something more, something deeper. He had been putting all kinds of names to his feelings for Amber this past week, desire, respect, admiration, and even friendship. Anything but that one four letter word: love.

Now that truth was laughing at him, right in the face, he hadn't a clue as to what to do about it.

Amber, who was still laughing, rolled herself to her feet, and reached for his hand. "Come on, we've got to get off the course before they think one of us is hurt and send down the paramedics or something."

He got to his feet and walked over to where their toboggan had landed. The wooden sled didn't appear to have suffered any damage from the wipeout. "There're paramedics here?" They got off the course and started the trek back up the hill, dragging the sled behind them.

He hadn't noticed any medical personnel standing around at the top of the hill. There had been three fifty-five-gallon drums, each burning a nice size blaze, to warm up a sledder or two. There were a few groups of teenagers. At least six or eight parents, with older children doing the sledding, seemed to be circling one of those blazes. The rest of the sledders seemed to be a bunch of adults trying to relive their childhood while hurtling down an ice-slick hill at an alarming rate of speed.

Having paramedics standing by might be the best idea he heard all evening.

"Half of Misty Harbor's volunteer fire company is here, Ian. I'm pretty sure they all have some kind of medical training." Amber grabbed the toboggan's lead rope out of his hand and hurried to the end of the line. "Hurry up, Ian, we need to discuss a very important subject."

"What's that?" He wondered what the odds were that Amber wanted to talk about the same thing he did—falling in love and the realization that he was supposed to be leaving Misty Harbor in the next day or two.

"Steering." Amber jammed her hair back up under her hat and pulled the knitted cap back down over her ears before she started to brush snow off her coat and mittens.

"Steering?" So much for love. The woman seemed bound and determined to break a bone or two.

"Well, it's more leaning than steering."

As the line moved forward, Amber proceeded to give him pointers on how they were going to make it down Suicide Hill in one piece.

Ian slowly pushed himself away from the snowbank. This time it was he who had ended up facedown in the snowbank with a mouthful of snow. During their second run he had figured out that by trying to protect Amber, by wrapping his body around hers, he could possibly cause her more damage. The second time they had slammed into the snowbank, she had elbowed him in the ribs after pulling her face out of the snow. Words had been unnecessary; he had gotten the message.

He didn't know how much they were improving as a sled team, but they surely were entertaining everyone left on the hill sledding. Some joker had started calling them the Jamaican Bobsled Team and wagers were being made if they would ever reach the bottom of the hill without wiping out.

He had already figured out what had gone wrong this time. Their second run he hadn't leaned enough. This run, he had overcompensated, and leaned too much. The hardest part was releasing Amber when they went tumbling out of control so his body wouldn't go smashing hers into the snowbank.

Amber hadn't looked like a woman wanting to eat anymore snow.

Ian slowly got to his feet and headed for Amber. The silly woman was spread-eagled in the middle of the course, flat on her back, and staring up at the stars. He could tell by the smile on her face that she wasn't hurt. He reached down and grabbed one of her mitten-covered hands. "Amber?"

Amber clasped his hand and laughed. "We almost made it that time."

He figured they had been about halfway through the turn before losing it. "We're definitely getting better." At this rate, he'd be eligible for Social Security by the time they make their first clean run down Suicide Hill.

"Ian?" Amber turned her head and looked at him.

"Yes?" This time they had both landed spread-eagled in the middle of the course. Above them, at the start of the course, he could hear laughter and a few, "Hey, mon! You two still breeding?" He turned his head and looked at Amber. They weren't that far apart. If he stretched his fingers, he might be able to touch her mitten.

"We made it through the curve that time." Amber grinned.

"I know." Amber's smile was infectious. He ignored the snow that had managed to get past the collar of his jacket and down his back. He grinned back at her. "Next time I promise to stop leaning once we make it around the curve."

Ian didn't know what surprised him more; the fact that they finally made it all the way down the hill, or that they hadn't ended up bathing in Sunset Cove. A couple of the hay bales had been nudged around a bit, but it really hadn't been that close of a call. Amber's snow boots had plowed up enough snow to cover the state of Minnesota the last fifty feet of the course. Someone should have warned him that sledding on a toboggan was like riding in the Flintstone automobile. You needed your feet to stop. He had been so used to crashing, he had forgotten to ask how they were supposed to stop, when they wanted to.

Cheers erupted at the top of the course as he slowly released his grip on Amber. He gave a casual wave of his hand to the audience above.

Amber quickly turned in his arms and practically knocked him flat on his back. "Did you see, Ian? We made it!"

He regained his balance by clutching at her hips. Amber was a breath away from being in his lap. Her hands gripped his shoulders and the front of her jacket brushed the front of his. The lime green scarf that had been slapping him in the face all evening was now twisted beneath Amber.

He never wanted to move again. He'd be content to spend the rest of his life sitting on a toboggan holding Amber close.

He smiled at the flush of victory coloring her cheeks, and the sparkle of excitement dancing in her eyes. His gaze dropped to her mouth, and his smile slowly faded. The strawberry ChapStick, that she had been applying throughout the evening, looked wet, inviting, and entirely too kissable for his peace of mind.

The scent of strawberries was driving him crazy. He wanted to kiss Amber, more than anything he had wanted before in his life. He needed to taste Amber. Just once. That was all he wanted, one kiss. His fingers tightened on her hips as he whispered her name and slowly pulled her closer.

Amber's hands slid off his shoulders and slowly wrapped their way around his neck. Snow-crusted mittens caressed his neck as she brought her lips closer.

Ian swore the entire earth shook beneath them, and they weren't even kissing yet. Amber's lips were close enough that he could feel her warm breath against his mouth, when all of a sudden they were both showered with flying snow. Another toboggan had raced down the course, only to stop two feet away from them.

"You did it, mon!" Ryan Albert and his sled load of friends joined them at the bottom of the hill to celebrate.

Amber's arms slowly slid away, along with his chances of finally kissing her.

Eight o'clock the next morning Amber sat on a stool, enjoying her second cup of coffee, and glancing around the workroom of the shop. She had to admit that ever since Ian showed up in town, the workroom was always neat and organized. Every order that had been sitting either on the table or in the fax tray last Friday when he had walked through the door had been packed and shipped.

The UPS man hated Ian with a passion that was bordering on psychotic.

Of course a new stack of orders had taken their place, but this pile wasn't nearly as big. The UPS man was going to have to transfer that hatred over to her Monday afternoon. Ian's vacation was coming to an end.

The feeling of being overwhelmed and totally frustrated with the business was gone. She was once again in control, and could handle whatever orders came in from now until the end of the holiday rush. Tiffany hadn't entertained the basketball team in the shop all week, and she had only been late by a couple of minutes once. Grace had curtailed her shopping sprees and had shown up to help out in the shop every day.

The biggest help had come from Ian. The man was a born jam packer, and he knew how to clean up after himself. Ian also wasn't as introverted as she had first thought. Back in their college days, she thought Ian was on the shy side. Even James had always referred to Ian as the shy geek.

James had been wrong. Ian wasn't shy, nor was he a geek. James had been right about one thing, though; Ian had been the creative one in their business. James had been average in the creativity department, but he had excelled at the sales end. What everyone took for shyness in Ian was in reality his ability to concentrate and to sink himself into an idea.

Yesterday afternoon, Ian had sat in front of her computer and practically redesigned the shop's entire Web pages. Notes, pages, and detailed drawings had littered the desk and half the worktable. Ian had even taken a trip over to Krup's and purchased some markers and colored pencils, to better illustrate his ideas.

She had busted her butt for months last winter designing and playing with those Web pages until she had been satisfied. In a matter of one afternoon, Ian had shown her just how lackluster they were, and how exciting they could be with some minor changes. It was amazing that anyone had placed an order on such a boring Web site. Ian hadn't done it to upset her, or to show off. He had done it because that was what he did for a living. Drawing little berry characters, which helped a shopper navigate the site and get to that all-important order page, had been Ian's idea of fun.

The tobogganing had been her idea of fun.

She had enjoyed herself immensely last night. Her only regret had been that *almost* kiss. They had been so close that she could still feel the slight trembling in his hands and the warmth of his breath bathing her lips. She had closed her eyes and leaned forward, only to be sprayed with a small cascade of snow.

The desire to toss Ryan Albert and his friends into Sunset Cove had been so overwhelming that she nearly succumbed to pushing their toboggan through a couple of hay bales. Only the knowledge that she would look like a fool stopped her.

After their one and only clean run down Suicide Hill, they headed back home. Where once again, Ian had acted like the perfect gentleman and walked her to her door. He hadn't accepted her invitation in for coffee or tried to kiss her again.

Ian McNeal had once again ruined a perfectly good date. After months of grieving, and then months of healing, she was finally ready to move on with her life. Now the problem was, the man she wanted to make those moves with didn't seem all that interested. Last night, for at least one fleeting moment, Ian had been more than interested. She had read it in his eyes, and felt it in the hardening of his body as he pulled her closer. She might have imagined it, but she would swear on a stack of orders that Ian had whispered her name with such need and desire that it had stolen her breath, right before they were both sprayed with snow.

Sometimes life sucked. She wanted that moment back, more than she wanted those orders she had spent the rest of her frustrating night downloading.

The back door swung open, and her aunt hurried into the room. "Do you know how cold it is out there?" mumbled Grace as she slammed the door behind her.

She recognized her aunt from her eyes, the only visible part of her body, and the hot pink, lime green, and bright orange plaid coat. There could only be one coat like that on the entire East Coast and only one person who had the courage, or the bad taste, to wear it. Grace's orange knit hat, scarf, and gloves would be a hunter's delight. Grace had knitted the trio last winter while working through her grief. Her aunt had knitted every member of the family something, from mittens to sweaters to afghans large enough for king-size beds. Knitting needles had been permanently affixed to her hands. Grace had been the Edward Scissorhands of the knitting world.

Grace put her giant-size tote on the floor and started the long process of taking off all her outer gear.

Amber thought her aunt's question was rhetorical, since Grace had to know that she was out in the weather at least once this morning. "What brought you out so early?" The store wasn't scheduled to open for another hour yet. The lights in her aunt's house had been lit last night when Ian and she had returned from the sledding expedition. Grace's date to the movies with Mac Pierce must not have gone very well. Mac's truck hadn't been in the driveway.

Grace stomped the snow off her boots and then stepped out of them. She pulled a pair of fur-lined moccasins from the large purple tote bag, and slipped them on. "I wanted to redo a couple of the displays out front before we opened." Grace hung up her coat and straightened her sweater. Today's outfit was a pair of khakis, black turtleneck, and a thick cardigan covered in poinsettias. The sweater clashed with her hair. Plastic Rudolphs dangled from her ears.

"What's the hurry?" Grace seemed to be unusually anxious to start the day.

"No hurry, I was planning on leaving an hour or so early today, if that's all right with you." Grace poured herself a cup of coffee.

"That's fine with me." She worked every Friday night until they closed at eight because Grace always went to the Misty Harbor Volunteer Fire Company's weekly bingo game. "Got a heavy date tonight?"

"No, just playing bingo." Grace sipped her coffee and warmed her hands around the cup. "I made an appointment at Estelle's to get my nails done." Grace frowned at her closely clipped nails. "I'm thinking about fake ones, painted a nice holiday red. Maybe get some of those glittery festive decals on the ends."

The last thing her aunt needed was glitter and more festive colors. "Don't you think that's a little extreme for a bingo game?" She didn't want to think about the logistics of handling all those plastic chips with two-inch nails.

"No, silly, it's for the holidays." Grace drummed her chipped and chewed nails against the cup.

"They'll be ruined before Christmas. It's only the third of December."

"So, I'll go and get them redone." Grace's fingers tapped faster.

She took a wild guess, and asked, "Who are you trying to impress?" She laughed at the guilty flush sweeping up her aunt's cheeks. "Oh, come on now, you've really got to tell me who's got you all in a twitter." She had never seen her aunt blush before. It was not only a shock, it was endearingly sweet. She had been so caught up in her own life this past week, she hadn't been paying her aunt's life enough attention. Her mother would have a stroke if she saw Grace blush like this.

Grace gave her a stern look and tried to look disapproving. "Once you're through menopause, there's nothing left to twitter."

She snorted. "Now you sound just like *my mother.*" She knew how much Grace hated to be compared to Gladys. "Besides, we both know you can still twitter all you want after 'the change,' you just don't have to worry about unplanned accidents."

"Isn't that one of those oxymoron things—unplanned accidents?"

"I know of a couple of those 'accidents' that were planned down to the day." She watched her aunt squirm for a minute. "You're trying to change the subject, Auntie."

"What subject was that?"

"Men." She couldn't believe this was the same women who sang praises to broad shoulders, square jaws, and big strong hands. Especially those *big* hands. Maybe her mother had finally worn her down.

"Good, I love that subject." Grace pulled out the desk chair and sat in it. "Let's start with Ian."

"Ian?"

"Yes, you know, the six-foot hunk who is clinging to you like blue on a berry."

"The only time Ian has been clinging to me was when we were barreling down Suicide Hill." That one brief moment at the bottom of the hill didn't count; besides, she had been the one clinging to him.

"How did the tobogganing go?" Grace gave her an innocent look. "I couldn't help but notice Ian didn't stay for coffee or anything else after he dropped you off last night."

"I couldn't help but notice you were home awfully early from your date with Mac Pierce," she countered right back.

"He's got big strong hands," said Grace with a deep romantic sigh.

"Mac?" Lord, she didn't want to hear about Mac's big strong anything.

"No, Ian." Grace shook her head as if she were disappointed that Amber hadn't followed the conversation, but there was a smile teasing the corner of her mouth. "Pay attention, dear, we're talking about Ian."

"Why?"

"Why what?" asked Grace.

"Why are we talking about Ian?"

"Because you wanted to talk about men, dear." Grace shook her head and then topped off her coffee. "You know I never had a daughter of my own." Grace's voice got serious, and her eyes held nothing but love. "In my heart, you are that daughter, Amber. You can ask me anything."

Grace wasn't playing fair. She knew her aunt loved her like a daughter, but it was totally unfair of her to use that to change the subject. Her aunt needed a little payback. "Thanks, Grace, but Mom's already had that talk with me, and she's answered all my questions."

Grace nearly snorted coffee out of her nose. "Lord, child, do you want to spend the rest of your life alone? That woman doesn't know anything about men. Do you know what she once told me about Bob . . ."

"Stop!" She slammed both of her palms against her ears. "That's my mother and father you're talking about." She closed her eyes and shuddered.

Grace's laughter had her lowering her hands.

"I'm sorry, Amber." Grace chuckled. "For a moment there, I forgot." She grabbed a paper towel and soaked up a spot on the floor where she had spilled some coffee. "Just never, ever listen to that woman when it comes to men."

"I don't know, she and my father have been together thirty-six years. Got married right out of high school."

"I know, I was there." Grace grinned.

"So you were." Sometimes she had trouble remembering that Grace and her mother were twins. Identical twins, at that. Grace was so different from her mother, not only in looks, but in attitude. Her mother's hair was its natural shade of light brown, now liberally streaked with gray. Her mother wore glasses, while Grace preferred contacts. Her mother watched her weight and obsessed over every extra ounce. Their attitudes about life were just as different as their appearance.

"Want to tell me about the lucky guy who finally has you worrying about your nails?" She couldn't imagine who had caught her aunt's eye. In the past three months, Grace had dated just about every single guy in the county.

"No." Grace didn't look apologetic about the refusal. "Want to talk about Ian?"

"There's nothing to talk about."

"What do you mean by 'nothing'?"

"Nothing. You know, nada, zip, zilch. Nothing." She had no idea how much clearer that could be.

"Are we talking about the same Ian McNeal who is here every day packing up jam and sweeping up Styrofoam peanuts? The same Ian who escorts you to gallery open houses, freezes his wazoo off listening to an off-key choir sing Christmas carols, and receives a black-and-blue eye from playing hockey with a bunch of Neanderthals? The same Ian who spends every evening and spare moment with you since coming to town a week ago?"

"That's the one." Listening to her aunt say all those things sounded great, except she forget a few important details. "The same Ian who was my husband's business partner, and who constantly reminds me of that fact. The same Ian who came here to check up on me, probably out of a sense of guilt." Her voice lowered to a whisper, as she said the one thing that had been playing on her mind all morning. "The same Ian who will be leaving tomorrow."

"He's leaving tomorrow?" Grace looked about as upset as Amber felt.

"I guess so." Ian hadn't come right out and told her that, but she wasn't stupid. "He said he was taking a week's vacation. The week's up. He has a company to run back in Boston." Tears were once again clogging her throat.

Grace and she stared at each other.

Ian and a blast of frigid wind came in through the back door. "Do you guys know how cold it is out there?" Ian slammed the door closed and stomped his feet to knock the snow off them.

"Cold as a witch's . . ." Grace looked at her and winked ". . . nose."

Ian chuckled as he started to pull off his gloves and hat. "You're bad, Grace. Did anyone ever tell you that?" Ian hung up his coat and ran his fingers through his already tousled hair.

"My sister does, about three times a day." Grace nodded to the rolled-up papers Ian held in his hand. "What's that?"

"Amber's next headache."

"Gee, nice of you to deliver it." She pushed her empty cup to the side. "What is it?"

"Your future, ladies." Ian seemed to hesitate for a moment before he finally unrolled the papers. "You can't just rely on Christmas orders for the business. You need a steady stream of Internet and phone orders coming in all year-round. A spring and summer ad campaign will help, but I think I figured out where your big orders will come from."

"Where?" Grace seemed so excited while she was getting this queasy feeling in the pit of her stomach. Visions of multiple fax machines spitting out orders twenty-four hours a day filled her thoughts.

"The health food industry. Blueberries are ranked number one in antioxidant activity and are linked to better eyesight and circulation and are a great source of vitamin C."

"Have you been listening to public service announcements?" She had known all that about the juicy little berry.

"People are always looking for healthy, delicious food. We just need to tell them where to buy it. We need to target the health-conscious market." Ian spread out a couple drawings of some health-conscious ads. "These are only some rough ideas, since I was doing them at two in the morning, but you can get the general idea."

"Two in the morning?" Grace stared at him as if he were nuts. "You didn't hit your head on anything last night, did you?"

"No, my head's fine." Ian looked at Grace and shrugged. "The idea came to me, and I had to get it down on paper as fast as I could."

"It's wonderful." Grace grinned. "Pure genius."

"Pure genius would have been me getting that idea last spring so we would have had the ad campaign out and in full swing come January. The whole country goes health and weight conscious for their New Year's resolution. As it is, we might be able to hit the swimsuit phobia season."

She knew what the swimsuit phobia season was without asking. If anyone dared to hand her a two piece swimsuit right now she'd wrap the top around someone's neck and not let up until all the oxygen was gone.

"I like." She liked everything Ian did. "When you get back to Boston, work up a contract, at your regular prices."

"I, ummm . . . wasn't planning on going back just yet." Ian's gaze was on the drawings he was rolling back up."

"You're not?" Amber refused to acknowledge the little jolt her heart had just felt. "I thought you'd be heading back tomorrow, or Sunday at the latest."

"I thought I'd stick around for a while longer. The office is fine without me. I've been checking in every day." Ian snapped a rubber band around the papers before looking at her. "You won't mind if I hang around for a while longer, will you?" Ian nodded at the stack of orders sitting in a tray. "You still are a little behind."

"You're welcome here for as long as you like. Don't worry about the orders, I can handle those." She couldn't read Ian's brown eyes.

"Glad to have you around, Ian," Grace said as she picked up her tote and headed for the front of the shop. "Amber needs someone like you to keep her out of trouble. She's been a terrible strain on my love life, demanding all my attention and time." Grace winked at her before disappearing through the doorway.

"You really don't mind me staying?"

"Of course not." She wasn't sure why he was staying, but she knew there had to be a second chance at that kiss. She'd make the chance.

"Good." Ian slipped the rolled-up designs into the pocket of the coat he had just hung up. "Ethan stopped over last night. They need me to play another two games of hockey this Sunday."

Chapter 8

Grace looked at the eight cards spread out before her and crossed her fingers. She was waiting two different ways for Bingo. N 43 would take it down the Ns, or a B 15 would give her a bingo across the bottom. She'd be happy with either number.

"O 65." Joe Clayton, tonight's caller, held up the ball for all to see.

Ruth Busby screeched, "Bingo," at the top of her lungs.

Ruth, Norma, and Priscilla were sitting clear across the other side of the room from where Grace was sitting. The trio seemed to be together constantly lately. She had to wonder if her sister was checking in with Ruth and Norma for progress reports, too. No wonder Gladys knew every move she made, but more upsetting, every move Amber made. If Gladys didn't watch her step, she was going to make her own daughter dislike her. Amber would be thirty years old soon. She was old enough to make her own decisions and to live with the consequences. Ian McNeal looked like one delicious consequence to her.

There were a few mutters and mumbles from disgruntled bingo players as Abraham Martin made his way up the aisle to Ruth.

She watched as Abraham picked up Ruth's card and started to call back the winning numbers to Joe. "O 63, O 65, O 66, O 71, and O 75." Abraham was looking mighty good tonight, for some old, grouchy lobster fisherman. It must be the fluorescent lighting.

"That's a bingo," shouted Joe.

Grace started to clear the green plastic chips off her cards with the side of her hand. Picking up each individual chip was out of the question with these nails. She was having enough problems getting the chips on the right numbers to begin with. But she was bound and determined to figure out how to maneuver the two-inch lethal weapons Estelle had glued onto the end of each of her fingers.

She liked how they looked, and she liked the clicking sound they made when she drummed them against the table. The shocked and appalled looks they had received from some of the old fuddy-duddies at the fire hall had been an added bonus. Estelle had done an outstanding job. The red was bright and so glossy, they still appeared wet. At the tip of every nail was a gold star with just a touch of glitter surrounding it.

"First number of the next game is, B 15." Joe held the ball up for all to see.

Figures. She muttered a word that would have caused her sister heart palpitations. It wasn't as if she needed the thirty dollars a game that the fire company paid out. She spent more than that every Friday night between the admission, the special intermission games, the drinks and snacks that the Women's Auxiliary served, and the fifty-fifty chances she was talked into buying every week. She just liked yelling "Bingo" at the top of her voice. There was something exhilarating in it. In the one brief moment, when her whole body clenched with excitement, and the "Bingo" came flying out of her mouth, it was almost as good as sex.

Or at least what she remembered about sex. Howard had passed away over two years ago, and she was old. Her memory wasn't as sharp as it used to be. All she knew was that it would have felt darn good to yell that word.

"Hey, Grace, how are you doing tonight?" Lenny Holmes had spiffed himself up tonight with a new pair of jeans and navy turtleneck with the fire company's name embroidered across the chest. A half dozen gray hairs were combed over his bald spot and if any woman had a gut that big, they would rush her to the nearest hospital and induce labor.

"Hey yourself, Lenny." She had gone out with Lenny twice.

"N 43."

She glared at Joe and then fumbled a chip into place. God obviously had a sense of humor. "I'm fine. How's it going with you?" She liked Lenny. He was a really sweet guy, but something had been missing. There hadn't been a spark. Or even a connection. There surely hadn't been any bingos yelled. It had been like dating one of her brothers.

"G 52." Joe kept the balls coming and the game hopping.

Grace smiled as she put five chips on her cards. *That's more like it.* The thrill of yelling Bingo grew closer with every chip that went down.

Anticipation had its own rewards.

She was praying that Lenny wouldn't ask her out again. Lenny had said he understood the last time she had turned him down, but he was still giving her those sad puppy dog eyes. Turning him down again would be like kicking a defenseless puppy. She could almost see that movie or dinner invitation in his big brown eyes.

"N 44."

Two more chips went down, but nothing was matching up. Just like her love life. There had been plenty of dates, but nothing had matched. Nothing had felt right. Over the past several months she had been to the finest restaurants, out dancing the night away, to plays in Bangor, and even a couple of concerts. Her calendar was full, her dates attentive, and she was the envy of the Women's Guild. She had enjoyed herself, but somehow she thought there would have been more. With Howard there had been more.

She wasn't *Sex and the City,* she was *Menopausal in Misty Harbor.* Being the hottest date in town, for the Centrum Silver set, was wearing thin on her old bones and playing hell with her beauty sleep. Whoever thought that dating would be such hard work?

"G 54."

Maybe it was time to pass the torch to someone else. Some woman who would appreciate the Lennys and the Mac Pierces of the world.

"I 27." Joe Clayton held the little white ball high into the air for all to see.

She carefully placed three chips down and crossed her fingers. She was waiting for O 71. She tried not to get too excited as she glanced around the hall. There had to be close to eighty players tonight, and a good ninety percent of them were female. Out of those females, a good seventy percent had to be forty years old, or older.

Bingo wasn't for the young. Younger women had either hot dates or a house filled with children. It was the older women of Misty Harbor who supported the fire company every Friday night.

"O"—she felt her body clench—"72"—only to deflate.

Thankfully, no one yelled Bingo. She shifted in her

seat and started to take inventory of all the unmarried women in the room.

Mamie Martin was single, but she was pushing her mid-eighties. She was happy to see her out and about and playing bingo with her usual flair. Mamie had a dozen good luck charms positioned in front of her and her twenty-four cards. Not only was she a seasoned bingo player, she took the game seriously. Ten bingo dabbers, for the paper throwaway intermission specials, were lined up in a row. Mamie had one of every color made and used some elaborate system to decide which color to use when. In the center, directly in front of Mamie, was her pride and joy: a fancy silver box with her name engraved across the lid that held five hundred silver-edged red plastic bingo chips. Abraham had bought his mother the set last year for Christmas. Grace thought it had been the sweetest thing she had ever seen. Whenever Mamie showed it to anyone, Abraham blushed.

"O 68."

She glared at Joe and carefully maneuvered a chip onto every O 68 she had. Her luck was still holding, but the longer she waited, the better the odds were she would be splitting that jackpot with someone. Yelling Bingo the same instant someone else did took all the fun out of winning.

Lenny stood beside her chair, shuffling his feet. Lenny's job was to wait until someone yelled "Bingo," go to them, and read the winning numbers back to Joe. If it was a good bingo, he paid that person their winnings. It was the same job Abraham and Paul Newman were doing tonight. She wished it was Abraham standing next to her, instead of Lenny.

"O"—she held her breath and squirmed in her seat as Joe announced—"65."

She had practically tasted that "B" forming on her

lips. She really needed to hit bingo tonight. It had been so long since she had last yelled.

She renewed her search for a single woman, one who was at least in Lenny's decade. Agnes McGee sat at the other end of her table, right in front of the caller, because her hearing was going. Agnes was pushing eighty and had already been through four husbands. Lenny wouldn't survive the honeymoon.

Her fingers started to drum on the table, and her left leg started to bounce as Joe pulled the next ball. Grace Winslow, the minister's wife, who was sitting next to her, frowned at her tapping nails. Grace Winslow was known as Grace I, while she was known as Grace II in the church social circle. She didn't like being the second in anything, but no one wanted to alienate the reverend or his wife, so she was stuck with being Grace II. When they were together and people called them by number she felt like Thing 1 and Thing 2 from the *Cat in the Hat* book.

"O 75," Joe's voice echoed throughout the room.

Two chips slipped from her fingers and rolled across the table. She almost had had it. She could hear the mumbling throughout the room. Too many Os had been called. At least a dozen people had to be waiting now. It was going to be a multiple bingo-winner game.

She covered the two O 75s that she had and glanced down at the other end of the table. A grin spread across her face as Joe pulled the next number. Her problem of Lenny had been solved.

"O"—she closed her eyes and visualized the number she needed—"71."

Her shout of "Bingo!" hung in the hall, alone and unchallenged. Relief washed through her and she could finally breathe again. She had done it.

"Gee, Grace, you sure get into this game." Lenny was leaning over her shoulder and picking up the card in front of her. He had been working bingos for so many years that he didn't need anyone to tell him which card was the winner.

Lenny called back the numbers and Joe declared there was a single winner, and to clear the cards for the next game. Lenny laid three crisp new ten dollar bills in front of her. "There you go, Grace."

She felt so cheap. She grinned at Lenny. "Thanks, Lenny." She felt so good. A quick swipe of her hand and she cleared her cards. "I need to ask you a favor."

"Anything, you name it, and I'm your man." Lenny, knowing he had a minute or two before he was needed again, sat in the vacant chair between her and Grace I.

"You know Evelyn Ruffles, right?" She lowered her voice to a whisper. Only thing faster than gossip spreading in the bingo hall was Erik Olsen's slap shot on goal at a hockey game.

Lenny leaned forward and tried to look around her toward the far end of the table, where Evelyn was sitting.

"Don't do that," she whispered as she moved in closer. "She'll know we're talking about her." As it was, quite a few people were staring at her and Lenny with interest. Including Abraham Martin, who didn't look too pleased with Lenny or her at the moment. Interesting.

She moved a few inches closer to Lenny as Joe called the first number. "B 6."

She placed her chips. "I'm beginning to worry about Evelyn."

"Why? Is she sick or something?"

"No, but the holidays are coming up, and I think she's lonely." Joe called the next number, but she only gave half her attention to the game. "Her kids are all grown, married, and scattered throughout the country."

"Holidays are the worst." Lenny frowned at his big work-roughened hands lying on the table before him.

She knew Lenny would understand. "I was hoping that maybe you would, I don't know, ask her out for coffee, or pay her a compliment or two." She cringed when Lenny's head snapped up and he stared at her. Subtle was not her middle name. "You know, nothing serious like a date or anything, just something to pick up her spirits a bit."

"Her husband just passed away," Lenny's voice was barely a whisper, and she had to lean in closer to hear him.

"He passed away two years ago, this month." She remembered it was a couple weeks before Christmas. Evelyn had joined her in the ranks of widowhood six months after Howard had passed.

"She's not interested in dating or anything else yet." Lenny snuck a quick glance down the table. "If she was, there would be plenty of guys willing to keep her company this holiday season."

That was what she was hoping for—a sweet distraction to draw the bees away from herself. Evelyn might not have been out on a date yet, but she was ready, or as near ready as any sixty-year-old woman would be. Grace knew the signs, and Evelyn was looking. Evelyn was the honeycomb, just waiting for the bees. "Lenny, I like you, so I'm going to let you in on a secret. Evelyn's not the type of woman to ask a man out."

Lenny snorted. "Women shouldn't ask men out, it just ain't right."

There was the reason she and Lenny had never connected. Lenny was a chauvinistic pig, while she had burned her bras back in the sixties with the best of them. Howard had supported her, and even offered to take the darn things off her himself. Lord, how she missed that man.

Lenny was also a little thick in the head at times and needed things spelled out for him. "Maybe the reason Evelyn hasn't been on a date since Ed passed is because no one has asked her yet."

"You think?" Lenny looked intrigued by the idea.

"Maybe." She automatically placed her chips as Joe called the next number. "Only problem I see is that once it gets out that she is starting to date, every guy in town will be courting her. It's a well-known fact that her German chocolate cake wins the Bake-Off every year."

Abraham Martin stood against the far wall of the bingo hall and watched Grace and Lenny conspire about something. For a moment there he thought Lenny was going to make a nuisance out of himself and bug Grace for another date. The darn woman was too soft-hearted for her own good. She probably would have said yes, and he couldn't really fault Lenny for trying.

Little Gracie Sullivan had grown up into one beautiful woman. As a young girl she had been all skinned knees and long brown braids. Even in grade school Gracie had challenged, and usually broke through every gender boundary set before her. Back when they had been growing up, girls weren't encouraged to play sports. They sure as dickens weren't allowed on any of the teams. Girls were supposed to dress their dolls, play house, and baby-sit their younger siblings.

Gracie had been able to outrun every boy on the Little League team, and out-bat most of them without really trying too hard. But she hadn't been able to join the team. She had sat on the bleachers and laughed at their pathetic attempts to finally win a game. Most of the boys on the team hated her guts, while he secretly thought she had been right. Their team had been pathetic and the rules that separated boys from girls were stupid.

If they would have had Gracie on their team, they might have actually placed in the top three of the four team division. Some guys took it as a threat to their masculinity if a mere girl could hit the ball over the outfielder's head. Not him. Joe Clayton could whack the ball just as far, and his masculinity hadn't been threatened by Joe or any other guy on the team. Some people were just better athletes, and Gracie just happened to be one of them.

By high school Gracie's attention went from sports to the guys who played them. One guy in particular, Howard Berry, caught and held her eye. They had been married the summer after graduation and from all accounts had a great, if childless, marriage. Everyone in town had known how desperately Gracie and Howard had wanted children. It just hadn't been in the cards.

Howard Berry had been a great guy. He had been a hard worker, and had treated Gracie like the princess she was. The community had lost a good man the day Howard was taken from them. Gracie had lost her prince. For months, he and the rest of the town had watched little Gracie Sullivan Berry grieve. It had nearly broken his own heart watching the shadow of the woman he had known his entire life, barely leave her own house. When she had ventured into town or church, she had looked and acted twice her age. She had become this different woman. A woman who just didn't care any longer. Gracie's hair had appeared gray almost overnight, she never wore jewelry, and she had been dressing either in black or grays.

Gracie, without her color or vibrancy, had been the most heartbreaking thing he had ever seen.

He knew exactly when Gracie's grieving had stopped, and the slow healing process had begun. The change happened when her niece, Amber, who had just lost her husband, arrived in town. Gracie had someone who needed her. The two women had been the walking wounded of Misty Harbor. Over time the color had slowly come back into Gracie's life. Gray hair turned a subtle brown. Black clothes turned into navy or dark green and then into lighter colors.

While he had patiently waited for Gracie to heal he had been making plans. Gracie Berry was too young and beautiful to go through the rest of her life alone. Females had always been in short supply around Misty Harbor, and he never had been one to exert himself in his youth. While other young men spent their money courting the ladies, he had bought a brand-new pickup truck and a lobster boat. While other young men got married, had children, and spent a fortune on food and orthodontist bills, he had pampered his boat and pulled in a nice living from the sea. Having a wife and possibly children of his own hadn't been important to him back then. A decision he deeply regretted now. He was lonely.

He was a fifty-six-year-old man who still lived with his mother. Not what anyone would consider a great catch, but not the worst either. He didn't drink, smoke, or run around. He worked hard, and made a decent enough living. He could have gone out and bought himself his own small house in town, but there hadn't been any point to it. He would have been stuck cutting two yards and maintaining two homes; his and his mother's.

His mom was getting up there in age. At eighty-three, Mom was slowing down some, but she was still one of the best cooks around. He did most of the cleaning at home now, while Mom handled the laundry and the cooking. He wasn't looking for someone to cook or clean up after him. He knew how to do both, and wasn't adverse to either.

He was looking for love, companionship, and forever. He had known Gracie her entire life. She was the one he wanted to spend the rest of his silver years and the future golden years with. He might not have exerted any energy when he had been a young man, but he had plenty of energy now.

Priscilla Patterson yelling "Bingo!" pulled him out of his musing about Gracie and away from the wall. He walked over to Priscilla and took the card she was waving in the air like a flag.

"It's down the Ns, Abraham, down the Ns." Priscilla fanned herself with one of the other cards. The way she was carrying on, someone might have thought she won thirty thousand dollars, instead of thirty.

He called the four winning N numbers out, waited until Joe said it was a good bingo, and then handed Priscilla her thirty bucks. "Now don't you go spending all of this in one place."

Priscilla giggled like a schoolgirl as everyone set up their cards for the next game. "How did your mother like the wreath you picked out on Sunday night, Abraham?"

"She said it had to have been the prettiest one there, because she couldn't imagine one prettier." His mother had made him hang it on their front door that night, before she would even let him warm up the soup he had gotten her.

"I see your mother must be feeling better." Ruth looked way down to the other end of their table, to where his mother and two of her friends were sitting.

"Whatever was ailing her didn't grab ahold. She was up and about like her old self the next morning."

"That's good." Ruth put a couple of chips onto her card as Joe called the first number of the new game. "I hear the flu season has already started and it's going to be a doozy."

"I haven't heard of anyone having the flu." He really didn't even think his mother had been sick, or feeling under the weather. He had chalked Mamie's staying by the fire and under a blanket the other night up to how cold it had been outside. His mother hadn't reached the age of eighty-three with barely a doctor's visit by being stupid. He, on the other hand, had known Gracie would be working the greens tent and he would have gone out in a blizzard just to see her smile.

"It was on CNN this afternoon." Ruth looked solemn as she relayed this important news. "Anderson Cooper says the flu's already in New York, Pennsylvania, and parts of southern Ohio."

Priscilla and Norma looked duly worried about the impending health situation. He thought they were all crazy. He seldom listened to the news. He was a Weather Channel junkie. He found it fascinating how they could predict the weather. When he had been a boy they would predict snow and only be right about half the time. Now they would tell you exactly when the snow would start and how many inches to expect. Darn if they weren't right ninety-eight percent of the time.

He glanced across the room to where Gracie was sitting. Lenny was finally standing back up. Whatever they had been discussing must have pleased Gracie. She was smiling. Lenny was looking down at the other end of the room.

"So, Abraham, when are you going to make your move?" Priscilla looked at him with open curiosity and a fake innocence.

"My move?" He didn't like the looks he was getting from the three close friends. There was a predatory gleam in their eyes. His gut told him he was about to become a victim of their matchmaking.

"With Grace." Ruth had played bingo enough over the years that she could place her chips, eat her hot dog and drink her coke, and hold a three-way conversation without blinking an eye. More times than not, Ruth had a crochet hook in one hand and a ball of yarn in the other. She was one of those women who constantly had to be doing something and had no clue as to what the word "relax" meant. Living with Ruth would drive him nuts.

"What about Gracie?" He knew where this was leading, but sometimes it was better just to play dumb.

"You're the only one who has ever called her Gracie," added Norma.

"She was Gracie back in kindergarten. Don't see a reason to change her name now."

"I heard she dumped Mac Pierce in the middle of their date the other night." Priscilla popped a potato chip into her mouth and smiled. "Walked right out of the theater, in the middle of the movie, too."

He had heard a rumor to that effect. He could only speculate as to what had gone wrong. Mac and he were going to have a nice long talk, the next time he ran into him. "Gracie's a big gal, she can handle herself." Gracie was handling herself quite well these past months. Too well.

Every unmarried man over the age of forty-five was making a damn fool of themselves over her. Gracie's dating life and a three-ring circus had a lot in common. They both had a lot of clowns running around in them.

"She's lonely." Ruth looked across the room to where Grace was sitting talking to the minister's wife and placing her chips. He hoped she'd hit bingo again. There was something special in the way she yelled "Bingo."

"She needs the love of a good man," added Priscilla.

"Well, she's got plenty to choose from." If he ticked off every man who was panting after Gracie, he'd run out of fingers before names.

"I don't think she can do any better than Clyde Davenport," Norma said. "The man's rich and good-looking."

He tried not to flinch. Clyde had been causing him some worries. He had this whole game plan figured out, and then Clyde had come along and thrown a monkey wrench into it. He was rich and sophisticated, and even his own mother had said if she were ten years younger, she'd give Gracie a run for her money when it came to Davenport.

Norma yelped, as if someone had kicked her under the table. She glared at Ruth and snapped, "Well, he is."

"Clyde's a dear, but he's just not right for our Grace," purred Ruth.

Abe tried not to laugh. Since when did Gracie become "Our Grace"? When Gracie first became a widow, Priscilla, Ruth, and Norma had clucked around her like they were all mother hens and Gracie had been some wounded chick. It had been Grace this, and Grace that. Now that Gracie had finally joined the living again, and was attracting all the male attention, the threesome were angry, petty, and jealous. They all acted as if she were going after their husbands, which would have been hysterical, if it wasn't so sad. Gracie wasn't the kind of women who went after someone else's man. There were already plenty of single men in town running after her. Besides, he knew Priscilla's, Ruth's, and Norma's husbands. If they were fish, Gracie would be throwing them back.

"Why isn't Clyde right for Gracie?" He was curious. So far as he could tell, Davenport had everything going for him. Maybe they were seeing something he wasn't.

"He's ten years older than she is." Priscilla popped some more potato chips into her mouth as she frowned at the cards before her.

"Lots of women go for older men." From what he could see, Priscilla had only two chips down on her cards. He glanced up at the lit board, above Joe's head. Over a dozen numbers had been called already.

"He likes opera," Norma said, as if this were a crime.

Ruth, not to be outdone, supplied what she considered the killing stroke: "He's a Catholic."

He chuckled and shook his head. "If Gracie liked

him, his religion wouldn't matter." He glanced across the room and watched as Gracie squirmed in her seat. Damn, the woman was waiting on a number. He could always tell when she was close to hitting bingo. Her face got flushed and she squirmed.

Joe called another number and he watched as Gracie rolled her eyes and wiggled some more. No one shouted "Bingo." Gracie had done something different to her hair, but he couldn't put his finger on it. It was the same brilliant red as the poinsettia plant his mother had bought last week. Gracie might have gotten an inch cut off, but it was hard to tell with the way it was sticking out all over the place. Tonight she looked like that famous country singer, Reba McEntire.

Gracie snapped a couple more chips down onto her cards and then her long red fingernails rapidly tapped a beat on the table. He liked the nails, but he hoped she didn't have to scratch anywhere important. The nails looked lethal.

He heard Joe call out a "G," and he watched enthralled as the flush in Gracie's face deepened, and her red lips formed the letter "B." He forgot how to breathe. He had never seen such a sensual sight in all his life.

Joe called, "52" and Gracie came out of her chair shouting, "Bingo."

He groaned in frustration and walked right out of the bingo hall. He could hear Priscilla stammering something after him, but he didn't slow down. He kept on walking right out into the foyer of the building, past the coat room, and right out into the dark parking lot.

The freezing December night air felt like a slap in his face. He braced his hands on his hips, closed his eyes, and took another deep breath. It didn't help much. He could still see the look on Gracie's face as she shouted "Bingo." It had almost been sexual, and he was surely losing his mind for even thinking that thought.

He had been waiting too long for Gracie. It was the

only explanation he could come up with for his strange reaction to her yell. The cold night air felt good, but not as good as Gracie's arms would feel.

It was time for him to get off his duff and go after the woman of his dreams, before Clyde, or someone else, took her out of the game. He took another lungful of frigid air, counted to ten, and then headed back to the hall and the job he was supposed to be doing.

Thankfully there were only two more games of bingo left tonight. He could at least last that long without making a fool of himself. What were the chances of Gracie yelling again?

Chapter 9

Amber stood at the end of the aisle and grinned. She had finally located her shopping buddy, the man she had talked into spending such a gorgeous and sunny Saturday driving to Bangor and hanging out in the overcrowded mall so she could start her holiday shopping. It seemed everyone in the state of Maine had had the same idea.

The toy store was so crowded that it had taken her a while to find him. Ian was standing in front of a large video screen zapping aliens with a laser gun. The six-foot hunk from Boston was surrounded by a group of nine- and ten-year-old boys cheering him on.

"Look out, on your right," shouted one boy.

"Use your grenades!" shouted another.

Ian was maneuvering the joystick and pushing buttons as fast as his fingers would fly. He obviously wasn't a novice to video games. "They're multiplying and I'm running out of ammo." Sparks and red streaks flew across the video monitor. Loud explosions rocked the foreign mountainous landscape. Aliens screamed in agony before melting into a stream of green smoke.

"Go into the tunnel," shouted a little boy tugging on Ian's jacket. "There's ammo down in the tunnel."

"Which tunnel? I see three of them." Ian continued to shoot the slimy-looking creatures. For a man who was squinting at the screen, and had his reading glasses perched on the end of his nose, Ian had amazing aim.

He looked so darn cute playing with the boys she didn't know if she should kiss him or treat him to ice cream.

"Go down the tunnel on the left," answered the small boy.

"No, the one on the right," said another.

"Straight, straight, straight," shouted another.

Ian laughed with murderous glee, zapped another alien into oblivion, and headed left.

Amber leaned against the shopping cart she had been pushing through the toy store and watched in wonder as Ian stole another little piece of her heart.

He had purposely headed left because of the little boy tugging on the bottom of his jacket. The kid couldn't have been more than seven or eight, and was surely the youngest and least experienced there. Ian could have very easily listened to the advice of the older kids, and improved his odds of surviving and winning the game. Instead he had chosen to listen to the little boy with the big eyes and adorable cowlick.

Was it any wonder she was falling in love with this man?

She watched as Ian's alien hunter entered the long dark, scary-looking tunnel. It looked more like a cave to her, but what did she know about planets that had four suns? She had seen a couple of her older nephews play these types of games, but she had never paid close attention to what they had been doing. Her money was on something really horrible happening to Ian's guy.

"Watch out, they come from above." One of the older kids leaned in closer.

Ian moved the joystick, trying to get a better view as to what was above him, but it was too late. In an instant the game was over. One huge, mother-of-all aliens dropped from the ceiling, right on top of Ian's guy. The guy gave one loud girly shriek, and then lay still in a pool of green slime.

The large alien made a slurping sound as it seemed to suck on the hunter's face.

"You're toast, man." The older boy shook his head. "He got you good. I told you to go right."

Ian's guy evaporated into ash, leaving only the alien hunter's slime-covered overalls and smoldering combat boots behind. The big slimy alien slithered back up the wall, to await his next victim.

"They're in the right tunnel, too," said another. "They're all over the place. You have to shoot them before they jump on you."

"But I couldn't even see them," complained Ian. He reached down and ruffled the little boy's hair, making the cowlick worse. "Doesn't seem fair to me."

"You've got to watch for the ooze." One of the older boys took the controller from Ian and got ready to restart the game. "The Gunks always slobber before they drop down from the ceiling."

"I'll remember that for the next time." Ian looked down at the little boy. "So, which do you think my nephews will like better for Christmas—Alien Hunter or the NFL game?"

"They are only allowed one?" The little boy looked torn by such a monumental decision.

"Yeah." Ian looked guilty. "I'm afraid I went a little overboard last year and got them too many toys. Their father says I can only buy them one game this year."

"But you said there were two of them. One's my age, and one's a year older."

"That's right." Ian glanced up, saw her standing there watching him, and flashed a killer smile. "Amber,

I would like you to meet my consultant, Kyle. Kyle's help-ing me pick out a really cool game for my nephews."

"Hello, Kyle, nice to meet you." She had a detailed list in her purse with everything already spelled out for her. Next to each of her nieces' or nephews' names was exactly what to buy them for Christmas. Make, model, and sizes were listed in detail. She could have gone on the Internet and done all her shopping. It just wouldn't have been the same, though. She loved walking up and down the aisles of a toy store, checking out all the neat toys. Of course she never got to pick out the toys. She was expected to follow the lists her brothers and their wives sent her every year.

Little Kyle had that bewildered look on his face, like he didn't know what "consultant" meant. "Hi." Kyle turned back to Ian. "Did their father say one game each or one game for the two of them?"

Ian slowly grinned. "He hadn't been real clear on that point."

"I would hate having to share my Christmas present with my brother." Kyle glanced at the older kid playing Alien Hunter. "He doesn't like to share sometimes."

She and Ian watched the older boy, obviously Kyle's brother, maneuver the hunter down the tunnel on the right. Gunks were falling fast and furious to their smoky deaths. She could sympathize with Kyle. Who would want to share a present with a sibling? She glanced back at her cart as she pulled her list back out of her purse.

There was no way her nieces and nephews had com-piled the list in her purse. Her brothers' and their wives' hands were all over the list. She glanced at the list and frowned. Justin, her eleven-year-old nephew might want a PlayStation 2 game, but no way did he want the cute little racing go-cart one listed by his name. Justin was an Alien Hunter, if ever there was one. Same with ten-year-old Brent.

"Hey, Kyle," she asked, "Do you like the Scooby-Doo game?" She had a sneaking suspicion that the game next to Brent's name was too tame for him.

"My little sister has it for her Game Boy. I don't play it, but she seems to like it." Kyle's grin showed the fact that his parents would be having one massive orthodontist bill.

She smiled back. "What's your brother's favorite game?" Kyle's brother looked about the same age as Brent.

"Zombie Killer." Kyle's smile grew. "I like it, too, but I can't get out of the first level yet."

"Can I ask you one more question?" Kyle's brother's Alien hunter must have been killed by a Gunk. Another kid was grabbing for the controls. "What would a girl your age want for Christmas?"

Kyle scrunched up his face. "She got a Game Boy?"

"Not that I know of." Amber glanced in the cart to where a big Barbie swan sat. The swan was stupid and really didn't do anything. She would rather buy nine-year-old Jessica the remote control car; at least that way Barbie could go tooling around the family room. "Don't girls play with Barbies anymore?"

"My sister does, but she's only five." Kyle pointed to the display shelf with all the Game Boys lined up in a row. "Older girls like the pretty-colored ones and all the fancy cases to carry them in."

Ian plucked a slip of paper out of Alien Hunter and the newest NFL game. "You talked me into it, Kyle. One for each of them."

"Boy, I wish I had an uncle and aunt like you two." Kyle made a funny face. "All my aunt buys me are stupid sweaters and dorky stuff my parents tell her I want, but I don't."

Amber plucked a slip out of Alien Hunter and

Zombie Killer, before walking over to the Game Boy display. "What do you think, Kyle: pink or purple?"

"Purple, pink is for sissies."

She thought about her nine-year-old niece. Jessica might be girl, but she wasn't a sissy. "Purple it is." She pulled the tag out of the clear envelope below the purple Game Boy.

"Are we done shopping?" Ian glanced at her cart.

"Not yet. There are a couple more things I need to pick up." *And some stuff I need to reshelve.* "Thanks, Kyle."

Ian ruffled Kyle's hair again. "Thanks for the help, kid. Next time I'll remember to watch for the Gunk drool and not use up all my ammo before heading into the tunnels."

Kyle shuffled his worn sneakers, and tried not to appear too flattered. "No problem."

Amber grabbed her cart, and headed back for the doll section. "This won't take long."

"No problem, we have all day," Ian said as he followed her through the store. He watched in amusement as she put all the pink Barbie stuff back on the shelves. "Did you change your mind?"

"Something like that." She didn't change her mind, because she wasn't the one to write out the list to begin with. She changed her mind about following the list. She didn't want to be like Kyle's aunt, and only give stupid or dorky gifts. She wanted to be the "cool" aunt.

She walked past the Barbie aisle, to where the Bratz were shelved. Bratz were hard rockin', motorcycle riding, punk-hair dolls that could kick the Swan Lake Barbie's butt, and her sissy prince Ken's butt, too. The Barbies of the world would go to the prom and become perfectly coordinated vets and mothers. Bratzs would backpack through Europe, never experience a dull moment in their lives, and play in a rock-and-roll band.

She picked up a blond streaked Bratz dressed in ratty

Zebra Contemporary

Whatever your taste in contemporary romance –
Romantic Suspense … Character-Driven … Light and
Whimsical … Heartwarming … Humorous – we have it
at Zebra!

And now Zebra has created a Book Club for readers like
yourself who enjoy fine Contemporary Romance written
by today's best-selling authors.

Authors like Lori Foster… Janet Dailey…
Fern Michaels… Janelle Taylor… Kasey Michaels…
Lisa Jackson… Shannon Drake… Kat Martin…
to name but a few!

*These are the finest
contemporary romances
available anywhere today!*

But don't take our word for it! Accept our gift of 3
FREE Zebra Contemporary Romances – and see for
yourself. You only pay $1.99 for shipping and
handling.

Once you've read them, we're sure you'll want to
continue receiving the newest Zebra Contemporaries
as soon as they're published each month! And you
can by becoming a member of the Zebra
Contemporary Romance Book Club!

As a member of Zebra Contemporary Romance Book Club,

- You'll receive three books every month. Each book
  will be by one of Zebra's best-selling authors.

- You'll have variety – you'll never receive two of
  the same kind of story in one month.

- You'll get your books hot off the press, usually
  before they appear in bookstores.

- You'll ALWAYS save up to 20% off the cover price.

SEND FOR YOUR FREE BOOKS TODAY!

If the FREE Book Certificate is missing, call 1-800-770-1963 to place your order.
Be sure to visit our website at www.kensingtonbooks.com.

To start your membership, simply complete and return the Free Book Certificate. You'll receive your Introductory Shipment of 3 FREE Zebra Contemporary Romances, you only pay $1.99 for shipping and handling. Then, each month you will receive the 3 newest Zebra Contemporary Romances. Each shipment will be yours to examine FREE for 10 days. If you decide to keep the books, you'll pay the preferred subscriber price (a savings of up to 20% off the cover price), plus shipping and handling. If you want us to stop sending books, just say the word… it's that simple.

FREE BOOK CERTIFICATE

Yes! Please send me 3 FREE Zebra Contemporary romance novels. I only pay $1.99 for shipping and handling. I understand that each month thereafter I will be able to preview 3 brand-new Contemporary Romances FREE for 10 days. Then, if I should decide to keep them, I will pay the money-saving preferred subscriber's price (that's a savings of up to 20% off the retail price), plus shipping and handling. I understand I am under no obligation to purchase any books, as explained on this card.

Name _____

Address _____ Apt._____

City_____ State _____ Zip _____

Telephone (____) _____

Signature _____

(If under 18, parent or guardian must sign)

Thank You!

Offer limited to one per household and not to current subscribers. Terms, offer and prices subject to change. Orders subject to acceptance by Zebra Contemporary Book Club. Offer Valid in the U.S. only.

CNHL4A

THE BENEFITS OF BOOK CLUB MEMBERSHIP

- You'll get your books hot off the press, usually before they appear in bookstores.
- You'll ALWAYS save up to 20% off the cover price.
- You'll get our FREE monthly newsletter filled with author interviews, book previews, special offers and MORE!
- There's no obligation — you can cancel at any time and you have no minimum number of books to buy.
- And—if you decide you don't like the books you receive, you can return them. (You always have ten days to decide.)

lll..l..lll...lll.l.l.ll..l.ll..l.ll.l..l.ll.l.lll..l

Zebra Contemporary Romance Book Club

Zebra Home Subscription Service, Inc.

P.O. Box 5214

Clifton , NJ 07015-5214

jeans and denim jacket. Colleen would love her, and her sister-in-law was going to have a cow. She picked up a miniature guitar, microphone, and a black leather outfit for the doll and added them to the cart. She wasn't buying Colleen's Christmas present to please her prissy sister-in-law, but she would try to remember she was buying for a seven-year-old. A pair of pajamas, a sleeping bag, and a package of hair products was added to the pile.

Amber was debating on the Bratz radical-looking motorcycle, when Ian held up a doll. "Hey, this one has Grace's hair."

She took the doll from him and laughed. Sure enough, the doll wearing a miniskirt and black fishnet tights had red spiked hair. "The pierced eyebrow is a nice touch, don't you think?" The skimpy T-shirt the doll was wearing left nothing to the imagination. "I should get her for Grace for Christmas. She'll fit right in my aunt's stocking."

"Don't give your aunt any ideas. She would pierce her eyebrow, and your mother would blame you."

Ian was right. Her mother would blame her. Ian had been privy to her side of the conversation during one too many phone calls from her mother. Considering her mother called her about three times a day to complain about Grace's dating life, and to interrogate her on Ian, the man knew her mother well. Extremely well.

"I don't know, Ian." She looked at the doll named Jewel. "Grace could do a lot with a pierced eyebrow."

"Yeah, like what? Hang a Hallmark ornament from it? Maybe hook her key ring to it, so she wouldn't have to go hunting through her purse every time she needed to go somewhere?" Ian grabbed the doll and shoved her back onto the shelf. "Are you done now?"

"Nope, I still need a doll for Lauren." She glanced up and down the choices, and picked up a brunette, with a blue streak running down one side. The doll was dressed in baggy camouflage pants, an olive drab tank top, and black combat boots. She would have made a heck of an alien hunter. The three diamond earrings, in one ear, gave her a classy, yet understated look.

Another black leather outfit, pair of pajamas, sleeping bag, and hair care products were added to the cart. Along with a totally cool drum set. Her nieces could now start their own band.

Ian looked in the cart and asked, "How old are your nieces?"

"Nine, seven and six." She pushed the cart out of the aisle and headed for the other end of the store. The newest electronic math game, for five-year-old Joshua, went back on the shelf, as she hurried to her final destination. She came to a stop in front of the item that had caught her eye, while trying to find Ian.

Ian had only one thing to say about the display: "Wow!"

She smiled and couldn't have agreed more. "Joshua is going to love it."

"I don't know who Joshua is, but I want one." Ian ignored the sign that asked customers not to touch the display, and picked up a brontosaurus. "This is so cool."

"It comes with twenty-four dinosaurs, thirty different trees, assorted bushes, rocks, and vegetation. There's also a mountain cliff, complete with pterodactyl perch, and nine square feet of a detailed land region." She picked up the box she had been reading from, from the shelf beneath the display. "The fire volcano actually erupts."

"Really?" Ian moved closer and studied the fourteen-inch-high plastic volcano. "Oh, I see." Ian sounded disappointed. "You put all these red painted plastic rocks in it, push this lever, and the rocks come flying out of the opening at the top."

"Joshua's five, Ian. I don't think he's ready for molten lava and brimstone." She shook her head and placed the box into her cart. Joshua was going to love it. What little boy didn't like dinosaurs?

Ian repositioned the stegosaurus so that it was now battling the triceratops, and the tyrannosaurus rex was devouring the diplodocus. "Want to tell me why you're exchanging all the gifts you picked out?"

"I refuse to become the dorky aunt who gives everyone slippers and stupid sweaters every year." She yanked up the strap of her purse, which had been slipping off her shoulder. "Ready to check out?"

"I see you took our little friend Kyle's words to heart." Ian glanced at the cart and she could see he was trying to control his growing smile. "I take it Elmo comes with us?"

In the basket of the cart, going along for the ride, was a three-foot-high, bright red, furry Elmo. Two-year-old Hannah's mom had only written down "stuffed Elmo." Nowhere on the list was a size mentioned. Hannah was going to love playing with her new Sesame Street pal. "Wouldn't dream of leaving without him."

"You didn't think I could do it, admit it." Ian grinned as he took another bite out of his dinner. Barbecued ribs wouldn't be his first choice of a meal when he was with a beautiful woman. They were way too messy and he always felt funny eating with his fingers, but Amber had picked the place. He had been all set to order their deluxe hamburger, until Amber ordered a plateful of ribs herself. He had handed his menu back to the waitress and ordered the same entrée as Amber.

If Amber didn't mind the mess, neither did he.

"What do you want, a medal?" Amber waved her forkful of baked potato at him. "It was only a couple of hours' worth of shopping, Ian. It's not like you just climbed Mount Everest or deciphered someone's DNA."

He waved a rib back at her, in a mock imitation of her habit of talking with her hands, no matter what was in them. "But I didn't complain once." He had her there, and he wanted her to admit it. Shopping with Amber had been an experience he wouldn't soon forget. The woman had a detailed list of what to buy for whom, and then she turned around and bought totally different gifts. The only gift on the list that matched what was in her SUV out in the parking lot, was the three-foot, furry red guy, belted into the backseat.

"No, you didn't complain, moan, or groan. You even got a workout today by carrying all the bags." Amber picked up a rib and took a bite. A drop of barbecue sauce clung to her lower lip.

"I didn't even protest when you purposely dragged me into Victoria's Secret." Oh, he had second, third, and fourth thoughts about being in that particular store with Amber. None of the thoughts had to do with being embarrassed by the scantily clad mannequins or the more erotic merchandise hanging around for all to see. He wasn't bothered by women's underwear.

His unease came from the fact that every article of clothing he saw, he kept wondering how Amber would look in it. It made for a very uncomfortable shopping experience. He had decided that Amber did not need a Wonderbra, and that green was definitely her color. He had still been debating if Amber would look better wearing bikini undies or a thong when she paid for her purchases and he had to leave the store.

That sweet mystery of life had kept him occupied for the rest of the afternoon.

"How do you know it was on purpose?" Amber grinned, and the tip of her tongue swiped at the drop of sauce at the corner of her mouth. "I did have to do some shopping in there." She took another bite of her rib.

The smear of sauce, still on her lower lip, kept drawing his gaze. He always was partial to hickory smoke barbecue sauce. "I saw the gleam of laughter in your eye."

"Maybe I was laughing at what my sisters-in-law's reaction was going to be when they open their Christmas presents." Amber dug into her baked potato.

"I still haven't figured out how you got silk pajamas and feathery little high heel slippers out of that list. From what I read, one wanted a new blender, one wanted dark blue bath towels, and the other wanted queen-size sheets, in light blue." Amber had purchased each of her sisters-in-law pajamas, and while not being overly sexy or see-through, they definitely would be sending out some signals to Amber's brothers.

"I'm tired of following that stupid list, year after year." Amber waved an empty fork. "I finally came to the conclusion that they must think I'm stupid. Just because I don't have any children of my own, doesn't mean I can't pick out things my nieces or nephews would like."

"I think you picked out some really cool gifts." He didn't want to bring up the fact that one of the Bratz dolls had a Celtic design tattoo around her bicep. He noticed it when he was helping Amber unload the cart at the register in the toy store. He wasn't too sure how appropriate the doll was for a six-year-old, but since he didn't have any children of his own, boys or girls, he wasn't about to make a judgment call.

His own brother, Sean, kept telling him to go out, get married, and have children of his own, so he would stop spoiling his nephews. "It's a sibling thing, I think." He dumped some sour cream onto his potato. "Maybe it's a parent thing. Once they have kids, they all start thinking they know what's best and that the rest of us are morons."

"They all think their brains must have grown in that delivery room." She gave him a teasing smile. "Maybe they passed out extra brain cells along with all those how-to pamphlets, free samples of diapers and baby formula."

He laughed along with her. "I know quite a few parents they forgot to hand those extra brain cells out to."

"That's true." Amber's smile faded as she concentrated on her meal. He knew the exact instant she wanted to say something. Her hand holding the fork started to wave. "So Ian McNeal, why haven't you grown a bigger brain?"

"Huh?" She lost him on that question.

"Why haven't you gotten married, settled down, and had a few video game–playing boys of your own by now?"

There were a lot of ways he could answer that personal question. He had dated plenty of women over the years. Most were just casual dates, a couple had been more serious, usually on his date's part. The one relationship that he thought had a great chance of amounting to something special ended with a job promotion on the West Coast. He should count his blessings that Jill had even thought about calling him to tell him good-bye, as she was packing her bags. "I guess the right woman never asked me."

Amber arched an eyebrow, and her fork stopped moving. "A woman's got to ask you?"

He shrugged. "I've been told that I'm usually buried so deep in work that I can't see what's directly in front of me." James hadn't been the only one to point out his workaholic tendencies. His own mother was threatening to start calling her friends to see who had available daughters hanging around Boston. Even his brother's wife, Abby, was getting that matchmaking gleam in her eye.

"Are you telling me that if a woman, one you found attractive or interesting and was definitely available, was standing in front of your desk, and you were working on, say, the Coca-Cola ad campaign, you wouldn't ask her out?"

He sadly shook his head. "Amber, if I had a shot at getting the Coca-Cola ad campaign, Catherine Zeta-Jones could tap dance that number from *Chicago* on my desk and I wouldn't even look up."

Amber chuckled. "James once told me you were married to the business, but I didn't believe him." Amber gave him a teasing smile. "So you like Catherine Zeta-Jones?"

He didn't want to think about Amber and James discussing him, and his lack of a love life. It sounded pathetic. He could have gone out and partied every night of the week, but he had chosen to concentrate on the business. Marketing the newest trend in sneakers or the hottest fashions to a bunch of zit-faced teenagers wasn't as easy as the television led one to believe. Advertising was a lot of hard, time-consuming work, so he figured he could be excused from not hanging out at the coolest bars looking for the woman of his dreams.

Besides, the woman of his dreams had been either at home or out partying with her own husband.

Amber McAllister had been the woman who had set the bar when it came to finding his perfect partner in life. Amber was not only beautiful, smart, gracious, and nice, she was funny and had a wicked sense of humor and adventure. She had also made the perfect wife. No man had ever been happier in their marriage than James McAllister.

James had raved about his wife to any and all who would listen, morning, noon, and night. He had been

"Amber this, and Amber that," to death over the years. Problem was, he was having a hard time reconciling the Amber James had constantly bragged about to the woman sitting across from him eating barbecued ribs with her fingers.

James had told him that Amber loved jewelry, and over the years he had seen many of the pieces James had given her. A diamond bracelet, a matching emerald necklace and earring set, and gold rings set with just about every precious gemstone dug from the earth. Yet, he had seen Amber wear jewelry only once, and that had been a simple set of silver teardrops. James also had said that Amber loved parties, plays, and anything else that she would have to dress up for. So far, the closest thing to a dress-up event had been the gallery open house. Piling on an extra layer of clothes, just to go sit on the sidelines and watch him play hockey, didn't count as a dress-up event.

He couldn't match the sophisticated social butterfly James had claimed she was to the woman who spent the entire evening getting tossed into snowbanks and freezing her butt off, just so they could finally claim a clean run down Suicide Hill. He just wished the real Amber would stand up.

He wanted to know who he was falling in love with.

"I've upset you somehow, haven't I?" asked Amber. "I didn't mean to." He saw the sadness dull her beautiful green eyes.

"I'm not upset." How was he to explain he didn't want to talk about James and their seemingly perfect marriage? "Catherine had to choose one of us, and I can't really blame her. Michael Douglas had a hell of a lot more to offer her than I could."

Amber's laughter lightened the mood. "I wouldn't know about that one."

"I don't know what you mean by that comment"—he

picked up another rib—"but I'm taking it as a compliment."

"It was one." Amber ate in silence for a moment. "So, you really are staying in town for a while longer?"

"Seems that way." He hadn't really been able to gauge Amber's feelings on him staying around. He liked to think she was happy about that news, but that might be wishful thinking on his part. "Olivia said there's no problem with the room and the office is going to be over-nighting me stuff that I need to be working on this coming week."

"So it's all set?" Amber seemed to be concentrating on her baked potato with a little more intensity than was required just to eat the thing.

"I figure I could work every morning at the bed-and-breakfast, spend the afternoons packing up orders for you, and in the evening . . ." He gazed into Amber's intense green eyes, and he would swear in a court of law that he heard the sound of ice cracking beneath his feet. If he had been out on Sara's Pond, he would have been hustling his butt back to solid land as fast as he could. As it was, he couldn't very well tell her the truth, that the evenings were the worst, yet the best part of his days. Time alone with Amber was a double-edged sword. "In the evenings, you can keep showing me around Misty Harbor."

"Ian, I hate to disappoint you, but you've seen all of Misty Harbor."

"Would you rather I head back to Boston?" Amber wasn't looking too thrilled about him staying.

"No." Plain, simple, and to the point.

"So you don't mind me hanging around?" He felt like he was back in middle school. Maybe he and Amber should be passing notes back and forth.

"Ian, when you look at me, who do you see?" Amber

placed her silverware next to her plate and wiped her fingers with a napkin.

"I see you, Amber."

"No, do you see an unattached woman who you might want to spend some time with, or do you see James's widow?"

That double-edged sword just went slashing over his head. How in the hell was he supposed to answer that question without losing a vital limb. "You're both."

Amber sadly shook her head. "You came to Maine to check up on me, didn't you? You wanted to make sure your friend, James's widow, was doing okay, and moving on with her life. Right?"

"That was part of the reason." The sword took another deadly swing.

"What's the other part?"

"I needed to deliver the check." Another half-truth.

"You could have dropped that into any mailbox, Ian. So why did you drive over five hours to get here? And don't give me that story about needing a vacation. Any sane, rational man would be sitting on some sandy beach, drinking drinks with paper umbrellas in them, and watching girls in bikinis walking by." Amber looked like she wasn't going to move until he gave her an answer. "So, why are you still in Misty Harbor?"

He shrugged. He couldn't very well tell her he was falling in love with her. They hadn't even kissed, and the only time she had been in his arms was when they had been flying down Suicide Hill. "I like the company."

Amber looked disappointed. "Okay, Ian, this is how it's going to be. If you're still in Misty Harbor because of some misguided sense of responsibility to James's memory, I want you to leave."

"You do?" The sword sliced deep and was merciless.

"I do." Amber's fingers crumpled her napkin. "But, if you're still here because of me and what almost happened at the bottom of Suicide Hill, then I would like you to stay."

"What almost happened?"

"You almost kissed me." Amber held his gaze.

He shook his head and felt the pull of a smile tease his mouth. "You were the one who almost kissed me."

"I think we need to work on perception." Amber's slow smile matched his. "Your perception."

Chapter 10

Amber watched as the UPS man took the last load of boxes out to his truck. It's the Berries Jam Company was well on its way to making a name for itself. The orders kept coming in, but thankfully they were now holding their own on getting them out in a timely manner. Between Ian, Grace, and herself they were only about two days behind in shipping out orders. The UPS man had taken one look at the towering stacks of boxes piled by the front door and Grace's proud smile, and wisely kept his thoughts to himself.

Now that the latest shipment of orders were on their way, Amber headed back to the workroom to handle some last minute details before she called it a day. Being Monday, the shop was open till eight, but Grace and Tiffany were scheduled to handle the evening hours. She had the night off, since Friday was her night to work.

Grace had really outdone herself this past weekend when it came to the business and packing up orders. Amber wasn't sure what had happened to Grace's Saturday night date with Joe Clayton or why her aunt was putting in all kinds of hours at the shop. Grace, in a totally uncharacteristic move, wasn't talking. The most she had gotten out of her aunt was that the work needed to be done, and she had the free time.

Since when did her aunt have any free time? Grace's schedule tired Amber out, just hearing about it. And she was twenty-five years younger than Grace.

By noon on Saturday, Grace and Tiffany had kicked Ian and her out of the workroom, so they could get an earlier start to the mall and their Christmas shopping. Tiffany had left when the shop closed at three, but Grace must have stayed long into the night. When Amber came in early Sunday morning, to do some work before going to see Ian play hockey, the place had been stacked with outgoing boxes. Instead of boxing up more orders like she had planned, she had spent four hours downloading more orders, printing shipping labels, and posting the inventory.

After freezing her butt off watching Ian and the rest of the men play two games of hockey yesterday, they had gone back to Olivia and Ethan's for dinner and penny poker. The newlyweds had behaved themselves, and she had managed to win a whopping eighty-seven cents. Ian had lost about two bucks. After the card game, Ian had driven her home, walked her to the door, and politely thanked her for showing him another good time.

Today was going to be different. The rules had changed. She was having her first real date with Ian tonight. It wasn't anything special, they were just going ice-skating out at Sara's Pond, but he had been the one to ask. Her days and nights of being Ian's personal tour guide had ended.

Ian was staying in Misty Harbor because of her, and hopefully no one would detect the subtle change in their relationship. The last thing she wanted was for her mother to hear about it.

It wasn't as if her mother objected to her dating and

getting on with her life. Gladys would be one well-contented woman if her only daughter got married again, bought a house down the street from her, and gave her another grandchild or two to spoil. Her mother's objection to her life was the location in which she had chosen to live. Gladys Donovan wanted her daughter back in Providence, or at least Boston.

Gladys had been born and raised in Misty Harbor, had gotten married two weeks after graduating from high school, and had moved away as fast—and as far—as she could at the time. Amber and her three brothers had been born and raised in Providence, Rhode Island. Her mom visited Misty Harbor about once a year, to see her twin sister and to catch up with childhood friends. Her mom felt the same way about the town now as she did at eighteen; it was small, boring, and who in the hell would want to live there?

Her mother hadn't understood her decision to move in with Aunt Grace and help with the jam business. Her mother hadn't understood when she fixed up the apartment behind Grace's house and permanently moved in there. Her mother didn't understand Grace's reemergence into the dating game and thought it was appalling that Grace was having some fun in life. It seemed her mother didn't understand anyone's decisions on anything she hadn't approved of first.

Gladys Donovan wanted everyone to live life by Gladys Donovan's rules. Amber knew she was too much like her Aunt Grace to idly sit back and let someone else dictate her life to her. Grace and she were the rebels of the family, and her poor mother was not only making herself nuts trying to control them, but she was driving herself into the poorhouse with her long distance phone bills.

Hearing that Ian and she were "dating" would have her mother seeing rainbows at the end of what she once termed her "stormy" period. Her mother would not only be mentally planning her wedding, but her move back to Boston, to where Ian's business was located. Her mother would hear about this "dating" business, and think all her prayers had been answered.

Nothing was farther from the truth. She liked Ian, really liked him. She thought he was handsome, charming, polite, and funny. With Ian she had a great time and he always made her smile. She also was very attracted to him and she was tired of waiting for him to make the next move in their fragile and shaky relationship. She would even go so far as admit there was a good possibility she was falling in love with him. But she wasn't thinking marriage and wedding receptions. And she definitely wasn't moving back to Boston or even Rhode Island. She was staying right where she was—knee-deep in blueberries and lobsters in Misty Harbor.

Tonight she had only one goal: to get Ian McNeal to finally kiss her.

Amber glanced up from the pile of paperwork she was supposed to be working on, to look at her aunt who had just walked into the back room. Grace started to gather up a bunch of candles from the storage shelves to take out front. Amber noticed the shelves had more space than candles. "I guess I need to call Karin and order some more candles." The candles had a nice markup, not a huge one because she had only been interested in offering the customer something that couldn't be poured, spread, or spooned out of a jar.

"Tell her the hollyberry ones are selling as fast as I can display them." Grace studied the two shelves holding the different size and scented candles. "You better get some more cranberry, mulberry, and the dark green ones."

"Pineberry?"

"That's the one." Grace carefully set a couple more candles into the box she was filling. "A lot of customers are just coming in for the candles. They're claiming they smell better and last longer than some of those high-priced glass jar ones."

"Karin's experimenting around with not only the glass jars, but some new scents for spring. A lot of the customers don't like the pillar style, and would feel safer if the flame was in the jar."

Karin Warner was about twenty-six years old, had two adorable little girls, and was in, if she had to guess, a horrible marriage. When Karin first hesitantly approached Grace and her about carrying the berry-scented candles, she hadn't the money to mass produce them on a scale the store would require. Amber had not only loved the candles, she had quietly bankrolled Karin's operation to get it off the ground. She was also silently funding Karin's experiments. Seeing the young mother's self-confidence grow, along with her business, these past several months was her reward for the no-interest loans.

"Will they be as pretty as these?" Grace's long red fingernails flicked at the festive gold bow and the two tiny pinecones tied around one of the pineberry candles.

"Prettier. Karin's working on a scent called seaberry. It will be a great seller, once she gets it down right." Amber shut down the computer for the night. "You need anything else before I leave?" Ian would be picking her up in about an hour and she needed to get home to change.

"Amber"—Tiffany waltzed into the back room looking fresh and vibrant, as only a seventeen-year-old could do—"you don't need me Tuesday or Wednesday afternoon, do you?"

Tiffany looked like she was about to beg not to work. "Not that I know of." Tiffany sometimes worked a couple of hours after school on those days, if they needed her. Because of Ian's help, Tiffany would be getting those days off and the begging could be averted to another time. "What about you, Grace? Do you need Tiffany for anything?" Grace had gladly, and willingly, handed over the reins of running the business to her, but she always tried to include her aunt in the discussions. After all, it was still Grace's business.

"Not that I can think of. The store's in great shape and I was planning on spending tonight getting more orders packed."

"Great." Tiffany did that girl thing of flipping her hair over her shoulder and smiling as if a photographer were standing by shooting pictures. "I hear you and Ian are going out on a *real* date." Tiffany glanced at Grace and tried not to smile at the woman who obviously gave her that information. Tiffany failed miserably.

"We're only going ice-skating out at the pond." If Tiffany knew it was a real date, so did the whole entire town, but worse, so did her mother. For over the past week she had spent many an hour on the phone with her mother, convincing her that Ian and she were just friends. She'd be lucky if her mother wasn't sitting on her doorstep with a *Brides* magazine in her lap when she went home to change.

"Derrick took me out to the pond skating Saturday night." Tiffany flipped her hair again and tugged at the hem of her black turtleneck sweater. The skintight sweater, that didn't quite reach the waistband of her jeans, looked new and expensive. A half inch of pale skin was visible above the jeans every time Tiffany raised her arms. "I hope you two have as much *fun*."

There was no mistaking the emphasis Tiffany had placed on the word *fun*. Tiffany's parents should lock her up until her thirtieth birthday. She didn't want to think what her employee had been doing out at the pond Saturday night. It wasn't the frozen pond that would have gotten her in trouble, but the nice heated cars everyone piled into to snuggle and get warm while taking breaks from the cold. Amber had been out to

Sara's Pond enough times to know that a lot of those breaks had been ridiculously long. The town's road crew didn't plow "Lookout Point," but they did do a rough couple of passes out at the pond if the ground was frozen.

"It's only skating, Tiffany." She ignored her aunt's snickers.

"If you say so." Tiffany looked at Grace and rolled her eyes. "Ian's hot, Am, so you better make your move before he heads back to Boston."

"What do you mean he's hot?" Tiffany's parents should lock her up until she was forty, and then throw away the key. Seventeen-year-old girls shouldn't be referring to thirty-year-old men as hot.

"I agree with Tiffany on this one." Grace put the box of candles on the worktable and grinned. "Ian's definitely hot."

Fifty-four-year-old aunts shouldn't be checking out guys young enough to be their own sons.

"So what are you waiting for, Am?" Tiffany asked. "You're not getting any younger."

Grace looked grave. "Her thirtieth birthday is in a couple of months."

"Quick, someone sign me up for Medicare," she snapped.

Tiffany and Grace both laughed. "I didn't mean that you were old, Am," Tiffany apologized. "It's just that life is short, and you only go around once. You should be going after what you want, that's all."

"How old are you, seventeen? What do you know about life being short?" *Heck, what could she possibly know about life, long or short?*

"Hey, I once again agree with her, Amber. Tiffany's right, life is too darn short," Grace said. "I think you should go after what you want."

"And what do I want?" Considering she didn't even know the answer to that question, she was curious as to what her aunt would say. Her Christmas list had one item on it, a coffee bean grinder. Grace's list was taped to her refrigerator door and had a dozen or so items listed. The list started with a Dolly Parton wig and ended with alligator boots, size eight, wide.

"You want Ian." Grace gave her a look that defied her to disagree.

"Don't worry, Am, he wants you, too." Tiffany gave her a knowing look.

"And how do you figure that one?" Back when she was seventeen, it took gossip and rumors floating through the school's hallways between classes, and a complicated phone chain system that the CIA is still trying to duplicate to learn who wanted to go out with whom. Considering the technology the kids had today, she wouldn't be surprised that babies were being conceived in cyberspace.

"I see the way Ian looks at you." Tiffany looked offended.

"How does he look at me? Before you answer, remember you're seventeen and I know your parents." She ignored Grace's uproarious laugh. The woman was crazy, anyway. She wanted to wear dead reptiles on her feet.

Tiffany thought about it for a moment. "You know that look you get in your eyes when you're over at Krup's and they set that thick chocolate shake in front of you?"

She could only imagine. If Brad Pitt stood between her and that shake, the actor would have her boot prints across his forehead. "Yeah." A person didn't jump two sizes in her jeans without obsessing about those milk shakes.

"Ian has that same look in his eyes when he's looking at you." Tiffany's smile was pure satisfaction. She looked like she just aced a geography test.

Amber wasn't sure, but her knees might have melted.

One thing she knew for sure, she had to be blushing the exact same color as Grace's hair. "That's ridiculous." She would have noticed that look, wouldn't she?

"She's absolutely right, Amber." Grace looked at the young girl with a great deal of respect and awe. "I had been trying to place that look in his eyes, myself. Tiffany has hit it on the head. You get that same feverish hungry gleam in your eyes every time you see one of those shakes." Grace shook her head and chuckled. "I had been hoping the memory of that look had been from one of my beaus, when he had been gazing into my eyes, but I guess not."

"I'm out of here. You're both nuts." She grabbed her coat off the back peg and tugged it on. She didn't want to hear about her aunt's dates or their heated glances. She pulled her hat low over her ears and wrapped her scarf around her neck before heading for the desk and her purse.

Grace turned to Tiffany. "I don't think I've been giving you enough credit, young lady." Grace picked up the box of candles and headed for the front of the shop with Tiffany in tow. "So what do you think is the best way to catch a gentleman's interest?"

She snatched up the purse and headed for the back door. She couldn't believe her aunt was pumping a seventeen-year-old girl for dating advice. The whole world had gone crazy. She stepped out into the cold dusk and started the short walk home while pulling on her mittens. A light dusting had coated everything with a clean, fresh blanket of snow. The entire town looked like a picture postcard.

As she kicked up the fresh powder with her boots, she waved to a couple of people who honked and felt the cold air cool her heated cheeks. She didn't want to think about what was being discussed back in the shop, but a disturbing question did remain. Whose interest was Grace trying to attract? As far as she knew, every single male above the age of forty-five had been panting at the heels of her aunt's fake Dalmatian fur-trimmed boots.

"I'm sorry for the sandwiches, but I couldn't figure out a way to keep anything hot." Ian handed her a plate piled with a thick roast beef on rye and a mountain of potato salad. The plate was fine china, and the fork antique silver. The green napkin lying across her lap was fine linen.

She grinned as she took the plate and moved her frozen feet closer to the heating vent. "This is perfect, Ian. I've never had a picnic while ice-skating before." She took a sip of wine, from a crystal goblet, and set it back into the cup holder between the seats.

"It's Olivia's picnic basket and dishes." Ian snapped the lid onto the container of potato salad. "The food's from Catch of the Day in town. I picked it up earlier." Ian closed the wicker basket and put it on the backseat. "There's a thermos of coffee, if you prefer something hot to drink."

"No, the wine's wonderful. We'll save the coffee for later." She snuggled into the heated seat of Ian's luxury car. The only part of her body that was still feeling the cold were her toes, but they were warming up by the minute. It was her own fault; she should have worn two pairs of socks, instead of just one. "I must admit that I'm impressed."

"By my skating?" A teasing smile curved Ian's mouth.

"No. You skate like a hockey player, all force and no grace." She smiled back before biting into her sandwich. If Ian was expecting false compliments, he was dating the wrong woman.

"Hey, I saw you on your butt a couple of times." Ian tried to sound offended, but his smile blew it.

There was no denying that truth. Her butt had hit

the ice more than a couple, but less than a hundred, times already tonight. Her loss of balance usually involved a wayward skate from a kid or two. It seemed every kid in town had had the same idea as Ian. Even though it was a school night, it was still early enough that the ice was crowded with shrieking children and harried parents. Ian had been roped into giving a few of the younger boys hockey lessons on the far end of the ice. She in turn had helped hand-hold a couple kids around the pond, and her now black and blue derriere was paying the price.

It hadn't been the most romantic date, until now.

Now it was just Ian and she. They were alone in his toasty car with a picnic basket full of food, and a bottle of fine wine. Through the windshield they could watch the skaters. A couple of the older boys were practicing making their shots at the far end of the ice. A few teenagers were paired up and pretending they were skating at the shadowy end of the pond. A couple of their moves would have been banned from the Olympics.

The spotlights, which were being run by a gas-powered generator, were lighting most of the pond. Either the farthest spotlight had burned out, or one of the teenagers had unscrewed the bulb. Teenagers grew up to have teenagers of their own, but the behavior stayed the same. They watched the skaters glide across the ice, moving in and out of the shadows.

"This was one of my favorite spots to come when we came to visit my aunt during the winter." She had fond memories of her brothers and all her cousins piling into cars and heading for the pond for an evening full of tumbles, bruises, hot chocolate, and Aunt Grace's famous oatmeal raisin cookies. Aunt Grace had always strapped on her skates to join them, while her mother either stayed back at the house, or went car-hopping, catching up the latest gossip with the other mothers.

"I thought Suicide Hill would have been your favorite." Ian's gaze was on her, instead of the skaters.

"It ranks in the top ten." She watched as some mother loaded up half a dozen kids into her minivan, and then drove away. Most of the little kids were now heading home. Homework and bath time were calling.

Ian leaned against his door, balanced his plate on his jean-clad thigh, and picked up his glass. "Name some of them."

"My favorite places?" She never had anyone ask her that before. Her favorite song, or movie, or even color, but never a place. She liked the fact that Ian was always asking her questions and actually listened to the answers.

"Only here, in Maine, and at this time of year." Ian picked up his sandwich and started to eat.

"The lighthouse has to be one. I love just going up there to sit, no matter what time of the year. There's something magical about the place, especially on moonlit nights. It's either the roaring thunder of the crashing of the waves against the rocks below, or the way the light strobes across everything." She gave a fleeting smile. "Aunt Grace used to take me up there for hours on end, but my mother thought it was one of the most boring spots in town."

"You did seem to like to stand on that cliff and stare out to sea the other night. The whipping wind didn't even faze you." Ian dug into his potato salad.

"There had been way too many people to truly enjoy it. The noise alone was drowning out the sound of the sea." She thought about all the visits over the years. "My favorite place of all was Aunt Grace's and Uncle Howard's den. In the winter, Uncle Howard always had a fire going in the fireplace and big, soft afghans were on every chair and usually two on the couch. While all my brothers were fighting over the television in the living room, I was curled up in a big chair reading a book."

"What kind of book?"

"Mysteries, mainly. The bloodier the better."

"Now that I wouldn't have guessed. I figured you for one of those love stories type." Ian chuckled. "What did you do, go looting through Grace's bookshelves every time you visited? Your mother must have been horrified at your reading material."

Now it was her turn to chuckle. "Grace passes out at the sight of blood, and wouldn't be able to sleep for a week if she watched *CSI*. Grace is so scared of the dark that I swear there is a nightlight plugged into every outlet in her house. I get my love of mysteries and horror from my mother. It's one of the few things we have in common."

"Really?" Ian turned the heater down a notch. "I thought you and your mother would have a lot in common."

"In some strange twist of logic, yet to be explained by the laws of nature and to the exasperation of my mother, I take after my Aunt Grace."

"Not in fashion sense you don't." Ian chuckled. "In case you didn't notice, today your aunt was wearing an emerald green velour jogging suit, sneakers with a moose on them, and a fake rack of antlers."

"I thought the antlers were a nice touch and coordinated beautifully with the pinecone earrings. I think she was going for the northern look today." She kept a straight face and managed not to choke on her next bite.

Her aunt was really outdoing herself this holiday season. Half the people who came into the shop only did it to see what Grace would be wearing. She would like to think that it was all a marketing ploy, but that didn't explain Grace's unusual collection of flannel pajamas and slippers. Her aunt had given her more than one fright at night. Grace hadn't been selling anyone blueberry jam while raiding the refrigerator wearing glow-in-the-dark flamingo pajamas and matching slippers at two in the morning.

"Any farther north and she would have to have been a polar bear." Ian chuckled. "Has she always been like this, or is this a recent development?"

"She went as Elvira to her senior prom. Howard had made a dashing Dracula. My mother still hasn't forgiven her for that one." She munched on a fat piece of potato. "Does that answer your question?"

"Howard was okay with it?" Ian seemed curious.

"Okay with it? No, he encouraged it." She laughed at distant memories of her favorite uncle. "Who do you think bought most of her wardrobe and accessories?"

"Tell me he didn't dress like her all the time."

"He didn't dress like her all the time," she deadpanned.

Ian laughed. "Seriously?"

"Seriously. Uncle Howard usually saved dress-up for Halloween. It was the one holiday that I begged and begged my mom to take me to Grace's for, but she never did."

"You never spent Halloween in Misty Harbor?"

"Not until I moved here. The last two Halloweens have been a real eye-opener for me. Let's just say, Grace is quite laid-back at Christmastime."

Ian softly whistled. "I can see why you love living here."

"Thanks." Her own mother couldn't understand, but Ian did. She finished off the last of her wine. "Dinner was excellent. Thank you." She now felt full, warm, and contented.

Ian loaded up the empty plates and glasses back into the hamper. "There're two thick slices of chocolate cake for later."

She groaned. The waistband of her jeans was already digging into her gut. "Let's go work off what we just ate." She reached for her coat and everything else she needed to pull on before heading back out onto the ice. If she ate another mouthful she would never be able to bend over to lace up her skates. "I'm betting you that I could beat you from one end of the pond to the other."

"You want to race?" Ian reached for his coat. "What are we betting?"

"Dinner tomorrow night. You win, I cook, but if I win, you cook. I'll even let you use my kitchen."

"That's mighty nice of you, but since I'm going to win I won't be needing your kitchen." Ian turned off the car, opened his door, and grabbed his skates. "Have I mentioned that I'm partial to Mexican?"

"No, but since we'll be having spaghetti I don't think it will matter." She bent over and started lacing up the skates Grace had loaned her the first Christmas she lived here. The skates were white with hot pink laces.

"Spaghetti?" Ian had already finished lacing up his one skate and had started in on the other.

"With meatballs." She finished lacing and then tugged on her mittens. "Come on, slowpoke." She shut the car door and hurried the short distance to the pond's edge. Ian was beside her when she stepped onto the ice.

There were still a couple of younger kids on the ice, but most had gone home. Older boys were now taking shots at one of the hockey nets at one end of the pond. A couple of teenagers were still taking advantage of the near darkness at the other end. "Let's start at that end." She pointed to the hockey net.

"That's fine with me." Ian slowly skated around two five-year-olds, who appeared to be holding each other up. "So are there any rules to this race besides first one to the far snowbank wins?"

"No rules." She stopped at the far end of the pond and eyed the distance to the other end. It hadn't looked that far from the car. Grace and style weren't going to win this race, speed was. She was toast. Ian's strength and speed were going to get him down to the other end of the ice faster. She started to count, "One"—she wasn't worried—"two"—she knew how to make tacos—"three!" She got a jump on Ian off the line, but that was going to be her only advantage.

Ian caught her before she was twenty feet out. By mid ice he had her by a good ten feet. She knew he was holding back so it didn't appear as if he had creamed her. She was laboring hard by the time they hit the shadowy darkness at the far end of the pond.

Ian skidded to stop mere inches from the snowbank and turned to face her. She was just starting to slow down when one of the teenage girls backed away from her boyfriend, laughing about something. Amber saw her coming, but the girl wasn't paying attention to what was behind her.

Ian and the girl's boyfriend shouted at the same instant. Amber knew she would never stop in time to avoid the collision, so she put on a burst of speed. The girl, reacting to her boyfriend's yell, turned one way. Amber turned the other and collided into a solid muscular wall.

The next thing she knew, Ian's arms were around her and they were both going down. The jarring impact wasn't too bad. She had landed on a soft, warm body— Ian's. Ian landed on his back in the snowbank.

She got her breath back and slowly raised her head. "You alive?"

Ian grunted.

She was hoping that was an affirmative. Her arms were wedged in between her chest and his. She braced her arms and pushed up. Ian grunted again as her hips pressed into his. Her legs were on either side of his and she was pretty sure she hadn't cut him with one of the sharp blades during their fall. She scooted up a little higher to get a better look at him in the gloom. "Ian, are you okay?"

Ian's arms tightened around her hips and held her still. One brown eye peeked open. Ian's hat had been knocked askew and a lock of dark brown hair was dangerously close to being in his eye. "Don't move."

She tried to wiggle higher, only to have him groan again. "Where are you hurt?" She tried to push off of him, but he held her fast.

Ian gave a rueful chuckle. "You don't want to know."

She was about to argue with him, until she saw the hungry gleam of desire in his eyes. Ian might be hurting, but his pain wasn't coming from the fall. She ignored the cold wet snow seeping into the knees of her jeans. "I see."

She stared down into Ian's handsome face and realized she wasn't getting any younger. Time marched on, and if she didn't go after what she wanted, no one was going to hand it to her on a silver platter. "Maybe this will help." She leaned down and kissed him the way she had been dying to kiss him. There was nothing tentative about the kiss. It was all heat.

Ian's arms slipped up her back and pressed her closer. His mouth opened beneath hers, and she sank farther into the kiss. She nipped at his lower lip, and then tangled her tongue around his.

The snow beneath them hissed from the steam, the ice on the pond started to melt, and she wasn't sure, but the world might have stopped spinning on its axis for a short space of time.

"Hey, man, are you two all right?" One of the teenagers had come skidding to a stop before them.

She frantically pushed away from Ian, the same instant he released her. She ended up in the snowbank, lying on her back, staring up at Ryan Albert's know-it-all smirk.

Chapter 11

Ian set the picnic basket down on Amber's kitchen table. "Would you like me to start a fire?" Amber's apartment was nice and warm, but a fire would be a nice touch. It was still early and they had yet to have dessert. Chocolate cake and coffee in front of a roaring blaze sounded like a perfect ending to their evening.

"That's sounds great. You know where everything is, right?" Amber was hanging up her coat and kicking off her boots. Her ice skates were already dumped by the front door and her cheeks were still red from the cold. "Let me go change into something dry." He could see that her jeans from the knees down were damp from their tumble into the snowbank.

"Go ahead. I'll take care of the fire." The back of his jeans might not be soaked, but they were definitely more than damp. Rolling around in a snowbank with Amber was going to give him pneumonia if he wasn't careful, but it had been well worth every frostbitten minute of it. He could single-handedly give a new meaning to the phase "rosy-red cheeks."

He had been waiting for over a week for that kiss. And what a kiss it had been. He wasn't sure what surprised him more, the heat that had ignited between them, or the fact it had been Amber who had initiated the kiss. One thing he did know, it had been truly embarrassing to be caught kissing by Amber's teenage neighbor. Ryan Albert hadn't come right out and teased Amber, but by the smirk on his face, he knew Ryan had wanted to.

Ian kicked off his boots, hung up his jacket, and reached down to scratch Light behind her ears. The cat had greeted him as soon as he walked into the apartment, and was now busy rubbing against his leg demanding some attention. Shadow hadn't made his appearance yet.

Amber disappeared into the bedroom closet, and then into the bathroom. With Light trailing behind him, he headed for the fireplace. Light sat beside him, washing her paws and watching his every move as he got a fire started. Shadow came out from under the bed to investigate what was going on, but he didn't stray too close. Shadow was still leery of him.

By the time Amber joined him, the fire was blazing, and Ian was standing in front of the flames trying to dry the back of his pants. Most women that he knew would have taken a good half hour or more in the bathroom changing and fussing with their appearance. "That didn't take you long." Amber looked beautiful, but there was nothing new in that. Amber always looked gorgeous.

She had changed from her jeans and sweater to plaid flannel pants and a matching, soft sage colored sweatshirt. Cream terry cloth slippers were on her feet, and her hair was brushed to a beautiful sheen. Amber's gorgeous hair was auburn, straight, and past her shoulders. To his frustration, most of the time she either wore her hair in a ponytail, or had a monster clip holding it up off her neck. Tonight she had left it down.

Amber's cheeks were still flushed from ice-skating,

and an assortment of freckles danced their way across her nose and onto her cheeks. It was her enticing mouth that still held most of his attention. A light sheen of gloss coated those luscious lips. He knew from experience that Amber's lips tasted like heated strawberries.

The desire to pull her into his arms and to taste wild strawberries once again nearly had him dropping the cat and reaching for her. There was no way that kiss had been as good as he was remembering. First kisses were usually soft, shy, tentative, sweet, awkward, or just plain passionless. None of those adjectives described Amber and his first kiss. Nuclear meltdown came close, but even that description was lacking something.

"I see you have company." She nodded to Shadow, who was sitting in the chair watching them, and Light, whom he had cradled in his arms.

"She likes the attention." He gave Light a couple more strokes and then set her down on the floor. "Shadow's still not too sure of me yet."

"The person who feeds him gets his affection." Amber gave Shadow a quick scratch on top of the head and then walked into the small open kitchen. "Are you ready for some coffee now?"

"Okay. You need any help?" He really didn't want to move away from the fire. His jeans had gone from wet to a warm, steaming damp.

"No, thanks, I got it." Amber dug into the wicker basket and hauled out the thermos and two mugs. Two little boxes, each holding a slice of Catch of the Day's famous triple layer chocolate cake came out next, along with two clean forks. "I can't believe you went to all this trouble for dinner." Amber piled everything onto a tray and carried it into the living room. "How about we sit on the couch?"

"No can do." He took a tiny step away from the fireplace. The back of his pants were definitely getting a trifle warm and if he wasn't careful something vital might get steam-cooked. "I don't want to get your couch damp."

"Oh." Amber stopped in the middle of the room and frowned at his pants.

Ian shifted his weight. Having a very desirable woman, with whom he had just shared the most passionate kiss of his life, stare at his crotch and frown was dispiriting to say the least.

Amber thrust the tray into his hands. "I have an idea."

He would bet a year's salary it wasn't the same idea he was having. Amber's queen-size bed was maybe a good twelve feet away and looked incredibly inviting.

Amber hurried into her bedroom closet and came out holding a quilt. He wondered what the chances were that she would fulfill every man's erotic fantasy and demand that he remove those wet pants immediately.

"Move out of the way," she ordered as she shook out the blanket.

He had to smile at her militant tone and his lack of luck. He moved to the right and watched as she spread the quilt in front of the fireplace. "Another picnic?" He set the tray in the center of the blanket and spread himself out in front of the blaze on his side.

"Tonight seems to be the night for them." Amber sat across from him and reached for the thermos. "It will be a long time before having one outside again."

"At least this way there're no ants or mosquitoes."

"True." Amber poured the coffee and stated the obvious. "It's got cream in it."

"And sugar." He reached for a cup, but Amber didn't pass him one.

"But you take it black."

"Amber, a little sugar and cream won't kill me." He leaned in farther and snagged up a cup. "Trying to figure out how to pack cream and sugar wasn't worth the headache. I mixed up the thermos the way you like it."

"I can go put on a fresh pot." Amber opened up the containers holding the cake, and passed him one, along with a fork.

"Amber, it's fine." He took a sip of coffee just to prove it to her and smiled. He clamped his back teeth together and tried not to gag. He hated cream in his coffee. Sugar he didn't mind too much, but the cream got him every time. Milk either belonged on his Cocoa Puffs, or in a nice tall glass with a mountain of Oreos next to it. "So tell me, what are you going to do with all your free time, now that the orders are nearly caught up?"

"Put up a Christmas tree and finish my shopping." Amber started in on her slice of cake. "I'm figuring we got another week of heavy orders and then it should taper down to the occasional rush order." Amber stretched out across the far end of the quilt and faced him. "Grace is helping out more. She's been in the shop every day this week, including Saturday night, packing up orders."

"I did notice that there seemed to be an awful lot of boxes being shipped this afternoon. Mark didn't seem too thrilled with the pickup." Mark was the UPS man, and Ian had met him on more than one occasion. Usually when Mark had an armful of boxes, a strained look upon his face, and a clipboard jammed into his armpit. "I thought Grace had a hot date with Joe Clayton Saturday night."

"Either he cancelled it, or she did." Amber gave him an amused look and chuckled. "Then again, Grace might have had him boxing up orders with her. My aunt wasn't very forthcoming on her evening."

"Grace told me she won sixty bucks at bingo on Friday night. She even offered to take me with her next Friday night if I get bored."

"Are you?" Amber piled her empty cake box back onto the tray.

"Am I what?" His box landed on top of hers. The back of his jeans felt toasty dry and warm. The back of his neck was starting to sweat.

"Getting bored?"

Over the rim of his cup, he gazed at her mouth as he finished off the coffee. Amber had to be out of her mind. He was the most "unbored" he had ever been in his life. Just looking at her made him excited, edgy, and all revved up. He was falling in love, and Amber wanted to know if he was bored. "Do I act bored?" He placed the cup on the tray.

Amber placed her cup next to his, and then slid the tray off the quilt and under the chair sitting in front of her computer. "No, but with you it might be hard to tell."

There was a good three feet of small blue cotton squares sewn into a patchwork design between him and Amber. The quilt felt soft and aged beneath his fingers. "Why would it be hard to tell?" He moved a couple of inches closer to Amber, and away from the heat.

"You're nice enough to just be acting interested." Amber's fingertip traced a seam in the quilt. Her gaze was on the blanket and her cheeks were pink. He couldn't tell if she was blushing, or if the color was from the heat pouring off the flames behind him. All he knew was it was getting awfully warm in the room.

Amber wasn't out of her mind, she was certifiable. "Oh, I'm interested, all right."

"Interested in what?" Amber raised her head and looked directly at him. Golden reflections of the dancing flames were in her bright eyes.

He moved closer and slowly brushed a lock of her hair behind her ear. The strands of her auburn hair felt like silk as they slid through his fingers. "I'm still in Misty Harbor, Amber."

"That means?"

It meant he had one hell of a lot of work either to do or look over back at the bed-and-breakfast. He couldn't believe everything the office had sent him. It also meant he wasn't ready to leave Amber. He wanted to explore this growing feeling between them. He needed to be here, with her. "My perception is just fine." The pad of his thumb skimmed across the dewy gloss coating her lower lip. He could smell a hint of strawberry. "You were the one to kiss me back in that snowbank."

The tip of Amber's tongue touched his thumb, causing a shiver of need to slide down his backbone. His jeans weren't the only thing steaming. Amber's light green eyes turned dark and shadowy as she whispered, "What are you going to do about that?"

He moved closer. "Return the favor." His lips brushed the side of her jaw to the corner of her mouth in a slow seductive caress. "I'm going to take my time, and return that wonderful"—his mouth skimmed her chin—"remarkable, toe-curling favor." His mouth brushed hers softly once, and then settled in for a long drink.

Amber wrapped her arms around his neck, urging him closer. She lost her balance, and rolled off her side and onto her back. He could feel her mouth tremble beneath his as he followed her down onto the soft aged quilt.

Heat, passion, and desire erupted with such force he was surprised the carriage house didn't shatter from the impact. The kiss he had remembered was tame compared to what he was feeling now. He groaned as her teeth lightly and playfully nipped at his lower lip. He returned that favor, too.

The feeling of Amber's small, delicate hands pulling at the back of his sweatshirt drove him over the edge. All pretense of being civil went flying out the window. He broke the kiss, pushed away from Amber, and yanked the sweatshirt over his head.

Amber's smile was pure sin as she reached for the hem of the long sleeve turtleneck he had put on under the sweatshirt. Obeying her unspoken wish and the flash of devilry in her eyes, he started to tug that shirt over his head, too. He felt Amber's palms stroke up his chest and her fingers thread themselves through the hair there before the shirt had cleared his head. For a moment he forgot how to breathe. The shirt ended behind him somewhere.

He leaned down and captured her strawberry-tasting lips with his mouth. Fingers tugged at his chest hair before sliding around his ribs to his back. Amber pulled him closer, and he went willingly. He was a drowning man. He was drowning in the taste, the feel, the heat of Amber.

The sweet curve of Amber's hip beneath his hand caused his fingers to tremble as they swept their way higher to her waist. Satiny skin warmed his fingers as he trailed his hand across her stomach.

Amber moaned into his mouth as he tenderly stroked the back of his fingers across one generously endowed breast. When he felt the hard pebbling of her nipple pressing against the lace of her bra, he moaned more than her name. He broke the kiss and very explicitly told her what he wanted to do with that ripened berry.

A wicked smile flashed across Amber's face. "I thought you would never ask." Both of Amber's hands pushed against his chest and with the momentum of her hips, she had him flat on his back. Amber straddled his hips as her hands pinned his shoulders to the quilt.

"I'm not asking." He felt his arousal threaten to burst the zipper of his jeans to get to the warmth cradling him. "I'm begging." Amber was leaning over him, and her breasts were dangerously close to his mouth. All he had to do was lean up a couple of inches and he would be able to capture one of those luscious berries. Sweatshirt, bra, and all.

Amber sat up, depriving him of the tempting fruit but heightening his arousal by putting more of her weight on a very sensitive—and highly charged—area of his body. He was ready to explode, and Amber hadn't so much as taken off her slippers.

Amber sat back and tried not to wiggle too much. Her every movement seemed to cause Ian pain. She could feel his thickness and hardness pressing against the junction of her thighs. Ian wanted her as much as she wanted him.

"Remember when we were shopping Saturday, and I had to run into the drugstore?" She knew Ian thought she probably wanted to buy tampons and such, and gave her the privacy to go into the store alone. For some reason, men avoided the feminine products like cooties would be popping out of the tampon boxes and attacking them in the aisles. She had picked up a box of tampons, but she also made another purchase.

Ian's hands gripped her hips and forced her to be still. "What about it?" Ian's jaw seemed to be locked, and he had to growl the words out.

"I did something that I've never done before in my life." She toyed with the hem of her sweatshirt and smiled at the way Ian's gaze became slightly unfocused as her weight shifted. "I bought a box of condoms." She looked across the room to her bed and tried not to blush. She had never propositioned a man before. "They're in the nightstand."

"Too far"—Ian flashed her a smile that would have done a pirate proud and caused her heartbeat to stutter—"I've got one in my wallet."

She trailed a fingertip down his chest and toyed with the brass snap on his jeans. "Confident, were you?"

Ian shook his head as his hands slid from her hips to her waist. "Not at all." The truth was in his words, and his eyes. "It's been in there for months."

She circled his belly button and the light dusting of

hair that surrounded it. An intriguing thick patch of dark hair arrowed its way downward, into the waistband of his jeans. "You always come prepared?" She knew in today's world it wasn't just an unplanned pregnancy you had to worry about. It could be your life.

"Boy Scout training." Ian played with the drawstring of her flannel pants. He concentrated on the simple bow as if he were untying the *Queen Mary* from its berth. "I even got a merit badge in knots."

She leaned down and quickly brushed his mouth with a fleeting kiss. Before he could respond she sat back up. "How are you at fires?" She liked the feeling of having Ian beneath her and totally at her mercy. Ian didn't look like he was going to complain.

"Fires?" Ian's thumbs were stroking the sensitive skin beneath her breasts and moving higher with every stroke.

"Are you as good at putting them out as you are at starting them?" The gentle rocking of her hips left him in no doubt as to which fire she was talking about.

Deviltry danced in Ian's eyes. "I haven't even begun to build this fire yet."

She wasn't sure how to respond to that outrageous statement. Ian didn't seem to be bragging, and in reality they hadn't even gotten to second base yet. But her heart was slamming against her ribs, and her breathing was shaky and rapid. The damp emptiness between her thighs was aching for Ian. Only Ian. If she got any hotter, she would spontaneously combust. Her hips shifted in need, and she could feel him grow harder.

He reached up, pulled her sweatshirt over her head, and tossed it in the general direction where his shirt had landed. His thumbs skimmed over the white lace of her bra and his smile widened as her nipples pouted further.

She reached behind herself, unhooked the bra, and then tossed the garment over her shoulder. She felt the shudder that coursed through Ian's body beneath her.

He cupped her breasts and whispered, "Beautiful," against one of the nipples before taking it into his mouth.

Desire spiked and coiled through her body as she bent forward. Her hair curtained Ian's face as she started to move her hips to the natural rhythm her body demanded. She closed her eyes and felt the pull of Ian's lips against her breast. Her hips moved faster as she climbed higher toward a climax that was going to blow her apart into a million pieces. She'd had climaxes before, but the climb had never been this intense.

Ian released her nipple and rolled her onto her back. Warm kisses trailed their way up her throat and teased the corner of her mouth. "Easy, love, we have all night."

She knew Ian was trying to slow them down, but she didn't want to go down, she wanted to go higher. She wrapped her arms around his neck and pulled his mouth back to hers. Her thighs wrapped around his waist. "Please, Ian." Her teeth nipped at his lower lip and she wasn't quite so playful as before.

Ian moaned as his hands slipped down her back and into the waistband of her pants. Warm, strong hands cupped her buttocks and pressed her closer to his arousal. "Please, what?" Ian's voice was gratingly harsh and he was having as much difficulty breathing as she seemed to be having.

"I need you now." She pressed a kiss on the side of his neck and another, lower. "Reach in and get it, Ian." Her lips nuzzled one of his light brown nipples peeking out from a few sprigs of hair.

Ian stiffened above her. "Uh, Amber."

It took her a moment to realize what had startled Ian, then she chuckled as she wiggled lower, trailing her mouth down his chest. "Not that, Ian." She pushed him over onto his back. Her tongue teased his belly button as Ian threaded his fingers into her hair. "Get out your wallet, and open the condom." Her fingers unsnapped his jeans.

Ian grabbed her hands as they started to explore. "You know those love scenes in movies that seem to go on and on forever? They go on for so long that you start to wonder if the guy is even human." Ian pulled away from her and reached for his wallet.

She kicked off her slippers and started to slide her pants past her hips. "What about them?" She couldn't care less what was in the movies. She wanted Ian, here and now. A wide smile spread across her face as he kicked off his jeans and underwear. Ian was definitely better than any movie she had ever seen. His white socks landed on top of her slippers.

Ian was watching the slow decent of her pants while trying to roll the condom on. He fumbled twice before completing the job. "This isn't going to be anything like them."

Her laughter filled the room as she kicked off the soft flannel pants. She was sitting in the middle of the quilt wearing nothing but a pair of white lace panties and a smile. Her fingers reached for the waistband of the panties.

"Don't." Ian reached for the delicate scrap of lace. "I want to."

She leaned back and allowed Ian to slowly peel the lacy triangle down her legs. Her gaze kept straying to his jutting arousal. Curious, she reached out and let her fingertip slowly travel the length of him. "Next time let me do it."

"Next time you can do anything you want." Ian cupped her jaw and kissed her hard. "If you touch me again, it's over before it begins."

She lightly scraped her fingernails down his back. "Sorry to disappoint you, but it has already begun." She kissed him back as his hand flattened against her stomach and then slowly inched its way into the curls nestled below. She arched her hips and urged him on.

Ian groaned as he slipped a finger inside her, testing her readiness.

She tightened around his finger and tried to think of anything besides the wondrous heat threatening to steal her sanity and cause her to go over the edge. She needed Ian with her, in her, when she took the plunge. "Ian, now."

A second finger joined the first, as Ian positioned himself between her thighs. "You're so wet for me," said Ian against her breast. "Do you have any idea what that does to me, knowing you want me as much as I want you?"

"No"—she raised her thighs and wrapped her legs around his hips—"show me." The tip of his penis replaced his fingers. She raised her hips and her breath caught in the back of her throat as she felt him start to enter her ever so slowly. She didn't want it slow or tame the first time. She wanted Ian as hungry for her as she was for him.

She was about to climax, and Ian was taking his own sweet time. With a soft cry she jerked her hips upward, and took all of Ian in with one swift move.

He groaned and tried to hold himself still. She wouldn't let him do that to her. To them. She lowered her hips and then slammed them upward again.

With a wild cry, Ian plunged, and then plunged again, sending her right over the edge. He kept thrusting as she convulsed around him, sparring on his own release and hoarse cry.

Amber lay in the middle of the blanket unsure if she was going to be able to ever move again. She had a feeling that she might have fallen asleep for a moment there.

The heat from the fire bathed her face with warmth and a soft golden glow she could see through her closed eyelids. Her eyelids were so heavy, she couldn't open them. But she could feel Ian still lying on top of her, bathing her body with his heat. Neither of their breathing or heart rates had returned to normal yet. She was beginning to think they might not.

She couldn't have cared less.

"Ian?" She knew he was awake because he kept nuzzling her breasts. He had a thick beard, and while he might have shaved again before picking her up to go ice-skating, it was definitely in the "shadow" stage now. She liked the bristly feel against her skin. She was going to have some very interesting scrapes against her skin come tomorrow morning.

"Hmmmm?" Ian's breath blew across her nipple, causing her to shiver. His arms immediately tightened around her.

She wanted to say something profound. Something special that Ian would remember for the rest of his life. Tonight hadn't been about two lonely people finding release in each other's arms. Tonight she had made love with Ian. There might not have been any words of love, or whispered promises, but that didn't matter. Her feelings for Ian went deeper than a quick roll across her living room floor. She had a hunch that Ian might be feeling the same way. He was still in Misty Harbor, after all.

Sleep pulled at her weary body and mind and she gave up trying to find the right words.

With a weary sigh she raised her head and kissed the top of Ian's head. "That was better than any movie I ever saw."

She fell asleep with his chuckle vibrating against her chest.

* * *

Ian carried Amber to her bed, and tenderly placed her on the sheet. He had already pulled down the quilt and fluffed her pillow. He also had seen to the dying embers in the fireplace, fed the cats, and turned out all the lights, except for the one above the kitchen sink. Amber's apartment was locked down for the night, and he knew he should be leaving. He wasn't sure if he had the strength to leave Amber, not after what they had just shared in front of the fire, but he was going to try.

Making love with her had been all that he had ever dreamed, and more. Much more. Amber was giving, sweet, funny, and so damn sexy his body had been hard and throbbing since he woke up in her arms a half an hour ago. He wanted her again, but she had been sleeping so peacefully he hadn't had the heart to wake her up.

It was close to midnight, and he needed to get back to the bed-and-breakfast. He didn't think Olivia would be doing a bed check, but Amber probably wouldn't appreciate having everyone in town know that he had spent the night in her apartment. In her bed. Then there was her Aunt Grace to consider.

He bent down, pulled up the blanket to Amber's chin, and then kissed her one last time on the mouth.

Amber pouted and slowly opened her eyes. "Ian?" Her voice was rough with sleep and sex.

"Who else would it be?" He tried to make the question light and playful when all he wanted to do was to rip off his clothes and join her under that blanket.

Amber stretched like a cat and asked, "Where are you going?"

He glanced down at the sweatshirt and jeans he had pulled on. "Back to the bed-and-breakfast."

"Why?" Amber brushed her hair out of her face.

"I wasn't sure if you wanted me to stay or not." The quilt he had pulled up to her chin had fallen halfway down her chest. He was having a hard time concentrating on the conversation with her nipples peeking up at him.

"You could have asked."

"You were sleeping." Ian tried not to laugh at the indignant look upon her face. "I banked the fire and fed the cats."

"You could have wakened me."

He bent and placed a kiss on her forehead. "Did you know that you're beautiful when you sleep?"

Amber frowned. "Are you saying I'm ugly when I'm awake?"

He chuckled at this side of Amber he had never seen before. "Are you always this argumentative when you first wake up?"

"Only when I find the man I just got naked with and rolled around on the living room floor with all night long sneaking out of my apartment like he was a thief."

The woman didn't have to ask him twice. Ian pulled his sweatshirt over his head and shucked his jeans in record time. "If you're going to be that upset because I was leaving, I won't." The bed bounced as he flopped down beside Amber and wormed his way under the blankets. "Just tell me Grace doesn't own a shotgun."

Heated skin brushed heated skin.

Amber turned into his arms and pressed her mouth against the side of his neck. "No can do." Amber's hands were busy rediscovering his body. His already aroused body.

He groaned when her warm little fingers wrapped around his straining penis.

Amber misunderstood his groan and chuckled as she nipped his shoulder. "Don't worry, Ian, I'll protect you from my aunt."

"I wasn't worried about Grace." He placed his hand over hers and tried to slow her down. "I'm more worried about you."

"Me?"

"Yeah, you." Ian removed her hand before he embarrassed himself all over Amber's clean sheets. "This time we do it my way."

"Your way?" Amber sounded intrigued as she scooted up in bed. The quilt was now lying across her thighs, offering her no protection, and no warmth. By the perkiness of her nipples, Amber was either very glad he was staying or was extremely cold. "What's your way?"

"Slow." He glanced to his left, and then to his right. There were nightstands on both sides of the bed. "Which nightstand?"

Amber grinned and then reached into the top drawer next to her side of the bed. "I bought the ultra sensitive ribbed kind." He caught the box she tossed him. "I hope they'll be okay."

Ian squinted at the box. In the dimness of the room he couldn't tell the make, but he knew by the size of the box there had to be at least a dozen in there. "I'm sure they're fine." He ripped into the box and pulled out a foil package.

Amber grabbed the little package from his hands. "Remember you said I could do it next time." She got on her knees in front of him and ripped open the package with her teeth. Her breasts bounced with her every move.

He didn't think this was such a great idea. Having Amber's fingers caress him the whole entire time she was rolling down that condom might be more than he could bear. He was only human, after all.

He snatched the condom out of her hand. "Maybe once we're on the third box, or so, I'll let you."

Chapter 12

Ian woke with Amber curled up beside him and a cat slumbering on his chest. Shadow had either finally gotten over his shyness or he had remembered who had opened the can of cat food last night for him and Light. A few strands of Amber's hair tickled his nose. He brushed her hair away from his face and squinted across her bare shoulder to read the clock. Six o'clock in the morning and it was still pitch-black outside. It wasn't much lighter in the apartment.

Shadow, obviously offended that his mattress had moved, stalked to the bottom of the bed and laid back down near Amber's feet. Light was curled into a ball and sleeping behind Amber's knees. Someone needed a bigger bed or a few less pets.

He settled back down to watch Amber sleep. Lord, she was beautiful. In the shadowy dimness of the bedroom he could make out the outline of half of her features as she slept. The other half of her face was buried into the pillow. Her lips were softly parted, and he could hear her gentle breathing. Amber didn't snore and he couldn't detect any drool spot, but she certainly liked to cuddle when she slept. Her one arm was wrapped across his waist and her thigh was draped over his in a most provocative manner. Amber had the face of an Irish angel, and a body built for sin.

He loved the way she slept and could very easily become accustom to waking up every morning with her in his arms.

In the darkness of the coming dawn the weight of guilt pressed heavy on his heart. Here he was thinking he was the luckiest guy in the world falling in love and being in Amber's bed, when the hard truth was, he wouldn't have been if James were still alive.

Last night he had made love to James's wife, not once, but three times. The third time, Amber had awakened him by stringing kisses down his chest. He had awoken drowsy, aroused, and with Amber's fingers rolling a condom on the part of him that had awakened long before his brain. The little witch had gotten her way, and he had enjoyed every agonizing moment of it.

The memory of his friend James squashed whatever joy he was feeling.

With slow, steady movements, so he wouldn't wake Amber, he slipped from the bed and walked over to the window. All he could see was darkness and the faint glint of lights down by the parking area by the docks. He knew in the daylight, the actual harbor wouldn't be visible from Amber's apartment. On the outside of the windows, a crystallized frost had formed. The cold harsh darkness matched his mood.

Making love with Amber had been the most incredible experience of his life. So why did he feel like he had betrayed his friend and business partner? James had passed away eighteen months ago. Surely after a year and a half it wasn't a betrayal to fall in love with his widow?

He pressed his forehead against the cold pane of glass and closed his eyes as the truth barreled its way into his heart and mind.

The horrible truth that was twisting in his gut and eating a hole in his heart was he probably had been halfway in love with Amber before she had even become James's wife. Was it any wonder that he was being consumed by guilt?

He never should have given in to the temptation to come see Amber in Maine. There hadn't been anything powerful enough in the universe to have stopped him once he had an excuse in hand. The need to see Amber had started to consume his life.

He sure as hell never should have allowed it to go this far. Now that he had touched Amber, tasted her, and loved her, he didn't think he would ever be able to let her go. He wasn't that strong a man.

With a disgusted sigh, directed towards himself, he walked away from the window and reached for his jeans.

The smell of brewing coffee pulled Amber from her sleep. Confused, she rolled to the side and looked out into the kitchen, and smiled. Ian was sitting at her kitchen table, reading a magazine and drinking a cup of coffee. He held the glossy magazine at arm's length and was squinting. He obviously hadn't packed his reading glasses for ice-skating. Light was curled up in his lap, and Ian's fingers were absently stroking the cat.

"I'm jealous," she called as she stretched. A few muscles that she hadn't used in a while protested.

"Of?" Ian asked as he lowered the magazine.

"The cat." She watched as Light stretched and purred beneath Ian's fingers. She didn't blame the cat. She had done more than stretch and purr beneath Ian's fingers last night. "What are you reading?" It was so nice and warm under the covers and she wasn't looking forward to the dash to the bathroom, where her robe was hanging.

Especially since she was naked and there were still

eighteen pounds of Krup's chocolate shakes adhered to her ass. Last night, in the heat of the moment, Ian might have overlooked a few extra pounds, but in the dawning light of the morning they were going to make quite an impression as she sprinted for the bathroom door.

She knew she would be paying for those extra thick, double chocolate shakes. She just wished it wouldn't be so embarrassing. After everything they had done last night she couldn't very well tell Ian to close his eyes or turn his head.

"I'm reading an article on how to redo my entire living room for under five hundred dollars." Ian chuckled and said, "Seems I made a faux pas by doing the room in beiges and browns. This article says I need at least one accent color, preferably, two."

"Go with two."

"Are you ready for some coffee?" Ian stood up and headed for the pot. "Hope you don't mind that I helped myself."

"Not at all, and I would love a cup." As soon as Ian turned his back to reach into the cabinet for another cup she sprinted for the bathroom.

Four minutes later she joined him at the table. "Thanks." Feeling halfway human now that she washed her face and brushed her teeth and hair, she reached for her cup. The thick chenille robe she had on was worn and in dire need of a replacement, but she could never bring herself to buy a new one. She loved the faded yellow robe that covered her from her neck to nearly her ankles.

"You're welcome."

The "morning after" was indeed a dangerous mine-field. Ian wasn't quite meeting her gaze and he seemed a little too polite. "Would you like some breakfast? I could scramble up some eggs." There was still plenty of time before the shop opened.

"Thanks, but I've got to be heading back to Olivia's. I've got a ton of work to do." Ian got up and put his empty cup into the sink.

If that wasn't a kiss-off she didn't know what was. What in the world happened between two in the morning and now? Her fingers trembled as they clutched the robe's lapels together. She tried not to let Ian see how much it hurt that he was treating her like a one-night stand. She was surprised he had bothered to stick around and make coffee. "I see," her voice was filled with the tears she refused to acknowledge. "Have a good one."

Ian came to a stop next to her chair. This time it was she who refused to meet his gaze. "Amber, that didn't come out right." He pulled her to her feet, and into his arms.

She felt his arms wrap around her as she buried her face into his shoulder. His sweatshirt smelled like the smoke from her fireplace. "How was it supposed to have come out?" She wasn't expecting a declaration of love or promises, but she hadn't been prepared for a brush-off, either. This was Ian, not some lobster fisherman she had picked up in The One-Eyed Squid after drinking way too many beers.

"Somewhere along the lines of a thank you for the offer, but if you want me in the shop this afternoon to pack up some orders, I really need to get some of my work done." Ian placed a soft kiss on top of her head. "Remember, we have a date for tonight. I won the race, so you have to cook me dinner." His arms squeezed tight. "The deal was for Mexican."

She pulled back and managed to get a couple of inches between them. "No." She was confused, not stupid.

"What do you mean no? I won the race, fair and square."

"I wasn't referring to the race or to dinner." She put

her palms against his chest and pushed. Ian released his hold. "I want to know what in the hell happened."

"When?" Now it was Ian's turn to look confused.

"This morning? Something happened between the mattress triathlon and 'would you like a cup of coffee?'. I want to know what it is." She studied Ian's face. His beard was thicker and rougher but there was a flush of guilt staining his cheeks. His eyes looked sad, but it was that sign of guilt that twisted her gut into a pretzel. What in the world did Ian have to feel guilty about?

Ian sat back down and glanced around the apartment. His gaze seemed to linger on the bed before coming back to her. "I keep thinking about James."

She jerked at hearing her deceased husband's name. Ian very rarely brought up James's name, so she hadn't been expecting that answer. "What about James?"

"I woke up, with you all naked and warm curled against me, and all I kept thinking was that I had just made love to James's wife."

This time she cringed. "I'm no longer his wife, Ian. James has been gone for eighteen months." She pulled out her chair and sat. She didn't think her knees would continue to hold her weight.

Ian ran his fingers through his hair and glared at her. "Don't you think I know that?" He gave a shake of his head and softened his voice. "Try to understand, Amber, I feel as if I betrayed him. James was my friend and my business partner. You are his wife."

"*Was* his wife." Amber tried not to flinch at Ian's words. "Shouldn't I be the one suffering from guilt? I was his wife, after all." What kind of person did that make her? She hadn't once thought of James last night.

In the faint morning light, James's ghost stood between them, and only Ian could see it.

What kind of wife did that make her? Hadn't she loved James enough? Her thoughts must have been splashed across her face.

"Amber, this doesn't have to do with you. You have absolutely nothing to feel guilty about." Ian came around the table and pulled her back into his arms. "It's my problem and I shouldn't have brought it up."

She felt the warmth of his arms wrapped around her and wondered who was crazier, Ian for thinking it had nothing to do with her, or herself for wishing Ian had lied about what was bothering him. How were they ever to have a relationship if every time Ian looked at her, he saw James's wife?

Amber shook out the jeans, neatly folded them, and then placed them into the plastic basket. Wednesday night was the night she did her laundry at Grace's. Tonight she had invited Ian to join them for dinner. Ian had driven all the way into Sullivan to pick up two pizzas. Grace had supplied a blender full of frozen margaritas and an eight-foot pine tree that needed to be decorated. Amber brought three laundry baskets of dirty clothes.

The blender was now empty, five slices of pizza were left in the box stored in Grace's refrigerator, and Ian was out in the living room stringing lights on the tree. Bing Crosby was singing about a white Christmas and she was alone in the kitchen folding pants, matching socks, and tormenting herself over Ian.

The man was driving her crazy. He had shown up at the shop yesterday afternoon with a bouquet of white roses for her and an apologetic smile. She had picked up all the ingredients she needed for tacos from Barley's Food Store on her way home from work. Ian brought the wine. The tacos had been wonderful but the evening had ended with Ian heading back to the bed-and-breakfast long before the evening news came on. They had shared one mind-blowing, melt your socks kiss, and then Ian had headed out the door like fire was licking at his ass.

He had changed the subject every time she tried to bring James up in their conversation over messy tacos and wine. Tonight wasn't much better. Grace had picked up on the strained atmosphere between them and not only kept the conversation going but had actually brought laughter to the table. Amber loved Ian's laugh.

She could hear her aunt out in the living room issuing orders to Ian. His reply was muffled by the distance, but she could pick up a chuckle or two. She matched two dark blue socks and thought about James and her growing relationship with Ian.

James had been her husband for four and a half years, and while she had loved him very much, he hadn't been without faults. Neither had she. There had been a serious problem looming on the horizon of her marriage and she would never know if their marriage would have been strong enough to weather that particular storm.

She had wanted children. Before they had gotten married, they had discussed children and James had agreed with her. They both thought two, maybe three children would be the perfect size of their future family. She had even agreed with James to wait a couple of years until his and Ian's business got off the ground so they could better afford their growing family.

M & M Ad Agency was a sterling success from the get-go, and after a year or two James started to hedge about starting that family they had agreed upon. He had pointed out she was only twenty-five, so what was the hurry. Then there was the need for a bigger house and that spring trip to Paris. Then came a new luxury sports car for James and the fall trip to the Caribbean. Another year went by, and then another. While she enjoyed all of the extras the success of the agency was providing, they weren't what she wanted.

She wanted to start their family, and James was looking over brochures for another fantasy vacation. She had loved James, but looking back, she could see it hadn't been a very equal partnership. Whatever James had wanted, James got. While she would have done—and did do anything—to make James happy, he hadn't been willing to do the same for her.

Part of the fault, she knew, had been her own. She should have grown a backbone and confronted James. She should have laid it all out on the table and told him how she felt. What she had needed to be truly happy was the knowledge they were trying for that family. That her husband had wanted the same thing she did.

James had been killed before she could test out the backbone she had been growing. One thing she did learn by becoming a widow at twenty-eight years of age, and that was there were no guarantees in life. She was responsible for her own happiness.

Right now her happiness came in a six-foot package out in the living room listening to Frank Sinatra crooning "It Came Upon a Midnight Clear" and untangling Christmas lights.

What she felt for Ian had nothing to do with what she had felt for James. They were two different men, at two different times in her life. They weren't entwined, even though they had been friends and business partners. When she looked at Ian she saw a man who knew how to laugh and make her happy just being himself. Ian wasn't out to impress anyone. He wasn't thinking about the next party or where he could go for his next vacation. He had come to Misty Harbor and seemed to slide right in with the lifestyle here from toboggan runs down Suicide Hill to filling in on the Sunday afternoon ice hockey games.

Here she had thought the problem in her and Ian's

relationship would be location. She lived in and loved Maine, while he not only lived in Boston, it was where his business was located. She had been trying to figure out the logistics of a long-distance relationship, while Ian was seeing a ghost from their past.

She pulled the last pair of pants from the basket and flattened out the wrinkles with the palm of her hand. She dropped the pants onto the stack of already folded laundry as the dryer's buzzer went off again. Her load of towels was dried. She headed for the small laundry closet, tucked in the far corner of Grace's kitchen. She transferred the dry towels into a basket, jammed the wet sheets into the dryer, and started the next load. She could still hear Grace and Ian out in the living room as she carried the towels to the kitchen table. Dean Martin was now singing about it being cold outside.

How could James have ever thought Ian was a shy geek? Ian was out in the living room singing along with Dino while Grace accompanied him on the female verses in the song. She chuckled as she started to fold the towels. Grace was the better singer of the two, and that wasn't saying much. Grace couldn't hold a note if someone tattooed one on the palm of her hand.

Ian glanced up from the box of ornaments lying at his feet as Amber walked into the room. He felt his heart pick up an extra beat or two and managed to stay where he was and not make a complete fool of himself by dashing across the room and pulling her into his arms. She had only been out of his sight for fifteen minutes, and already he missed her. She looked gorgeous tonight, but he still noticed the small signs of fatigue etched onto her face and beneath her eyes. He had a feeling Amber wasn't sleeping any better than he had been lately.

He never should have opened his mouth about her

being James's wife. The awkwardness between them now was almost physical. He didn't know how to breach that barrier or how to disregard the feeling of guilt that still assaulted him whenever he thought of Amber and the night they had shared.

The most wondrous, passionate night of his life and he had ruined it. If he wasn't careful, he was also going to destroy whatever had been growing between Amber and him. Amber was giving him the space he needed to figure it all out in his mind, without pushing him away. He didn't know what he had ever done in his life to deserve her, but he wasn't going to walk away from her without a fight.

His opponent, for the woman he loved, was a ghost who only he could see. How did one battle a ghost of a dear friend without destroying those wonderful memories?

"There you are," Grace said as she looked at Amber. "There's more laundry detergent in the cabinet above the washer if you need it."

"Thanks, but I have plenty," Amber said as she walked over to the tree. "I see you went with all white lights this year."

"I'm going to do it in white, pinks and gold." Grace held up a gold foiled box of fancy and obviously expensive ornaments. There were over a dozen delicate, pink feathered birds with gold beaks and tiny feet nestled in the box. "I found these in that little craft shop I love in downtown Bangor. I've decided to do the whole tree around them."

Amber picked up one of the tiny birds. "They are gorgeous, Grace."

Ian held up a bag of gold beads. "What goes on next, the beads or the birds?" He hadn't had a lot of practice decorating Christmas trees, and this was the second one he had been roped into helping with since coming to Maine.

The one back in the shop had been easier. He only had to set it up in the antique tree stand and string the lights. He had a feeling he wasn't going to get away that easy on this one. Grace's living room was piled with boxes upon boxes of delicate antique ornaments that looked so fragile they would break if he picked them up. He was scared to death to touch them.

"Beads go on first." Grace frowned at the string of gold beads in his hands. "But not those yet. Somewhere in this mess is a box with my mother's milk glass beads." Grace started rooting through the boxes. "Amber, in one of those shopping bags"—Grace pointed to the small army of assorted bags by the pocket doors leading into the den—"are pink beads I picked up in Sears last week."

He put the gold beads back in the bag for now. "Grace, I don't think all of this stuff is going to fit on one tree." By the amount of decorations littering the room, Grace would need a tree the size of the one they just put up at Rockefeller Center in New York City. Grace's Douglas fir was a good eight feet tall and filled the corner of the room nicely, but no way was even an eighth of this stuff going to fit on it.

"It's not all for the tree, silly." Grace smiled with delight as she pulled an aged wooden box from one of the cardboard boxes filled with decorations. "Here they are." Grace opened the box and lovingly caressed the beads. "These were Amber's grandmother's favorite decoration. I can't remember the family Christmas tree that didn't have them on." Grace handed him the box.

He held the box as carefully as he had cradled his nephews when they had first made their appearance into this world. String after string of white glass beads were nestled in the pine box lined with worn black velvet. "How fragile are they?" He had visions of a busted string and hundreds of glass beads bouncing and shattering as they hit the floor.

"Don't worry, the strings won't break." Grace started to dig though another box. "Years ago I reinforced them with fishing line."

"Amber, I think you should help me with these." He wanted her closer to him. He needed her closer.

"Sure, I'll be right there." Amber pulled five strands of pale pink beads from a bag.

The ringing of the phone pulled Grace away from whatever she was hunting for, and she hurried toward the kitchen.

Amber laid the pink beads onto an overstuffed chair that was done in a horrible shade of green with a row of gold tassels circling the bottom. Amazingly, there was even a matching ottoman. "We need to start at the top," Amber said.

He set the short stepladder Grace had given him earlier near the tree so he could reach the top branches. "Can I ask you a personal question?"

"What?"

He could see the uncertainty in her gaze and knew he had only himself to blame. "Is this wallpaper as ugly as I think it is?" He didn't want to insult Grace's taste, but the room was beginning to freak him out. The huge, ghastly pink flowers covering the walls looked menacing.

Amber's laugh lightened his heart and his mood. "Try being a kid with an overactive imagination who had to watch television in this room late at night." She wrinkled her nose at the walls. "My brothers used to fill my head with stories of killer roses that ate little girls and then they would sneak out in the middle of a television program and leave me all alone in here."

"I'm torn between laughing and punching your brothers out." Ian handed her the wooden box. "I didn't have any little sisters to torment, but it sounds like something my older brother would have done to me.

Of course, we would have to have had an aunt who bought her wallpaper at the Norman Bates hardware store."

"Grace might have helped hang the wallpaper, but she didn't pick it out. My grandmother did when she was sick and everyone knew it was only a matter of time. Grace and Howard redid the room just for her. Everything in this room was hand-picked by my grandmother."

"Did your grandmother like it?" He studied the basketball-size flower, not three feet away from his face. If he squinted real hard, the damn thing looked like it had evil eyes and a mouth that was open in a silent scream. The room didn't need Martha Stewart, it needed an exorcism.

"She loved it." Amber shook her head. "She spent the last months of her life either upstairs in her bed or in this room."

"Why hasn't Grace changed it yet?"

"Sentimental reasons, I guess." Amber shrugged. "I'm going to try to convince her to take down the wallpaper this spring, but I'm not holding out much hope. If Uncle Howard couldn't make her do it, I doubt if I can."

Ian glanced around the room. He couldn't picture Grace designing or living in such a room. The furniture had seen better days about a century ago. The area rug was worn and faded, and he could detect a hole or two. The pink velvet curtains had been bleached to a sick cotton candy color by the sun. Doilies, yellowed with age, were on the sofa and chairs. Even the few pieces of artwork hanging on the walls were dark and depressing.

This room didn't match the other rooms he had seen in the house. Grace's kitchen was large, warm, and welcoming. Modern appliances blended seamlessly with the glass-front cabinets and tiled countertops. The blue and yellow color scheme made a person want to sit down at the big country table and enjoy another cup of coffee.

The formal dining room, right off the kitchen, had been tastefully done in mismatched dark cherry furniture that spoke of good taste, but not deep pockets. Grace had pulled the whole room together with style and taste suitable for any magazine cover.

The foyer, with its sweeping curved stairway and pale golden walls, was grand and elegant, if one didn't look too closely. The grandfather clock wasn't working and the area rug was beyond worn. Nothing could persuade him to flip the light switch to see if the crystal chandelier, that had to be five feet across, actually worked. The wiring in the dusty antique would probably set the house on fire if someone turned it on.

So why was this room so different?

"Show me your favorite room." He nodded in the direction of the partially open pocket doors that led into the den. He had only gotten a glimpse inside the dark room and he couldn't see much. He was curious to see a slice of Amber's past. A slice of her past that didn't include James.

Amber headed for the den and slid the doors all the way open. She crossed over to a table, and flipped on a light. "It hasn't changed much over the years." She glanced around the room. "My aunt had the couch reupholstered about five years ago, and Uncle Howard's leather recliner was a new addition about four years ago." Amber walked farther into the room and flipped on another light. "The television was moved into this room about ten years ago because my uncle refused to sit in the living room any longer."

He chuckled at the mental picture of Amber's uncle being afraid of those intimidating flowers. He didn't blame the guy.

Amber glanced around the room. "Let's see, more

books had been added to the shelves since I was a little girl, and Grace's knitting basket seems to have gotten bigger."

He studied the dark walnut bookshelves that were custom-made for one entire wall of the den. Someone had money at one time or another. The fireplace had a marble hearth and a hand-curved mantel, and it matched the ones in the dining room and in the horrible living room. Money had built this house.

He walked over to Amber and lightly brushed a lock of her hair behind her ear. "I can almost see you as a little girl curled up in the corner of the couch reading your bloodthirsty tales. A fire would be blazing, and you have one of Grace's afghans pulled up over your legs." The back of his fingers caressed her jawline. "I want to say you had on one of those white cotton nightgowns down to your ankles and your hair was in braids, but I'm betting I'm wrong."

She smiled and seemed to lean into his touch. "I can't remember owning a white flowing nightgown. I was more into flannels. But you might be right about the braids. Grace loved brushing and braiding my hair whenever I visited."

"So I was half right?" This was the Amber James's ghost couldn't touch. The pad of his thumb stroked her lower lip. He could feel the slight tremor that went through her body at his touch. He tried to ignore the hot desire pooling in his gut.

"You forgot about the hot chocolate and cookies." Amber stepped closer and pressed the palm of one of her hands over his heart.

"What cookies and hot chocolate?" His thoughts definitely were centered on her mouth, but not the words coming out of it. He was remembering what that mouth had done to his body the other night.

"My aunt always made me a cup of hot cocoa when I read." The tips of Amber's fingers traced his ear and the hard column of his throat. "She also made more batches of cookies than the Keebler elves. Didn't you have an aunt who made you hot chocolate on cold winter days?"

He chuckled at the thought of his Aunt Eleanor fixing him a hot drink on a cold day. She probably would have added a splash or two of brandy. "My aunt started drinking martinis at noon and fell asleep in her chair before nine every night. All day long she used to give me toothpicks with the two gin-soaked olives speared onto them. At least she used to, until my mother found out one day."

Amber frowned, but her eyes still sparkled with amusement. "What did your mother do?"

"I wasn't allowed to see Aunt Eleanor unless it was at church on Sunday morning or family dinners."

"Do you see her now?" Amber's fingers teased the ends of his hair.

"I see them occasionally. Aunt Eleanor and Uncle Tony still drink like fish and bowl every Saturday night with one of the leagues. They wear matching pink polyester shirts and have matching bowling balls that sparkle. There are about a hundred bowling trophies in their living room and they still drive around the old neighborhood in a big fat old Cadillac with fuzzy dice hanging from the rearview mirror."

Amber's laugh gently soothed his soul. That was why he loved her. She made everything in his life seem better and brighter. "I would love to meet them one day."

"That can be arranged." The very thought of Amber wanting to meet his family filled him with hope for the future. Uncle Tony worked down at the docks and knew every dirty joke known to mankind. He had the tendency to tell them all when he was drinking, and he drank a lot. His aunt could shake a martini that would have James Bond applying for American citizenship. Amber would probably love them.

He wrapped his arms around her and pulled her closer. Their lips were so close he could feel her breath. "Have I told you how beautiful you look tonight?" He could feel his body respond to her nearness and he wondered how he was ever going to leave her alone in her apartment tonight. He wanted to love her, truly love her, but to do that he needed to get his head on straight. Amber's bed wasn't big enough for her, him, two cats, and James's ghost.

"I'm wearing the same clothes I wore at the shop all day. I dripped pizza grease on my blouse, and what little makeup I did manage to put on this morning was gone by lunchtime."

"As I said"—his lips brushed hers—"breathtakingly beautiful."

"You don't have your glasses on." Amber smiled against his mouth and wrapped her arms around his neck.

"There's nothing wrong with my eyesight when it comes to you." His hands slipped down her back and cupped her bottom. Memories of being buried deep inside her ignited his blood and caused him to groan as her hips cradled his arousal.

His mouth covered hers in a kiss that left her in no doubt what he thought about her pizza-stained blouse and lack of makeup. He might not be taking her to bed tonight, but there was no doubt in her mind that he wanted her.

Chapter 13

Grace was in a horrible mood, and she knew it. Her usual Friday night bingo cheer had gotten up and left, and the first number hadn't even been called yet. She hadn't felt this mean-spirited since she went through menopause a couple of years back. Well, she didn't have raging hormones to blame on this mood, only some stupid twig, branch—or was it an herb called mistletoe? What in the world was mistletoe, anyway?

It was all Joe Clayton's fault, and if he wasn't sitting up there on the platform getting ready to call bingo she would personally introduce him to what Howard used to call a "five knuckle sandwich." Joe could call every number she needed tonight to win every game, but she still wouldn't forgive him. The man was a menace.

Who would have thought that easygoing, always smiling Joe could be such a pain in the butt? Who would have thought that stopping in Krup's General Store to pick up an outside extension cord for the lights she wanted to put up on her porch could cause such a commotion? There she had been, standing by the cash register with an orange electrical cord in one hand and a battery operated singing Elvis—complete with a Santa hat and a choice of five Christmas carols—in the other, when Joe walked right up to her and kissed her. She had been so shocked that she hadn't moved until the kiss had ended. When she had opened her mouth to tear a strip off of Joe, he had only chuckled and then pointed upward.

How was she supposed to know that Harvey Krup had mistletoe hanging all over his store? He had hung enough mistletoe that she was darn lucky not to have walked back out of his store pregnant. Harvey had either turned into a voyeur or he was hoping to get lucky himself. Who in their right mind looked up at the ceilings while shopping for extension cords? She had almost forgiven Joe, because it had been a harmless kiss. It hadn't been like they swapped spit or even played tonsil hockey. It had been a closed mouth, okay-I'm-an-idiot-for-standing-under-the-mistletoe kind of kiss.

That was until she spotted Priscilla Patterson standing four feet away with her eyes bulging out of her head and her mouth hanging open so far she could count the silver fillings in her back teeth. Priscilla had looked at her as if she had just stripped naked, jumped up on the counter, and did the hokeypokey. Priscilla, true to form, had wasted no time rushing home and calling Gladys.

Grace had spent over an hour on the phone with her twin calming her down, and assuring her she wasn't involved with Joe Clayton. The lights on the porch had never gotten up. Gladys hadn't believed the part about the mistletoe at first because Priscilla hadn't bothered to fill her in on that part. Gladys had been too worried that her baby sister, by a whole six minutes, had been caught in a compromising position.

She informed her sister that it wasn't the eighteen

hundreds and no one was forcing her to marry Joe Clayton or anyone else for that matter. She held her tongue and didn't tell Gladys that had she wanted to see what a compromising position really looked like, she should have been over at her house Wednesday night when she had finished her phone call and walked back into the living room to decorate the tree. Ian and Amber had been in the den trying to set off the smoke detectors with their kiss. After one quick glance, she had turned right around and headed for the kitchen. Once there she started banging around in the pots and pans cabinet and making as much noise as possible.

She wasn't a fool. She had noticed that Ian had spent Monday night in Amber's apartment. That didn't surprise her considering the heat those two had been sparking off of each other since Ian came to town. What did surprise her was the fact that Ian hadn't spent a night there since. She didn't know what had gone wrong, or what had put that sad look in her niece's eyes. But she did know whatever was causing Ian to leave Amber's apartment long before even she got ready for bed, wasn't because he didn't want her niece. That quick flash of the kiss she had seen had relieved all doubts of that lamebrained theory.

Amber wasn't ready to talk about whatever was bothering her, or she didn't want to. Her niece was not only smart, she was independent and could make her own decisions, but Amber also knew that her aunt's door was always open. There had always been a special bond between them that Amber's mother resented.

Gladys, after having three boys in quick succession, ended her childbearing marathon with a daughter, Amber. Gladys had smothered poor Amber in frilly dresses, play kitchens, and ballet lessons. Amber had hated it all, but Gladys kept on pushing. It hadn't surprised her in the least when Amber preferred spending her summers and every other chance she got in Misty Harbor with her Aunt Grace and Uncle Howard. Grace allowed her niece the freedom to be who she wanted to be.

The loving bond Grace and Amber had always shared grew into something even stronger when she moved back to Maine and took over the business. They might not have age in common, but they did have one thing: grief. Both of them were grieving for their husbands they had just lost. They were both beyond sad, they were pitiful.

One evening she asked Amber to watch Howard's favorite war movie with her. They both had cried throughout it. The next evening they watched an action thriller that James had loved, and ended the evening bawling their eyes out once again. Every week, for months, they watched one of Howard's and one of James's favorite movies and cried. One week they were standing in Blockbuster deciding which movies to rent when Amber reached for a romantic comedy and said she always wanted to see that one. They had rented the comedy and a movie Grace had wanted to see. They had ended up laughing their butts off through the movies, but sobbing afterwards because they hadn't cried once during the film. Eventually the waterworks had dried up, and they only rented movies they wanted to see, but the weekly experience had strengthened whatever bond had been between them.

Amber's mother had always been jealous of their relationship. She didn't understand that the bond had been formed by mutual respect. Grace had allowed and encouraged Amber to be herself. Gladys, on the other hand, was always harping on her daughter for this, or criticizing her for that. Gladys wanted to run Amber's life, but Amber wasn't allowing it.

Grace was proud of Amber, and furious at her sister. Their telephone conversation had gone from bad, Joe Clayton, to worse, Amber. Grace's temper had snapped, and she had let her sister have more than an earful. A very loud earful. It was one thing for her sister to tell her how to live her life, after all, they had been butting heads their entire life and they still loved each other. But she couldn't bring herself to sit silently by and watch her sister destroy her relationship with her daughter any longer. Amber deserved better than that. She had told her sister the way things were, and Gladys hadn't appreciated it one bit.

She was beginning to wonder if her sister would ever talk to her again. All day long she had been waiting for Gladys to call. The phone never rang, and even Amber admitted her mother hadn't called her in two days. Amber was getting ready to call her mother to see what was wrong. Grace had had to tell Amber about the fight. They both agreed to let Gladys cool down a couple of days before calling her.

Between Gladys, nosy Priscilla, and Casanova Joe, she was at the end of her rope. The sadness in Amber's eyes had her worried and Clyde Davenport was pestering her to go dancing with him tomorrow night. Ever since Howard had passed away life had gotten complicated; really complicated.

She didn't want to go dancing with Clyde, or driving with Mac. She didn't want Lenny bringing her another bouquet of roses, and she really didn't want to get caught under anymore mistletoe by Joe Clayton. The man who could put the merry into her Christmas or the kringle in her Kris hadn't so much as asked her out for a cup of coffee.

Grace glared across the bingo hall to where Abraham Martin was leaning against the wall shooting the breeze with the mayor. Abe was driving her crazy. The man had barely glanced at her when she walked into the hall, yet her stomach had dipped to her knees.

Ever since he delivered the cup of clam chowder and hot chocolate to her at the lighthouse fund-raiser, she had been waiting for him to call. She had waited in vain. Almost two weeks had gone by and Abe hadn't called once. Enough men had dialed her number that she was beginning the think her phone number was written on the men's room wall in the firehouse. She was getting too darn old to be waiting by the phone hoping that a certain man would call.

She could still remember Tiffany lecturing Amber on life being short and that you had to go after what you wanted. Well, it was good advice then, and it was good advice now. She wanted a date with Abraham, just to see if her stomach dropping to her knees every time she saw him was attraction or a bad case of acid indigestion.

Bingo would be starting in another five minutes. Plenty of time to make a fool out of herself.

She sucked in her gut and headed across the room. She was thankful when the mayor walked away, leaving Abraham by himself. Abe raised a brow when he saw her heading right for him, but he didn't run. She leaned against the wall next to him. Close enough that she could smell his aftershave. "Evening, Abe."

"Evening, Gracie." Abraham kept his gaze directed out across the hall. He seemed to be sizing up the crowd tonight and looking for rowdy players.

"You're looking mighty fine tonight." Abraham was wearing a brand new flannel shirt, in various shades of brown, and a pair of khakis that were new enough to still have the crease down the legs. There was a tiny nick under his chin where he had cut it while shaving and his boots were new. Abraham had dressed to impress someone, but the million dollar question was, who?

"You're as beautiful as ever, Gracie." Abraham's mouth kicked up in the corners, but his gaze never wandered from the tables before them.

"How would you know? You're not even looking at me." She loved getting compliments as well as the next woman, but she wanted them meaningful and honest.

"This body might be old, but my eyesight is perfect." Abraham nodded his head to Ruth Busby as she hurried past to join her friends before the game started. Ruth did a double-take at Grace standing next to Abe, but she didn't stop to chat.

"If it's that good, what color are my fingernails?" She placed her hands behind her back and smirked. Over her lunch hour she had her nails done again and got caught up on the latest gossip. Most of the gossip being spread around town was about Joe Clayton kissing her, and Amber and Ian, and both of those subjects had been changed very quickly once she walked into the shop. The rest of the talk was about Doctor Sydney. Rumor had it that the doc was pregnant.

The corners of Abraham's mouth kicked up higher. "White."

That surprised her. "It's Crystal Frost, but white is close enough." She hadn't seen Abraham since she left Estelle's and walked into the fire hall. He had barely glanced at her, yet he noticed the color of her nails. "What decal did I get on them this week?"

"Decal?"

"On the tips of six of my nails I've got a tiny little decal. What is it of?" Abraham had to have the eyesight of a hawk to have seen the decals from where he was standing.

He finally turned his head and looked at her, or more accurately, he looked for her hands. They were still behind her back. "Rudolph?" he guessed.

She shook her head. Tonight she had dressed in brown thermal leggings, brown suede boots that came to her knees, and a baggy yellow sweatshirt with big bold fancy letters that proclaimed, "Well-Behaved Women Rarely Make History." Earrings shaped like pear trees, with a partridge perched on one of the branches, dangled from her ears. She had taken extra care with her makeup and even added a touch more gel than usual to her hair. She thought the spikes made her eyes look wider.

"Santa?"

"You're guessing, Abe." There was a teasing glint in his gray eyes that made her stomach do that dip thing again. Talking with Abraham was like riding a roller coaster.

Abraham flashed a grin before turning his gaze back over the hall. "So, Gracie, what's on the nails, or are you planning on keeping me in suspense all night long?"

She was tempted to walk back to her seat and let him think about her all night long, but she hadn't done what she had set out to do when she crossed the fire hall and started all those tongues awagging. She held out her hands and wiggled her fingers. "See."

Abraham scowled at her moving fingers. "Hold them still, so I can see."

She held them still and inched her way closer to him.

Abraham squinted at her inch-long nails. "Holly leaves and berries."

" 'Tis the season." She had to wonder why the fire hall didn't hang mistletoe. It would definitely add some excitement to their Friday night bingo game.

" 'Tis the season for a lot of things, Gracie." Abraham jammed his hands into the front pockets of his pants and seemed to be studying her mouth.

Her stomach clenched as it went down another one of those dips on the roller coaster. "I seem to owe you a cup of soup and hot chocolate, Abe."

"You don't owe me a thing."

"I would like to take you out and buy you that cup of soup."

The surprise on Abraham's face would have been comical, if her heart wasn't in her throat pounding away. "Are you asking me out, Gracie?"

"I guess I am." She held her breath and waited for Abraham to say something. The stubborn man refused to comment and she nearly gasped for her next breath. "Is that a yes or a no, Abe?" There was no way he could be that thick in the head.

"It's a no."

"No?" She lowered her voice, "What do you mean no?" Abraham was the first man she had ever asked out, and he was turning her down flat. Humiliation burned in her cheeks.

"Don't get me wrong, I want to go out with you in the worst way, Gracie girl, but it's not going to happen until you finish sowing whatever wild oats you got bugging you." Abraham leaned in closer, so their conversation wouldn't be repeated through the fire hall. "I'm not going to join the horde of men vying for your attention and time. I'm too damn old to play those games."

"Games?" She was having a hard time following Abraham. He wanted to go out with her, but he wouldn't.

"The only time in my life that I have taken a number and got in line, has been at Barley's Food Store and he had been running a weekly special at the deli counter." Abraham's eyes gleamed with laughter. "I happen to think you're better than sliced smoked ham or turkey breast. When you're done playing the field, give me a call."

Grace snapped her mouth shut, took two steps away, turned and said, "You think I'm lunch meat?"

People craned their necks to hear his response. Abraham laughed. "I think you're beautiful, now go play bingo and win a few games." He gave her a flirtatious wink. "I love how you yell Bingo."

She wasn't sure who had been more shocked, her or the crowd of bingo players who had overheard their last exchange. One thing she did know, Abraham Martin was turning into one very interesting man.

Amber watched as Ian body-checked Erik Olsen, of the Viking God fame, and stole the puck. She was impressed, but also secretly fearful for Ian's well-being. Erik didn't look like the kind of guy you wanted to steal a puck from, but when the big Viking threw back his head and laughed, she drew a deep breath and relaxed. Ian might live to the end of the game after all.

Something had gotten into Ian today. He was playing like a man possessed, or a man taking all his frustrations out on the ice. What did he have to be frustrated about? He was the one who chose to walk out of her apartment door every night. She was the one who needed to be out on the ice body-checking Vikings and whacking the heck out of a puck. She had done everything but strip naked and shout "Take me!" Talk about frustration.

A girl had to have some pride. The little ounce left in her was the only thing that prevented her from begging. That and the fact she knew Ian's leaving every night wasn't any easier on him. James's ghost was still haunting him.

As James's widow, what was she supposed to do about it? Stop living? Stop loving?

"Want to talk about it?" Olivia Wycliffe was huddled under enormous blankets.

She glanced at her friend sitting next to her and tried not to laugh. Olivia, who had been originally from sunny California, looked like a frozen popsicle. "Be careful you don't suffocate in there." Only a small portion of Olivia's face was visible peeking through layers of blankets. She heard the chattering of Olivia's teeth and frowned. Being from hearty New England stock, the cold didn't bother her too much, but her fair-weather friend wasn't holding up very well against the brutal December winds. Poor Olivia was going to be totally miserable come January.

"Come on, let's go warm up in Ian's car." It was ridiculous for them to freeze their butts off when the men were out on the ice, killing each other, and working up a nice sweat.

Olivia jumped to her feet without being asked twice. "Let's use mine. We'll have a better view of the game." Olivia, still clutching the blankets, waddled her way to her car.

Amber tossed the blanket she had wrapped around her shoulders into the backseat and slid into the passenger seat just as Olivia was cranking the engine and reaching for the heat controls. "If you were that cold, Olivia, why didn't you say something? We could have been sitting in here for the past forty minutes."

"Ethan thinks I'm turning into a wuss. Last winter didn't bother me nearly as much as this one is starting to." Olivia had tossed her blankets into the backseat. Her still gloved hands were in front of the heater vent. "This way I can tell him you suggested it."

Amber nodded at the heater. "You have to give it a minute to warm up." She tossed her knitted cap onto the dashboard and unzipped her coat. The inside of the car was at least thirty degrees warmer, and there wasn't any wind. It felt like Florida.

She glanced at her friend and her smile slowly faded. Olivia looked like hell. "You've been sick?" Amber couldn't remember Olivia being sick, but her friend was looking awfully pale and thin. There were even dark smudges of fatigue beneath her eyes. She glanced out the windshield and saw Ethan in the middle of the last quarter of the game staring at his car and not paying attention to what was going on around him on the ice.

"Not really." Olivia looked out the windshield and cringed when Ethan got creamed. "Ethan didn't want to play today because of me, but I thought the fresh air would do me good."

"If this is doing you good, I would hate to see what you looked like this morning." She was growing concerned for her friend. In her mind, a thousand illnesses started screaming their names. "Have you seen Doctor Sydney?"

There were tears in Olivia's eyes as she shook her head. "I don't need to see the doctor."

Fear clutched at her heart. She had known Olivia for over a year, and she had never seen her friend so fragile-looking. "Yes you do, Liv. First thing tomorrow morning you will be calling Doctor Sydney, or I will do it for you." Something was telling her that Olivia's husband wasn't going to let it go that far. Ethan's mind definitely hadn't been on the game.

Olivia's smile was on the watery side. "I know what's wrong, Amber."

"You do?"

"I wanted to give Ethan an extra special Christmas present this year." Olivia dug through the console, found a couple of tissues, and blew her nose. "I just didn't think it would be this hard."

"What are you talking about? What does Ethan's Christmas present have to do with you being sick?"

Olivia took a deep breath and said, "I'm three weeks late."

"Late?" The goofy smile curving Olivia's mouth told her how dumb that question had been. "Oh, my God, you're pregnant!"

"I'm not a hundred percent sure, but I can't keep hiding certain aspects of it from Ethan. Tossing up one's cookies every morning is kind of hard to hide from a husband. I sleep constantly, and I still look like hell."

"Ethan doesn't suspect anything?" Ethan never struck her as being dumb.

"Of course he suspects something. He's driving me nuts. He thinks I'm sick. He's hovering over me constantly and jamming vitamins down my throat. If I have to drink another glass of orange juice, the man will be wearing orange." Olivia wiped her tears. "I don't think I can hide it from him for another twelve days. That's all I wanted, Amber, just another twelve days."

Amber watched out the windshield as Ethan talked to a couple of guys on the team, and then headed for the car. "I don't think you can, either. He's heading this way, and I've got a feeling he knows something is wrong."

"Nothing's wrong, except he's going to be mighty disappointed Christmas Eve when he doesn't get to open that home pregnancy test I bought him." Olivia reached for another tissue. "It's wrapped and under the tree already." Her smile wobbled. "I swear he shakes that package every time he walks by it, trying to figure out what it is. I hinted at it being the best present of the bunch."

Amber watched as Ethan made his way around the hockey game. Ethan's gaze never wavered from the car, and she would wager the hot chocolate left in her thermos that he was only looking at one thing: the woman sitting behind the wheel, his wife and soon-to-be mother of his child. "Liv, I hate to break this to you, but I think you're going to have to give Ethan his present in about two minutes. I don't think he can last another twelve days."

"It's at home under the tree." Olivia watched her husband approach and wailed, "It was supposed to make him happy, not this upset."

"He's upset because he thinks you're sick." Amber pulled her hat back on, and zipped up her coat. "It's time to put the poor man out of his misery." She low-

ered her voice. "Let me know how the test turns out."
She opened the car door as Ethan reached for the
handle.

She bit her lip to keep from smiling. "Hi, Ethan.
Good game."

Ethan grunted a reply as he got into the seat she had
just vacated, ice skates and all, and slammed the door.

Amber walked over to where her and Olivia's folding
chairs still sat. She jammed her hands into the pocket
of her coat and cursed the wind. Her blanket was still in
the backseat of Olivia's car, but there was no way she
was interrupting that conversation.

Ian sat and stared across the candlelight at his dinner partner. Thankfully, the hostess of the Catch of the
Day restaurant had sat them at a very discreet corner
table. Amber went beyond gorgeous tonight. He didn't
think she had any more "stops" to pull out, but she had
surprised him yet again. Amber wasn't playing fair. The
low-cut black dress she was barely wearing had caused
the heat in his blood to simmer and the ache in his
groin to intensify. Amber hadn't dressed for sophistication, she had dressed for seduction.

He was a dead man. He wasn't sure if he had the
strength to walk away from her tonight.

He was leaving for Boston before dawn. He was
needed back at the office and he had to go. He was the
boss. He had responsibilities and a business to run. It
would only be for one week. He was coming back to
Maine on Saturday. Coming back to Amber.

Amber dipped a piece of lobster into the melted butter and then popped it into her mouth. He tried not to
groan as he watched her lips close around the fork.

"This is delicious, Ian. Thank you for inviting me."
Amber smiled politely, but the teasing light in her eyes

told the real story. Amber knew exactly what she was doing to him. Driving him insane.

"You've been feeding me all week, it's the least I could do." If they were back in Boston he would have cooked her a meal or two. He wasn't helpless in the kitchen, but he didn't think Olivia would appreciate him taking over the one at the bed-and-breakfast.

"So this is a payback meal?" The teasing light in her eyes faded.

"No, it's a date." He knew his voice sounded rougher than he intended it to, but she knew exactly which buttons to push. Amber was not happy that he was heading back to Boston. This was not the sweet even-tempered woman James had filled his head with stories about over the years. This Amber had bite and she wasn't afraid to let him know it. This Amber also had his heart.

"A date? I thought this was a very expensive good-bye dinner." Amber took a sip of her wine and looked around the restaurant as if she had never been in it before.

"I told you I'll be back Saturday afternoon." He didn't know if he should feel happy that Amber was obviously upset he was leaving, or upset that she didn't believe him when he said he'd be coming back.

"Boston's a long distance away."

"I can drive it in five hours, if the traffic cooperates."

"As long as you don't mind the speeding tickets." Amber stabbed at another piece of lobster.

He pushed his steak around his plate. He wanted to ask Amber to come with him. Boston had been her home for years. Surely she had friends she could visit and places to go while he was tied up in meetings. Three major ad presentations were scheduled for the upcoming week. He had to be there. He should have been there last week.

Then there was the small matter of a partnership to

consider. He had scraped together everything he could to pay Amber for James's share of the business. He was now the sole proprietor of the M & M Ad Agency. He owned it, lock, stock, and barrel, along with the bank. In the past year he had been approached by three different individuals who all wanted to buy into the partnership. He had stalled from giving them an answer as long as he could.

He didn't know if he wanted to be in another partnership. He employed plenty of people, some whom had taken over James's end of the business extremely well. The problem with being a sole proprietor was, he was spending more time being the boss, and less time on what he loved, the actual hands-on creative end of the business. He'd rather spend hours at the drawing board than hours in the board room.

He'd be back in Misty Harbor before Saturday if he could, but he couldn't. Friday evening was the company's Christmas party, and he had to be there. He was tempted to ask Amber to come with him, but Friday night was Grace's bingo night, and Amber always worked the store.

He could just imagine the look on some of the employees faces if he walked into the party with Amber. He couldn't care less what anyone thought, but Amber might.

He watched Amber as she halfheartedly ate her dinner. This wasn't what he had in mind for his last night in town. He wanted to see her smile. He wanted to hear her say that she was going to miss him.

"So, do you think Ethan has calmed down yet?" he asked. As a subject change, it was a good one. This afternoon, with one minute to play in the game, and the scored tied two to two, Ethan Wycliffe had charged out onto the ice and announced he was going to become a father. Paul Newman, the acting referee, had been about to give Ethan's team the win, in honor of the upcoming event, but Erik Olsen announced he was going to be a father, too, and his wife was due before Ethan's.

Doctor Sydney was furious that her husband, Erik, had announced the news to the town, because she hadn't even told her parents yet. She was waiting for their visit at Christmas. Olivia had been furious that Ethan had told everyone because she hadn't even peed on the Christmas present, whatever that meant.

Paul Newman had to call a face-off between Ethan and Erik. The last minute of play had been wicked, but Erik did manage to score the winning goal, hoping to ease the friction between him and the doc. It hadn't helped. Sydney had been running around swearing everyone there to secrecy until after eight o'clock Christmas Eve. By then, her family would know.

Erik was in the doghouse, and Ethan had been laughing hysterically, until Olivia got nauseous. Olivia had been clutching a plastic bag to her chest and breathing deeply, while fending off advice from the horde of women surrounding her. Ethan couldn't get within ten feet of his decisively green wife.

Through all the commotion he had watched Amber. She hadn't been jealous, but there was a strange expression on her face whenever she glanced at Olivia or the doctor. If he had to guess what it was, he would say envy. Amber seemed envious of the pregnant ladies, even the green one. He had to wonder if she had wanted children. In all the years he had known James, his friend and partner had never mentioned the desire to have any.

Amber's first real smile of the evening lit up her face. "I think every man should be that excited when he finds out he's going to be a father for the first time."

"A man should be that happy when he finds out he's going to be a father, period. It shouldn't matter if it's his first child or his sixth. I would think they all would be worth celebrating."

Amber's fingers faltered and her fork clanged to her plate. She looked stricken as tears pooled in her eyes and she fumbled for her napkin. "Don't say stuff like that."

His heart jolted in mid-thump. "Why?" What had he said that upset her so?

"Because every time you say something sweet like that, I fall in love with you more."

Chapter 14

Grace checked the oven for the third time. Anyone looking at her would think she had never cooked a pot roast in her life. The one thing she hadn't done was cook a roast for anyone besides Howard. With all the dating she had been doing for the past several months, she never once invited a man over for dinner. Tonight was different. Tonight Abe was coming for dinner.

There was something personal and intimate about a man sitting at your kitchen table, enjoying your cooking. None of the men she had dated would have fit into her kitchen, into her life. They had been fun, flirtatious, and great for her ego, but she had wanted more. Lord help her, but she honestly thought Abe was the "more" she had been looking for.

Last night she had stayed up till midnight cooking an apple pie and a chocolate cake. She wasn't sure which one Abe would prefer, so she had baked both. She had even set the formal dining room table with her good china. The candles were lit, and Sinatra was softly crooning Christmas carols on her CD player.

Howard would have been jealous at all this special attention she was pouring into one meal, but he would have laughed his butt off at how nervous she was in her own kitchen. Last night, while the cake was cooling, she had wrapped herself in a blanket and stood on the front porch, staring up into the night sky. Her one-sided conversation with Howard had eased her mind. It was time to move on with her life.

A knock on the back door announced Abe's arrival. Her life was about to move on. She ran her trembling fingers over her hips and smoothed out her tunic-length blouse. Tonight she had gone for elegance and simplicity—dark velvet pants and a shimmering, lighter purple silk blouse. She had accessorized the outfit with gold. Gold flats, three gold bracelets, a string of matching necklaces, and huge hoop earrings that brushed her shoulders added the flare she had been looking for. Her hair was gelled, and her lipstick fresh.

She opened the door and gave a startled laugh as Abe handed her the bouquet of flowers he had been hiding behind. The flowers were breathtaking, but it was the man that caused the sudden dip in her stomach. In the soft glow of the porch light she realized that Abe was truly handsome.

"Evening, Gracie."

"Hi." She was nearly speechless. Abe either had someone dress him, or he had been flipping through the pages of *GQ*. Black dress pants and a soft blue sweater made him look younger, but the new black leather jacket made him look dangerous. She took a step back and smiled. "Come on in." There was something about a dangerous man she always found exciting.

Abraham stepped into her kitchen and closed the door against the wind. "Something sure smells good."

"I hope you like pot roast." She reached into a cabinet for a vase.

"I wasn't talking about food, Gracie." Abraham give her a wink as he took off his jacket and hung it on one of the pegs by the door.

"Courting those younger women has taught you some tricks, Abraham Martin." She turned her back and started arranging the flowers. She didn't want Abe to see the blush burning in her cheeks. The man was incorrigible, and all of a sudden she felt like she was back in high school.

"You mean the Fletcher gals?" Abraham chuckled. "I wasn't courting them, Gracie."

"What do you call bringing them flowers and your mother's carrot cake?" She had heard all the stories, and had a good laugh about it with the rest of the town. Abraham hadn't been the oldest man to try to date the Fletcher sisters, but he was the one she remembered.

"I was observing."

"Observing what?" She positioned the irises in with the rest of the mixed flowers and then stood back to study the arrangement.

"How the guy won the girl." Abe chuckled at his memories. "Why would I want to catch a gal twenty some years younger? Then the question I would have to ask myself is, what in tarnation would I do with one, once I caught her?"

She laughed with delight as she set the vase in the center of the kitchen table. She moved the poinsettia that had been there to the counter. "Abe, surely you haven't forgotten?" she teased.

Abraham flashed her a smile that sent her stomach into another dive. "Time will tell."

Those schoolgirl flutters were still beating against her stomach. She didn't think there was a safe way to respond to that comment. "There's some wine in the refrigerator; why don't you pour us a glass while I put the biscuits in the oven."

"We might want to hold back on the wine."

"Why?" She had picked up the inexpensive bottle while at the food store. It was her favorite, and tasted a little fruity. Maybe she should have picked up some beer for Abe while she had been there.

"I thought we could go for a drive after dinner."

"A drive?" There was no way she was getting into Abraham's truck. The thing was a biohazard on wheels. It was a death trap that smelled of rotten fish and dried seaweed. She didn't want to hurt his feelings, but a woman had to have some principles. "We can take my car."

Abraham shook his head and reached for her hand. "I've got something to show you."

If any other man had said that to her, with that same gleam in his eye, she would have taken it as a pass. A badly thrown pass. "What?"

Abraham opened the back door and pulled her out onto the back porch.

"Abe, I don't know what . . ." Her voice trailed off as she stared at the shiny, brand new, silver mid-size SUV parked in the driveway. "Whose is it?"

"Mine. I picked it up this morning." Abe looked so darn proud of himself. "I can't go courting the prettiest lady in Misty Harbor in the truck. I'll save her for work. She has a good couple of years left in her."

"You bought this SUV just to take me out?" She had never heard of anything so romantic or sweet.

"Yeah, but don't tell my mom." Abraham winked. "She claims she's finally written me back into her will now that she doesn't have to ride in old Betsy any longer."

Grace slammed the lid of her trunk and quickly moved to get into the car. She was in a hurry, and she needed to get the chicken stuffed before she could even put it in the oven. Abe would be over in a couple of hours, and she wanted everything ready for him.

Who would have thought she would fall head over heels in love in just four days? Not her, but it had happened anyway. They had spent every evening together and things had just kept getting better and better. As the saying went, today was the first day of the rest of her life, and darn, it was looking good.

On the drive home from the food store she cranked up the radio and listened to those dogs bark out the classic "Jingle Bells." She loved those old mutts. As she turned into her driveway her good mood deflated like a bad stock option. Her sister's car was parked behind the house. Gladys had driven up from Rhode Island, and hadn't given anyone a heads up about the visit. Not a good sign. She hadn't talked to her sister in nearly a week.

Determined not to let her sister ruin her evening, she unloaded the food and headed for the kitchen. She dumped the bags on the table and yelled, "Gladys?" Her sister had a key to the house and had always been welcome there. Today she wasn't too sure.

"In here," called Gladys from the living room.

Grace headed in that direction and tried not to smile as she watched her sister slide a couple of brightly wrapped presents under the tree. Gladys had come bearing presents. Maybe tonight wasn't going to be a total disaster.

Gladys stood up and brushed off the knees of her fine wool pants. She was dressed like she was going to lunch at a country club, all grays and pink with an expensive pearl necklace draped at her throat. "The tree needed some presents under it."

"Thank you." She glanced down and spotted her name on a tag or two. "I haven't gotten around to wrapping my gifts yet." She had been too busy getting to know Abe.

Gladys straightened a gold bow on one of the branches. "How come your trees always look so beautiful while mine look like a bunch of second-graders did them?"

She didn't have the heart to tell her sister she just made the bow crooked. She busied herself by taking off her coat instead of straightening the bow. "Practice, I guess." She tossed her jacket onto a chair. "What brings you into town? Everything okay at home?"

"Everyone's fine." Gladys walked around the room scowling at everything in sight. "This room is ugly."

She bit her tongue. She wanted to agree with her sister, but couldn't. "It has its charm."

Gladys snorted. "So do toads."

Grace took a deep breath. She wasn't getting into that discussion again. She plopped herself down on the couch. She'd been on her feet all day at the shop. Walk-in business was booming, but thankfully the mail orders were finally slowing down to a manageable pace. "You drove a long way to admire my tree."

Gladys gave the couch a discerning glare before lowering herself onto it. "I came bearing gifts and apologies."

"For?" Gladys had caused her more than a headache or two recently, so she wasn't about to help her out here.

"For being a pain in the posterior." Gladys had her hands folded in her lap.

She shook her head. "You used to call a posterior an ass, Glad."

"I've grown up." Gladys looked uncomfortable with the subject.

"Haven't we all." Grace leaned back, kicked off her shoes, and propped her feet up on the coffee table. "Are you going to stop pestering me and Amber? Are you going to allow your grown, very intelligent daughter to make her own decisions about where she wants to live, who she wants to date, and what she wants to do with the rest of her life? Are you going to stop listening to Priscilla or anyone else in town? Are you going to stop calling four times a day?"

"Yes."

"Are you going to apologize and make amends with your daughter when she gets home from work?"

"Yes." Gladys's shoulders were stiff and unyielding.

"Good, she misses you." She gave her sister a wide smile. "Are you going to stay for dinner? Spend a night or two visiting?"

"If I'm invited." Gladys's shoulders started to relax.

"Of course you're invited." She slouched farther into the overstuffed sofa. "Lean back and put your feet up."

Gladys slowly leaned back and gingerly put her feet up onto the table. Somewhere along the way, she had lost her shoes. "This table is ugly, too."

Her sister would get no argument from her. "We're having chicken tonight, if I ever get it in the oven."

"I'll help."

"We also will be having company." This was where Grace would see how honest that apology had been.

"Who?"

"Abraham Martin." She waited for the explosion of questions and opinions.

Gladys gave her a long look before saying, "That's nice, I like Abraham." Gladys smoothed the crease in her trousers. "So, am I forgiven?"

She nearly choked on her astonishment. Her sister really had meant it. "Say 'ass.' "

"What?" Gladys looked shocked.

"Say the word 'ass' and I will forgive you."

"It's a vulgar word, Grace, and there is absolutely no reason why I would have to say it."

"I've seen you eat worms, sister dear." Grace chuckled at her sister's cringe. "I also know you stuffed your bra with tissues in the seventh grade."

Gladys crossed her arms and glared. "Ass," Gladys whispered.

She smiled. "Louder."

"Ass!" Gladys shouted.

Grace's smile grew. "Now you're forgiven."

"You're horrible." Gladys relaxed into the couch. "This room is still ugly. Why haven't you thrown all this stuff out?"

"It grows on a person." She ran the tip of a nail over a frayed doily.

"The only thing it's growing is uglier by the year." Gladys scowled at the walls. "How can you stand being in this room? I swear, before you got home I felt like I was being watched."

She chuckled. She knew that feeling well. It was like one of those paintings whose eyes followed you around the room. On more than one occasion she would have sworn the roses had been tracking her every move in the room. "You're just being paranoid."

"Did you promise Mom never to change the room?"

"What?"

"You heard me." Gladys looked right at her. "I know you hate this room, Grace. I also know this is not your taste or style. I've been giving it some thought and the only thing I could come up with was some kind of deathbed promise you made to Mom. She was the one who loved this room. She was the one who paid for every ugly piece of furniture. Maybe with all the medications she was on at the end she made you promise never to change it."

"Howard paid for it all." Maybe it was time she told someone. She had protected Gladys and her brothers, Tom and Steve, twenty-seven years ago from some hard realities of life.

"I thought Mom paid for it all. Isn't that where all her money went?" Gladys didn't seem so relaxed now.

"Mom's money was gone before she redecorated this room. Mom used up everything she had on doctors, hospitals, and medicine." She shrugged. "In all honesty, she didn't know the money was gone. I had power of attorney, and paid all her bills for her."

"You were also living here and taking care of her twenty-four hours a day. That was something Tom, Steve, and I appreciated more than we ever told you and Howard. Mom wanted to stay in her house, and because of you, she was able to."

"Howard and I were paying the taxes and all the other expenses while trying to save up for a house of our own one day."

"How much did you save?"

"Put it this way, if I didn't inherit a quarter of this house, we never would have gotten it. All the money we had saved over the years was gone by the time Mom lost her battle with cancer."

"You spent it all on Mom?" Distress etched Gladys's face.

"Just about." She reached over and held her sister's hand. "Howard never complained. He loved Mom as much as I did. We only fought once in all that time."

"Because of this room, right?"

"Right. To him it was a waste of money. Not that Mom didn't deserve a nice room, but because what she picked out was so darn ugly. Howard couldn't see anyone wanting it, and he sure as the devil didn't."

"Why didn't you come to me? Or to Tom or Steve? We would have pitched in and helped. She was our mother, too."

"Because you had four little ones at home, and Tom and Steve had their growing families. Money was tight for everyone." She squeezed Gladys's hand. "Besides, I had been trying for years to get pregnant, and it wasn't happening. I figured Howard and I were the best equipped to handle the financial burden. We, at least, had a nest egg."

"We'll get back to the financial end of things later." Gladys gave her a look that clearly stated that discussion was far from over. "What I want to know is, why haven't you changed this room?"

"Because I lied to Howard." She gave her sister a small smile. "I begged, cried, and looked my husband dead in the eyes and told him I loved everything our mother had picked out. I told him it was exactly what I wanted, and I would never change the room."

Gladys glanced around the room and laughed. "He believed you?"

"Enough to let me drain the rest of our savings out of the account." Grace wrinkled her nose at the room. "This nightmare on Spruce Street is my penance for lying to my husband."

Amber grabbed the huge, wrapped-in-plastic poinsettia plant out of the backseat of her car just as her mother came out of Grace's kitchen door. She had seen her mother's car in the driveway, but she wanted to get the plant inside her apartment where it was warm. Ian had the plant delivered to her at the shop today. There had to be at least two dozen blooms on the thing. "Hi, Mom."

"Hi, yourself." Gladys Donovan looked at her only daughter with love in her eyes. "Good gracious, that has to be the biggest poinsettia I've ever seen. Can you manage it?"

Amber tossed her mom the keys to her apartment. "If you unlock the door, I can carry it." She followed her mother up the steps and into her place. She was breathing hard by the time she set it on her kitchen table. She striped the plastic sleeve off the plant. Big whitish blooms stuck out farther than the table edge. The plant dwarfed her table.

Her mother laughed at the sight and gave her a kiss on the cheek. "What possessed you to buy one so big?" Her mother hung her coat up by the door.

"I didn't buy it. Ian sent it to me." She waited for the bombardment of questions. The whys, the whats, the wheres, and that all-important question—when the wedding was going to be.

"That was very nice of him."

She couldn't help but stare at her mother in worry. Gladys wasn't acting like herself. Granted, her mother had become more of a worrywart, opinionated know-it-all after James had been killed in the car accident, but still, this complete turn-about was troublesome. "Is everything okay at home? Everyone okay?" She couldn't imagine her mother leaving Providence if everyone wasn't okay.

"Everyone is fine. Your father sends his love." Gladys bent down and scratched Light behind the ears when the cat had come over to investigate the stranger. "She's grown a lot since I saw her last."

"You should see Shadow. He's at least ten pounds heavier." She glanced toward the bedroom. "He's probably hiding under the bed."

"They must like it here if they're growing."

"Are you here for a visit?" It was Thursday evening and Ian was due back Saturday afternoon. She loved her mother dearly, but there was no way she wanted her here when Ian got back. She had plans for Ian, and they didn't include leaving this apartment all weekend.

"Just for a night or two. I'll be staying over at Grace's since you don't have the room and she has plenty."

She had to wonder how Grace had taken that news. The last she heard, which was about two hours ago, her mother and aunt weren't speaking to each other. "Is everything okay between you and Grace?"

"No." Her mother smiled to soften the harshness of her reply. "There's a family matter that needs to be straightened out, but that's between her, your two uncles, and me."

"Let me know if you guys will be needing a referee."

Her mother laughed. "Which reminds me, you're invited to Grace's for dinner. We're making chicken. I just slid it into the oven before you pulled up, so it's going to be a while before we eat."

"Great." She glanced around the kitchen and wondered what she might have to offer her mother. "How about I make some coffee?" She opened the cabinet above the stove. "You're in luck, I've got a few Oreos left." Ian had polished off most of the bag with what appeared to be a gallon of milk. She'd nibbled on a few, but mostly she'd kept thinking about all those extra chocolate milk shake pounds on her hips.

"Coffee sounds wonderful."

"Great, make yourself at home."

"By the way, there will be a fourth at dinner. It seems Abraham Martin will be joining us." Her mother sat on the couch and tossed Light the catnip toy that had been lying there.

Light caught the toy in midair, and started rolling around the floor with it clutched in her paws.

"Abraham's sweet on Grace."

"So I hear."

She stopped measuring the grounds and stared at her mother. "Are you okay with that?"

"Grace can date whomever she wants." Her mother's cheeks looked flushed. "The reason for this impromptu visit is I came to apologize in person."

"To Grace?" Her aunt had been hounded unmercifully by her mother the past month or so. Grace deserved more than an apology, she deserved the Silver Star Medal.

"I already apologized to her, and she accepted it gracefully." There was a smile teasing the corners of her mother's mouth. "Now it's time to apologize to you."

"For what?" She knew what she would like to hear, but sometimes what you like and what you get are two different things.

"For being an ass."

The shock of hearing her mother utter a profanity jolted Amber's heart. "Oh, my God, you're sick! What did the doctor say?" She put the can of coffee on the countertop and hurried to her mother's side.

Her mother laughed. "You should see your face."

"Mother!"

"I'm fine, Amber," Gladys stood up and hugged her daughter. "I'm perfectly healthy and I haven't seen a doctor in months."

"You said 'ass.' " Amber hugged her mother tighter and suddenly realized how tiny she was. She had a good four inches over her mom, and more than a couple pounds. Gladys Donovan hadn't drunk a chocolate shake in over thirty years. "Grace made you say it, didn't she?"

"Yes." Gladys laughed and kissed Amber's cheek. "But the word fit the occasion."

"I see." There was no way she was going to forgive her mom for being an 'ass,' because there was no way she could say that to her.

"No, you don't." Gladys released her, walked into the kitchen, and finished making the coffee herself. "My only excuse is that I love you, and I want to see you happy."

"I am happy, Mom." She put the plant on top of her bureau in the bedroom. It was the only large spot cleared enough for it.

"In Maine? In this town?" Gladys looked doubtful. "There's nothing here, Amber. Job opportunities are almost nonexistent and the nearest hospital is forty minutes away."

"Mom, just because you didn't like living here when you were growing up, doesn't mean it's a bad place. Plenty of people love Misty Harbor, I happen to be one of them."

"What about family?"

"What about family? Just because you and Dad live in Providence, I should, too?"

Her mother smiled. "Your brothers, their wives, and all your nieces and nephews live there, too."

"True, but Grace is here."

"You have two uncles in Boston."

"I probably have a distant cousin five times removed living in Toledo, Ohio, but that doesn't mean I should go move there."

"True." Gladys got down the cups as the coffee dripped.

Amber arranged the few remaining Oreos onto a plate. "I love it here, Mom. I'm actually quite happy with my life." There were a few things in regards to Ian that needed to be worked out, but things were looking better. When he'd left her place Sunday night she had been in no doubt on how much he wanted her, but he still hadn't relieved her growing frustration.

If she had a chance to think about it, she never would have blurted out that she was falling in love with him in the middle of the restaurant. She would have waited for a more intimate surrounding. Ian's reaction to her words had been priceless. She had seen the desire and the need burning in his gaze, yet he had been powerless to act on that emotion.

At first she had been disappointed that he hadn't said those words back to her, or any other words that might describe his feelings. She knew he was having a hard time separating her from the Amber who had been the wife of his friend. She was holding out the hope that when he finally did say those words, they would mean so much more. They would mean he was ready to let go of the past, and step into the future, with her by his side.

"I understand that things could be getting serious

between you and Ian." Gladys filled both cups and carried them to the table.

Amber grabbed the sugar bowl and an extra spoon and joined her mom. "Could be." Her mother wasn't pushing her but she would be more comfortable talking about Ian with her aunt. Maybe it was time she tried to breach that rift that always existed between her mother and herself. She took a deep breath and opened her heart. "He's having a hard time."

"The business?"

"No, the business is great." Amber poured milk into her cup and then put the container back into the refrigerator. "He still sees me as James's wife. He's seeing the feelings that are growing between us as a betrayal to his friend."

"Oh, my." Her mother looked dazed. "I hadn't thought of that."

"Yeah." She took a sip of her coffee and echoed her mother's words, "Oh, my."

"We all loved James, dear, but he's been gone for eighteen months. What does Ian expect you to do? Life does go on."

"I know. It's not as if I started having these feelings for him while James was still alive and I was a married woman."

"Of course not." Her mother glanced over her shoulder and into the bedroom where the plant was dominating the bureau. "I see he's not too conflicted."

"He's working it out." She didn't tell her mother about the box of candy that had arrived Monday, that was still back at the shop. Or the new pair of ice skates that arrived Tuesday, or the stuffed animal that was a perfect likeness of Light. A note claiming that he was still looking for the likeness of Shadow had accompanied the stuffed cat. She had no idea what, if anything, would be arriving tomorrow. All she knew was that Ian had better arrive by the time she got off work on Saturday. Before leaving the restaurant Sunday night, he had made reservations at Catch of the Day for Saturday night. She had called and cancelled them yesterday.

"You do realize that Ian's business is in Boston. If you two get serious that could be a problem."

"I know." She didn't want to leave Misty Harbor, or move back to Boston. The alternative was to live without the man she loved. It wasn't a difficult decision. Aunt Grace could hire someone to help her with the jam business. "You would like that, wouldn't you?"

"No." Her mother's gaze was direct. "I would prefer for you to live in Providence, closer to me and your father. There's a nice split-level down the street that just went on the market." Her mother's mouth turned up at the corners. "But, what I really want is for you to be happy. Live where you want to live. We'll visit."

"Okay, what catastrophe occurred to make you do this one-eighty? A lunar eclipse? Did you win the lottery? A near-death experience? Alien abduction?"

"Worse."

"What's worse than an alien abduction?"

"Your father."

"Dad? What's wrong with Dad, he's a big old pussy cat." She chuckled. "You've got him wrapped around your finger so tight the man can barely breathe."

"Well, he came unwrapped with a vengeance."

"What happened?"

"Priscilla Patterson's husband called the other day and talked to him. Seems Priscilla ran up their long distance phone charges to an astronomical amount. Roy claimed that Priscilla was spying for me, so we should be paying the bill, not him."

"What did Dad say to that?" She could just imagine what Priscilla's phone bill must have been.

"He told Roy he'd call him back, and then he pulled our past phone bills."

She winced, but kept her mouth shut.

"Let's just leave it at we fought, and then we sat down and talked all night long. I told him about the fight I had with Grace, and how you were seeing Ian and how Grace was running around town dating anyone who asked her out. I told him how worried I was about you living here and my fear that you would marry some poor fisherman and spend the rest of your life struggling to make ends meet. I asked him if he wanted to see our future grandchildren raised here, in a town we both wanted to get out of since we were teenagers."

"What did Dad say to that?" Only her mother would have her married with a crop of toddlers at her knees struggling to put food in their bellies.

"He said Grace was a grown woman and could date whomever she wanted, do whatever she wanted, and I should be supporting her, not trying to run her life."

"If it makes you feel any better, Grace has very good taste in men. She's finally starting to live again, and is happy." Amber reached over and held her mother's hand. "She's smart, and she knows what she's doing."

"It took your father's shouting to get it through my thick head, but it's there now." Her mother squeezed her hand back.

She could count on one hand the number of times she had heard her father shout in her lifetime. If Robert Donovan was shouting, it must have been one whopper of a fight. "No more reports from Priscilla?"

"If I want to know something, I'll ask." Her mother finished her coffee without touching the cookies. "Your father was upset with my silliness concerning Grace, but he was furious over my stupidity about you. He threatened to sell the house, buy a boat, and sail away to Tahiti without me if I don't make things right with you."

She knew her father well enough to know he had

been bluffing on that one. Robert Donovan could get seasick in the bathtub. "Was it stupidity, or a mother's love?" In her heart she knew her mother wouldn't have been such a pain if she didn't love her or Grace.

"Love, definitely." Her mother's eyes swam with tears. "I'll admit I went a little overboard after James had died. His death made me realize how short and precious life was. All three of your brothers were older than him. The thought of losing one of you caused me to lose more than one night of sleep. I wanted to lock you up in a safe and secure place where nothing bad would ever happen to you again."

"If I was locked up, Mom, what kind of life would that be for me?"

"Rationally I knew that, but sometimes a mother's love isn't rational." Gladys chuckled. "Ask your father." She blinked back the unshed tears. "When you lived in Boston, you were only an hour away, but once you moved to Maine I felt lost, left out of your life."

"You'll never be out of my life." She walked around the table and pulled her mother into a hug. "I will always love you."

Gladys squeezed her back. "You're going to make me cry, and then my makeup is going to smear."

Amber kissed her mother on the cheek. "The horror."

Her mother's smile was radiant. "So you forgive all my foolishness? I promise to butt out of your life, as long as you keep me in it."

"Deal."

"You're not going to make me say a profanity, are you?"

"Grace made you curse?"

"That, and something far worse."

"What's that?"

Her mother's hand came up and lightly patted her elegantly styled hair. Gladys's brown hair, which was

heavily sprinkled with gray, was cut in a sleek, sophisticated bob that actually made her look older. "She made
an appointment for me tomorrow morning with her
hair stylist."

Amber looked at the distress in her mother's eyes
and laughed.

Chapter 15

Amber walked the couple of blocks to her apartment. The morning had been cold, but clear. Perfect walking weather. Ian was due back any time. He had left a message on her answering machine last night, and she had been disappointed to have missed his call. Her mother, Grace, and she had gone out for dinner at Catch of the Day to celebrate not only their truce, but Mom's new hairstyle.

Estelle's had done a wonderful job of restoring her mother's hair back to its original color, but they also added a few sun-kissed highlights and shagged it up a bit. The Meg Ryan haircut looked wonderful on her mom. Gladys was so pleased with the change, she even allowed Grace to take her to Claire's Boutique in town. Grace was having a ball either corrupting or blackmailing her sister. Amber wasn't sure which it was, but it didn't matter. Her mother had driven away this morning looking relaxed, happy, and ten years younger.

She started the walk up Spruce Street and chuckled. She would love to be a fly on the wall at her parents' house when her mother walked through the front door. Her father was in for the shock of his life.

She was halfway up the stairs to her apartment when she heard a car pull into the driveway. She turned around as Ian parked near the bottom of the stairs. Her heart picked up an extra beat as he got out of his car and stared up at her. He looked exhausted.

"I missed you at the shop. I was going to offer you a ride home." Ian started up the stairs.

"I closed five minutes early." She smiled when he stopped on the step below her and they were eye to eye. "For some reason I was in a hurry to get home."

"I bet you not half as much as I was to get back." Ian's gaze was riveted to her mouth.

She climbed to the next step backwards. She couldn't pull her eyes away from him. Her gaze devoured every inch of him, from his wind-tossed hair to the strong curve of his jaw. She wanted to lock away the memory of his face just as it was: hungry for her. "I missed you." She climbed another step and forced herself not to touch him. If she touched him now, they would never make it off the stairs.

Ian followed. "I'm a fool."

She blindly tried to put her key into the lock. "Why?"

"For leaving you here." Ian took the key out of her trembling fingers and opened the door. "I'm giving you two seconds to get into the apartment, Amber."

"If I don't?" She could see flare of hunger darkening his brown eyes to a near black. She wanted to drown in that darkness.

"We are definitely going to shock the neighbors."

She stepped into the apartment and grinned. At least they were on the same page. "Is this the part where you ravage me?"

Ian closed and locked the door behind them. "You want to be ravaged?" His grin was wicked.

She dropped her coat to the floor and tugged off her hat. "More than I want one of Krup's chocolate shakes."

Ian's coat landed on top of hers and then he pulled her into his arms and finally kissed her.

Heat exploded between them. Fiery and intense, it burned out of control. Everything within its path was about to be destroyed. She wrapped her arms around his neck and melted into the flames consuming them both. This was where she belonged. In Ian's arms.

She nipped his lower lip just to hear him moan.

He retaliated by cupping her hips and pressing her against the front of his jeans. It was her turn to moan as she felt his swift and powerful arousal.

Her fingers trembled as they tugged at the buttons on his shirt. Her mouth opened wider for the invasion of his tongue. The fire grew stronger and the need burned hotter. Two buttons slid through their holes.

Ian broke the kiss and wrenched her sweatshirt over her head. His mouth started to trail kisses down her throat. Her hand clenched as he hit a particularly sensitive spot. She laughed and looked down as one of Ian's buttons fell off and dropped to the floor.

Before the button made its second bounce on the tile, Light had caught it with her mouth. "Stop, stop, stop." She pushed against Ian's chest. Light was going to choke on the thing.

"What?" Ian stepped back and looked quite dazed by her outburst.

"Light's eating your button." She reached for the cat, who faked to the left.

Ian swept up the cat and pried the button out of her mouth. He put the button on the counter and the cat on the floor before pointing a finger at her. "Don't move."

She stood there in her jeans and bra and grinned. "Wouldn't dream of it."

Ian washed his hands and then finished taking off his own shirt. He tugged his T-shirt over his head and dropped it, along with his shirt, on the kitchen table. He bent over and started to unlace his boots.

She kicked off her sneakers.

"I thought I told you not to move." Ian cocked his head and looked up at her.

"It's only my shoes."

"I wanted to do that." Ian toed off his boots and started to yank at his socks.

"You got a foot fetish I should know about?" She looked at his toes. "By the way, in case I didn't mention it before, you have very sexy toes." Ian had wonderfully masculine feet.

Ian glanced down at his bare feet and wiggled his toes. "I do?"

"I wouldn't say it if it wasn't true." She liked how Ian was comfortable with his body without being over-confident.

Ian came toward her and she backed up against the wall. "I have a confession to make." Ian's mouth skimmed down her throat. His tongue ran a line around the lace trim of her black bra before trailing a path to her belly button.

She might have worn jeans and a sweatshirt to work, but she had put on her sexiest undergarments, hoping for such a welcome home celebration. "What's your fetish?" She prayed for something deliciously sinful.

The snap of her jeans came undone. Ian growled against her stomach, "You." Denim slid over her hips and down her legs. Ian's hands tugged the jeans and her socks off. "I'm obsessed with you." His mouth skimmed the lace band on her panties as his fingers inched their way up the inside of her thighs.

She closed her eyes and felt the heat wash over her like a wave. "That's good," she groaned as his fingers slipped under the edges of her panties and found her wet and ready. She felt her legs widen, but she was unsure if he did that, or if she moved them on her own.

Ian's teeth nipped at her hip bone as the panties slid down her legs. Hot fingertips trailed back up her thighs.

She bit back a scream as one long finger slid inside her, bringing her to the brink. His name was a plea, "Ian."

His mouth brushed the top of her thigh. "Tell me what you want."

A second finger joined the first. She clenched her back teeth and prayed for strength. "You," was gritted out between her teeth. "Now."

"Soon, love." Ian's fingers moved her thighs wider, and then cupped her bottom and tipped her hips forward.

Amber gave a strangling scream when Ian's tongue touched the place his fingers had been. She felt the climax hit her with such force she would have fallen to the floor if he wasn't holding her.

A moment later, while she was trying to see straight, Ian's mouth captured one of her nipples through the lace of her bra. Amazingly she felt the pull of desire tighten. She wrapped her arms around him and tugged him closer.

Ian fumbled with his jeans and quickly rolled on protection.

Her breathing spiked again, before it even had a chance to slow. Ian picked her up and she instinctively wrapped her legs around his hips.

"Take me inside you, love." Ian's jaw clenched as he slowly started to lower her onto him.

She felt him fill her and another edge of a climax rushed toward her. She felt him start to pull back out and clinched around him.

Ian closed his eyes, groaned, and plunged.

Her second climax was more powerful than the first. She felt herself convulse around the length of him. He shouted against her shoulder as his release shook his body.

Twenty minutes later she pressed a kiss in the center of Ian's chest. "You have a thing against my bed?"

"Yeah." Ian ran his fingers through her hair, separating the strands. "It's too far away."

She chuckled. "We didn't even get the fire lit."

"Oh, we had a fire lit all right." Ian shifted his weight and pulled her closer. "You cold?"

The afghan she had grabbed from the couch was soft against her skin. "Not in the least." How could she be cold when she was lying in his arms? She trailed a finger over his flat stomach and smiled when his muscles clenched and quivered beneath her touch. "Did I tell you how much I missed you?"

"If you missed me any more I would have been dead." Ian chuckled and skimmed a finger down her spine. "In case you didn't notice, we never made it out of the foyer."

"I was half surprised we made it off the stairs."

Ian kissed the top of her head. "I didn't touch you on the stairs." He had purposely made sure not to touch her on those stairs. By the time he made it into Misty Harbor his control had been shot. He had worked like a man possessed to get back here this afternoon. The company's Christmas party had been agony to get through. Torture would have been better. He had suffered through hours of socializing with his employees and their spouses, or their dates. He had been the only one at the party without a date. It was bad enough he had to suffer everyone's questioning looks, but he had missed Amber horribly.

He had called himself every known name for "fool." Amber had told him she was in love with him, and what did he do? He left for Boston the next morning. He never even told her how he felt.

"My neighbors thank you for your restraint."

He lightly slapped her bottom. Amber's humor had a wicked slant to it. One he appreciated and enjoyed. "Can I ask you a question?"

"Sure." She trailed a fingernail up his thigh. "But you might not like the answer."

He captured her hand before it reached a very appreciative part of his anatomy. "What smells so good?"

"Passion, it's a different perfume for me. You like?" Amber leaned up and smiled down at him.

Pale full breasts brushed his chest with her every breath, and her smile was contagious. Strands of auburn hair teased his jaw and the tightening in his gut told him that he wanted her again. Soon. Now. Forever. "I love the perfume, but I was referring to something cooking in the kitchen."

Amber shook her head and then playfully nipped at his chin. "It's meatballs. I started them in the Crock-Pot before I left for work."

"We have dinner reservations for seven o'clock." He remembered making them before they left the restaurant Sunday night. He had purposely made sure Amber heard him make those reservations so she would know he was coming back. It was his way of planning the future, even if it had only been a week away.

"I cancelled them." Amber straddled his hips and wiggled. "I stocked the refrigerator yesterday, and they're predicting at least ten inches of snow by morning."

His hands held her hips still. "So I heard." It was one of the main reasons he had hurried like hell to get back here to her. He had been fearful that the storm would hit before the Weather Channel had predicted. He might have been trapped in Boston for an extra day or two.

"So. Mister Creative Genius, prepare to be snow-bound. I'm sure you can think of some creative things to do to keep us amused."

Abraham paced Grace's living room like a caged tiger. "What's with you tonight, Abe? You seem a little edgy. Is it the approaching storm?" Some people were just more sensitive to the weather than others. Maybe Abe was one of the sensitive types.

"I'm fine, Gracie." Abraham reached for the water bottle and squirted more water onto the half peeled wallpaper. "Any particular reason this wallpaper has to come down tonight?"

"Let's just say I couldn't live with it another day." She scraped off another four inches of the aged paper and tossed it into the trash bag. Old wallpaper was the worst to get down. It was usually stubborn as all get out. The garden of evil roses was no exception to the rule; in fact, it was being unusually difficult. It was like the roses were clinging onto the walls for their very lives. She had started this project around four this afternoon. It was now close to nine, and not even a quarter of the room was done. By this rate it was going to be New Year's Eve before she had it all down.

Thankfully her sister Gladys had still been there this morning when the truck from the used furniture place got there and cleared out the room. She got a whole sixty bucks for everything in the room except the man-tel and her tree. They had even taken the old, worn area rug. Gladys had taken down the curtains and threw them away.

The sixty bucks was just enough for a couple gallons of paint.

The only problem she had had so far was Abraham. He didn't seem too thrilled with having to cancel their dinner reservations, but he did offer to pick up pizza and help her strip the paper off the wall. Something was up with Abe tonight, but she couldn't quite put her finger on it.

"Sorry to ruin your plans for this evening."

Abe looked startled for a moment. "Nothing's ruined. I'd rather be here with you scraping paper vegetation off your walls than anywhere else without you."

She preened and tried to suck in her gut. Maybe wearing bib overalls wasn't the smartest choice in clothing while trying to impress a man. The flannel shirt she had worn under them was one of Howard's old ones. She looked like a hillbilly. At least she had taken the time to fix her hair and add a fresh coat of lipstick before Abraham arrived.

"Abe, you say the sweetest things." It still didn't explain why he had been so nervous during dinner. Abe hadn't been that nervous the night Gladys and Amber had joined them for roasted chicken and garlic potatoes. Her sister had offered to clean up the kitchen, and she and Abe snuck out the back door like a couple of teenagers. They had even driven up to Lookout Point, but there had been two other cars already up there.

Her sister's arrival had put a crimp in her love life. Not that she was having an actual love life. A few heavy-duty kisses that left her wanting more was all she had shared so far with Abraham Martin. The man knew how to kiss, she'd give him that. She wanted to take it to the next step, but wasn't sure how to proceed. The only man she had ever made love with had been Howard. After thirty-two years of marriage to the same man, she had forgotten what it was like in the beginning.

She knew what century it was. She knew times had changed, and it was perfectly all right for a woman to make the first move, to have desire, to have needs. She had even seen an episode of *Sex and the City* once. Knowing and doing were two different things.

She looked over at Abe. The man looked miserable

as all hell. "Abe, sit for a while with me." She placed her scraper on a windowsill and sat in one of the two kitchen chairs she had dragged into the room.

Abe sat in the other.

"What's wrong?" She couldn't stand the sad puppy look on his face any longer. This was not the same man she had fallen in love with. "Is your mom okay?"

"Mom's fine and you know I'm not a momma's boy, Gracie." Abraham bristled at the thought.

"I know you're not, Abe." Him living with his mother made perfectly good sense to her way of thinking. No one made fun of her because she lived in her mother's house and took care of her until the good Lord saw fit to take her. "Didn't you ask about Gladys and Amber during dinner? Didn't you ask about my family? Why can't I ask about yours?"

"Sorry for jumping down your throat." Abe's expression actually got sadder.

"Okay, that's it, Abe. Out with it. What in the world is wrong?"

Abe shuffled his boots on the bare hardwood floors, but didn't say a word.

"If you really wanted to go out to dinner that bad, you should have said something." Abraham didn't seem like the type of man to pout.

"You seemed to have your heart on striping wallpaper tonight. I didn't want to disappoint you."

"You are disappointing me by pouting because you didn't get your way." She unbuttoned a cuff on the flannel shirt and started to roll up the sleeve. Scraping walls wasn't an easy way to pass the night, but the desire to be rid of the wallpaper had been burning in her gut for years. Now that she'd made up her mind to finally change the room, she wanted it done yesterday. "Next time you have to speak up."

"There won't be a next time."

She stopped rolling in mid arm. "What do you mean?" Was Abe breaking up with her? How could they break up? So far as she knew, they weren't going together. Back when she was younger, a lot younger, if a girl and boy were dating seriously they went "steady." What in the world did young people do nowadays? That topic wasn't covered in the one episode of *Sex and the City* she had seen.

Abraham must have picked up on her distress and quickly reached for her hands. "No, Gracie, it's not like that. There will be plenty of other times, but tonight was going to be special."

"What was going to be special about it? Are we celebrating my sister heading back home?"

"No, I planned for a nice romantic evening. Candlelight, fine wine, and the best meal money could buy at Gwen's."

"Sounds nice, Abe. How about we do that tomorrow night, if the weather isn't too bad?" The poor man had the whole evening planned, and she went and ruined it.

"It won't be the same."

"Sure it will."

"The meal wasn't the 'special' part, Gracie."

She loved surprises, and "special" sounded a lot like a surprise to her. "What's the special part?" She practically bounced in the chair.

Abe gave her a long look before reaching into his pants pocket and pulling out a small box. He got down on bended knee and cleared his throat. "I was going to wait until Christmas Eve, but I'm not known for being a patient man, Gracie. I know what I want, and I want you."

She stared in shock at the tiny, black velvet, jeweler's box. "Oh, my!" She clutched her chest and then stared in horror at her bib overalls. The man was going to propose and she looked like a farmer!

Abe cleared his throat again and said, "Grace Berry, will you do me the honor and become my wife?" Abe flipped open the lid of the box.

"Leprechauns and leotards! Is that thing real?" The diamond gleaming in the bed of black velvet had to be at least a carat. The white lights of the Christmas tree in the corner of the room were reflecting off the round cut diamond. Abe's hand was trembling so badly the ring was shooting rainbows across the room.

"Of course it's real." Abe looked offended.

She pulled her gaze away from the ring and saw the uncertainty in Abe's eye. The man was scared she was about to say no. He was a hopeless romantic who wanted to marry her. Was it any wonder she was so in love with him? "Abe, love, close the box for a moment. You can't be flashing a ring that size in front of a woman's eyes and expect to get her full attention." Her hand fluttered against her chest. "At my age, a rock that big could cause a coronary."

Abe slowly closed the lid and slid the box back into his pocket as he stood. "Sorry, Gracie"—his hand was still trembling as it ran through his thinning hair—"I didn't mean to give you a fright."

She had hurt his feelings. It was the last thing she wanted to do. "You didn't frighten me, Abe. Surprised me, definitely." She reached out and took his hand. She wasn't exactly sure how to go about this, but straightforward and to the point had always served her well in the past. "Please, come with me."

She led him from the room and up the stairs. Abe was quiet as she walked him into her darkened bedroom. There was no way she was turning on the bedroom light. There was plenty enough of it coming in from the hallway. The room was all her, from the creamy pink walls to the antique lace at the windows. None of Howard remained in the room, he was only in her heart.

Abraham didn't look around the room. He only looked at her. "Gracie, are you sure?"

"I'm sure you never should ask a woman to marry you when she's looking like a reject from that *Trading Spaces* show." She unhooked the straps on the overalls.

"Is that what had you so upset? That you looked like you were puttering around the garden?" Abe cupped her chin and looked into her eyes. "I think you're beautiful no matter what you're wearing, Gracie girl." He lightly brushed her lips with his. "I love you."

"Ah, Abe." She wrapped her arms around his neck. "That's what I wanted to hear." She placed a string of kisses up his jaw and playfully nipped at his ear. "I want to hear that at least once a day."

Abe's work-roughened fingers fumbled with the buttons on her overalls. "Every day, I promise, and sometimes twice." Abe's fingers were trembling so bad that he couldn't get the button through the hole. "Tarnation, woman, how many buttons you got?"

She chuckled and stepped out of his arms. She worked the buttons and slid the overalls over her hips and down her legs. The flannel shirt came to mid thigh. Standing in front of Abe wearing nothing but an old shirt and a pair of socks with moose printed on them, she must have looked a sight. But she never would have guessed it by the gleam of appreciation burning in Abe's gaze.

Abe's fingers were a lot more coordinated as he took off his own shirt and yanked his T-shirt over his head. She watched in wonder as he undid his laces and yanked off his boots. He danced around on one foot before bracing himself against the wooden post of her bed. His pants hit the carpet before her shirt.

The next instant she was naked and sliding between pink flowered sheets. Abe slid in after her.

Abe stayed on his side of the bed without touching her. "Gracie?"

"Shut up, and come here." She reached out her arms for him.

Abe came into her arms as if he had finally found his way home.

Grace played with the thatch of gray hair covering Abe's chest. Weak morning light was trying to filter its way into the room. It was still snowing outside. There had to be a good ten inches of the stuff already on the ground. It looked like Abe would be staying for breakfast.

"You never answered my question, Gracie." Abraham's fingers were drawing circles on her back.

"What question was that?" She knew darn well what question it was. She just wanted him to ask again. She didn't want the memory of Abe proposing to her while she looked like a sharecropper. Abe proposing while they were in bed was a much nicer memory.

Abe rolled them over. He stared down at her and grinned. "Lord, woman, you're even beautiful in the morning."

She didn't even want to think about what her hair looked like. "Ask me, Abe."

The smile slowly faded from his weathered face. "Will you marry me, Gracie? Will you make me the happiest man in the world?"

She reached up and kissed him. She put her heart into that kiss. "I will be honored to become your wife."

Abraham playfully slapped her bare bottom. "Tarnation, woman, why didn't you say so last night?" Abe nearly fell out of bed reaching for his pants. He pulled the jeweler's box from the pocket and tossed the wrinkled pants back on the floor.

Grace sat up and stuffed a couple pillows behind her back. She modestly tucked the sheet around her ample breasts. "Maybe I was in shock."

Abe snorted. "Maybe you wanted to try the merchandise out before you bought it."

She snorted back. "Maybe I did." She tried to appear offended. "Would you buy a pair of shoes without trying them on first?"

A wicked gleam flashed in Abraham's eyes. "Are you sure they fit okay?" He tossed the box onto the bed behind him and reached for the sheet covering her. "I think maybe you need to try them out again. You don't want to go through the rest of your life with your toes pinching now, do you?"

She tried to smack his hands and grab for the sheet at the same time. She failed in both attempts. "Abraham Martin!"

Abraham's mouth nuzzled the valley between her breasts that he had just uncovered. "What? Can't you see I'm busy trying out shoes?"

Grace felt the pull of his lips against her nipple and groaned. "I'll give you till dinnertime to stop." She pulled his mouth up to hers and said the words she had only said to one other man in her life. "I love you."

Chapter 16

Amber laughed as Shadow fought to get out from the tangle of ribbons wrapping him up like a steer at a rodeo. "Be still, and I'll help you." She reached for the red ribbon and the cat.

"He's making more of a mess than helping." Ian took the roll of green ribbon away from Light and scowled playfully at her. "You're not helping either, young lady."

She shook her head at the disaster the cats were making out of the room. Ian and she hadn't helped matters. Rolls of wrapping paper, ribbon, tags, and tissue paper were everywhere. Shadow had attacked the crinkly tissue paper as if it were a live animal. Shreds of the white paper were still floating around the room. Only half the gifts were wrapped, and they had been at it for two hours already.

Ian was a meticulously precise wrapper. She slammed a box on the paper, a cut here, lots of tape there, slap a bow in the middle, stick on a tag, and presto, one wrapped present. Ian wrapped each present as if it contained world peace. The paper had to be lined up just so and he even made sure the pieces of tape were the same length. He didn't slap on pre-made bows, he tied elegant ribbons into fanciful bows and patiently curled miles of ribbon. His creative artist talent was showing.

She had wrapped ten packages to his two.

"You can turn on the television if you want." She was happy with the silence, but she knew from experience with James, her Dad, and her brothers, men liked to watch TV. Especially if there was a game on. Didn't matter to them what kind of game—football, baseball, basketball, or hockey. They watched them all.

"Are you trying to tell me that I'm not holding up my end of the conversation?" Ian paused in the middle of tying a bow and looked at her.

"No, I just thought you might want to catch a game." She rescued the plastic tape dispenser from Shadow's jaws.

"I find this much more relaxing." Ian finished the bow, and slid that present under the tree with the rest. "We're almost done, anyway."

"Remind me to thank you properly when we're done." She reached for one of the video games she had purchased for her nephews and started to wrap.

"Will this thank you be in the same form in which you thanked me for helping you decorate the tree the other night?" Ian looked mighty interested.

She grinned. "Might be." Ian had spent the last five nights straight in her bed. Christmas Eve was two nights away, and she still had no idea if he would still be in Misty Harbor for Christmas. She had been too busy enjoying the past several days to worry about the future. There was plenty of time for them to work out their problems. "I've got to warn you, I still have a carpet burn in a very delicate spot. What do you have against beds, anyway?"

Ian pushed aside the present he was working on. "Want me to kiss it better?"

"The last time you tried that we ended up naked rolling around this room." She blushed at the memory. They had almost knocked down the Christmas tree.

"It was the only way for me to reach that particular spot." Ian yanked his sweatshirt over his head and started to crawl toward her on his hands and knees. He was pushing paper and scissors out of his way and clearing a path.

The sight of his bare chest slowed her thinking. Ian had a magnificent body, one she never tired of exploring. "I see that gleam in your eyes." She tried scooting backwards. She loved that gleam and hadn't seen it since this morning in the shower before work. They hadn't made it to her bed that time either.

Ian tracked her across the carpet. "You know what firelight does to me." He grabbed her ankle and pulled her toward him.

She halfheartedly fought as they rolled closer to the burning fire. When he had her pinned under him she had to laugh. A green bow was stuck in his hair, and the red ribbon she had just untangled from Shadow was snaking around one of his arms. A To-and-From tag was stuck to his chest. Ian looked like a partially unwrapped Christmas present. A present she definitely wanted under her tree Christmas morning.

Her fingers teased their way down his chest. "What does firelight do to you?"

Ian pulled her sweatshirt over her head. "It makes me want to see you naked." He pressed his lips to the hollow of her throat. "It's the sight of the firelight playing across your skin that makes me crazy."

Her hands fluttered against his chest. "Then we're even." She cupped his jaw and brought his mouth back up to hers. She needed to taste him. She needed him to hold her like he was never going to let her go.

Ian's mouth teased the corner of her lips as his

hands unfastened the front clasp of her bra. "How's that?"

"Because I'm crazy for you." She wrapped her arms around his neck and brought his mouth down to hers.

Amber woke from a delicious dream of Ian and their future together. She kept her eyes closed and could almost still hear the birds singing and smell the spring flowers. Life in her dream world had been perfect. She turned and reached for the real Ian, the one who'd ravished her in front of the fire, and then again in her bed, just to prove he had nothing against mattresses and sheets.

The spot beside her was empty. Cold sheets greeted her fingers. She opened her eyes. Ian wasn't there. She sat up and saw him standing at the bedroom window staring out into the approaching dawn. Ian was dressed.

She pulled the blanket and her knees up to her chest and rested her chin on them. She stared at Ian's strong, straight back and wondered how long he had been standing there? How long had he been thinking of James?

The ghost of her husband was there in the room between them. She could practically feel James's presence. With trembling fingers she pulled the blanket higher and wrapped her arms around her legs against the chill. It was like a strange version of a Dickens novel. The ghost from Christmas past was not only threatening her Christmas present, but all her future Christmases as well.

"You're awake?" Ian's voice was soft and low. She barely heard him because he didn't turn around.

"Going somewhere?" He might not have his coat on, but he had his boots on. Ian didn't appear to be staying for breakfast.

"I dreamed of James last night." Ian's voice shook. "He was sitting on the edge of my desk, back at the office. It was the end of April and he was already tanned, and his blond hair was streaked by the sun. You two had just gotten back from five days in the Caribbean. I forget the name of the island, but it was the one James told me that you loved. There was something about the secluded beach and the private bungalow that reminded you of your honeymoon."

She felt tears pool in her eyes. Two months before the accident they had flown down to the Caribbean. Ian wasn't retelling a dream he just had, he was telling her a memory. A memory he carried of James.

"James had barged into my office looking like a schoolboy who had found the most wonderful surprise. He couldn't have cared less that I was in the middle of a very important project. He had been out to lunch and happened upon a jewelry store. To hear James tell the story, it had been divine intervention that he had happened to walk down that particular street on that day."

Ian's voice cracked. "Anyway, there in the front window of this little shop was a diamond necklace. James took one look at the necklace, and no lie, Amber, he told me it called out your name. He even admitted to maxing out his favorite credit card to get you that necklace." Ian shook his head. "He couldn't wait to show me that necklace he bought for your birthday that was coming up. It was gorgeous."

She felt the tears roll down her cheeks, but she didn't bother to wipe them away. James had been so proud of that necklace. She had no doubt that James had shown that necklace to anyone who would look. She had worn it a total of two times. It was now tucked away in a safe deposit box, along with the rest of the expensive jewelry James had gotten her over the years.

Ian turned around finally and looked at her. "James loved you very much. You were his entire world."

"Yes, he did." What else could she possibly say to that? James had loved her.

"I've never seen a married man so darn happy. In all the years I've known him he never once complained, even jokingly, about marriage." Ian's hands clenched. "You made him very happy."

"Yes, I did." It was another truth. She had always put James's happiness first.

Ian sighed and his shoulders dropped. "You two had a perfect marriage. How am I supposed to compete against perfect memories?" He looked defeated by the very thought. "I promised my parents and brother that I would be there by Christmas Eve."

"That's tomorrow." She didn't want Ian to go, but she didn't have any right to ask him to stay. She had told him she was falling love with him, but he never said how he was feeling. Over the past couple of nights she thought he was feeling the same way, that he was falling in love with her. She had allowed herself to hope and to dream of a future. A future that held Ian. Now she wasn't too sure. How could he be falling in love with her, when James's ghost had such a strong hold on him?

"I have to leave in the morning." Ian jammed his hands into the pockets of his jeans. "I just want you to know one thing before I leave."

"What?" The tears were still flowing. The tears weren't for the memories of James, they were because her heart was shattering.

"I love you." Ian stood there straight and proud.

"But?" She heard that "but" loud and clear. She had been praying for over a week for Ian to say those three magical, wonderful words to her. Now that he had, she wished he would take them back. If he walked out the door now, she was going to end up hating the memory of James. Ian would walk away from her because of James. The loss of Ian would tarnish the memories of four and half years of marriage and the man she had loved at one time.

"I've been halfway in love with you for nearly seven years."

She used the sheet to wipe at her tears and clear her vision. Ian didn't look like he was joking around. He looked serious. How could that be?

"I wanted to ask you out back in college, but James asked first. Next thing I knew, you guys were engaged, and then I was the best man at your wedding. I stood at that altar and watched the most beautiful, fascinating woman I ever met marry my friend. Life went on and I dated, and even had a few relationships, but none of those women ever measured up to you, Amber. Day after day I heard James tell me how happy you made him and what a wonderful wife you were. I was envious as hell but thankfully you didn't come around the office all that much and I wasn't one for socializing in your circle of friends. Our paths didn't cross that often.

"Do you know how frustrating it was never to find a woman who made me one tenth as happy as you made James?"

She shook her head in wonder. Ian was serious. He had been jealous of James.

"Is it any wonder I'm being eaten alive with guilt over James? I've been in love with his wife for years." Ian turned his back on her again. He faced the window and rested his forehead against the glass.

She didn't know what to think. She never would have suspected that one. Ian had never once acted inappropriately toward her in all those years. His being in love with her all those years explained why he had driven all the way to Maine to deliver that check. She couldn't fault him for that. If he hadn't come she never would have fallen in love with him. There had to be a way for them to work this out. To put James's ghost to rest.

She slid from the bed and pulled on the robe that

had been lying across the footboard. She walked to the other side of the bed and sat. She wanted to wrap her arms around Ian's waist, press her cheek to his back, and never let go.

"Ian, how well did you know me?"

"What do you mean?" Ian turned and leaned against the window frame.

"Before you came to Maine, how well did you know me?"

"I thought I knew you pretty well."

"Was I the woman you thought you knew?" She tugged the belt on the robe tighter, and made sure it was covering as much of her as possible. She was about to expose herself and her marriage to Ian; she didn't need to be exposing her body as well.

"Not exactly." Ian gave a rueful smile. "You were better."

She tried not to smile at the compliment. "So after years of hearing James talk about me, I wasn't quite what you thought."

Ian nodded. There was a frown pulling at his mouth. She knew he was smart enough to see where this was heading.

"So if you were wrong about me, what makes you so sure you know the truth about James's and my marriage?"

"Don't for one minute try to tell me your marriage had been bad, Amber. I won't believe that." Ian looked mad and offended on James's behalf.

"Our marriage wasn't bad, Ian." She wondered if Ian realized how loyal he was to the friend he thought he was betraying now. "No marriage is perfect, just like no human is perfect."

"James loved you."

"I loved James with all my heart." She wanted Ian to understand the complexities of a marriage. The merging of two people into one unit took a lot of give and take. "In his own way, James had loved me back, just as much."

"James did nothing but talk about you, Amber. I swear he thought you walked on water."

"Ian, marriage is about two people. It's about their wants, their desires, and their needs. It becomes a partnership. James's and my marriage had been about James. It had taken me a long time to realize the truth. James had been so deliciously happy in our marriage because he had always gotten his way. His desires, his wants, and his needs came first, second, and always."

The tears were back and she couldn't control them. "To my shame, I allowed it. I thought that was what the perfect little wife did—made her husband happy, no matter the cost. If James wanted to go to a party, we went to the party, no matter how tired I was. If James wanted a new sports car, he got a new sports car. If James wanted a bigger house, we got a bigger house. James got everything he ever wanted out of life." Her voice rose with years worth of pent-up emotions that she'd never gotten to express. "James had every right to be deliriously happy. I had handed him that happiness on a silver platter."

She closed her eyes but the tears kept coming.

Ian didn't say anything for a long time. When he did he was far more perceptive than she thought he would be. "What did you want Amber?" he asked softly. "What did you need that James didn't give you?"

"A family." She wiped away the tears with the sleeve of the robe. "I needed a family and all I got was another round of parties."

"Family?"

"Our marriage was heading for a cliff, Ian. The bitter truth is that I will never know if it had been strong enough to survive the fall. I loved James, and I believe with all my heart he had loved me back, but I still will never know if the marriage would have lasted." She nervously played with the belt of the robe. "We were heading in two different directions."

"What direction were you heading in?"

"Do you know what I wanted for my twenty-eighth birthday? James did. We discussed it while we were in the Caribbean. In between James's private scuba lessons and his afternoon fishing trip he gave me his undivided attention for five whole minutes." There was a bitterness in her voice she couldn't soften.

"The one he bought you that diamond necklace for?"

"I didn't want a necklace, diamond or otherwise." She spread her hands. "In case you didn't notice, I don't tend to wear a lot of jewelry."

"What did you want? What was your birthday wish?"

"I wanted to throw away my birth control pills." Tears poured down her face. "I wanted to start trying for that baby he kept promising me we would have."

She hiccupped. What was the use of crying over something that never happened? She got up and headed for the kitchen. She needed a glass of water and a bottle of aspirin. She hiccupped twice more before downing half a glass of water.

Ian would never understand the devastation she'd felt the night of her birthday when James had handed her that necklace and a promise about waiting for next year. What was the rush, right, they were both young and healthy.

She wanted to tell Ian she loved him, but she didn't think he was ready to hear that again. How could he be, when James was still between them? Only Ian could exorcise that particular ghost.

After all those years of marriage she had finally developed a backbone, only to lose James before she could strengthen it. Well, it was strengthened now, and she wasn't afraid to use it. She deserved to be happy, and her happiness didn't include any ghosts.

She could hear the rustle of Ian's jacket as he slipped

it on. His duffel bag was already packed and ready, sitting on the kitchen table. Ian had been a busy boy while she had slept. She stared out the kitchen window and wondered how a man who claimed to be in love with her could walk out the door. How could he walk out on them? *So much for happy endings and the magic of Christmas.*

"I've got to get back to Olivia's. There's a project that I have to look over and approve before noon." Ian stood right behind her.

She could feel his breath on her neck, but he didn't touch her and she didn't turn around. If she faced him now she would make a fool out of herself and beg him to stay. "Have a safe trip to your parents'." There wasn't a reason in the world for him to come back this evening, only to rip out her heart again by leaving.

Ian was quiet for so long she thought he'd left without her hearing, or fallen asleep standing up. Finally he said, "I'll call."

She bit her lower lip to keep from calling his name as the front door closed softly behind him.

Ian paced the antique-filled bedroom at Olivia's bed-and-breakfast and uttered a string of curses that would curl the hair on an orangutan. He had to be the world's biggest idiot for walking away from Amber this morning. His only excuse, besides stupidity, was he had been in a state of shock. James's marriage hadn't been as perfect as he had let everyone believe.

He had spent the entire morning and most of the afternoon finishing up last minute details for the office. It still felt like the outline of his cell phone was imprinted on his ear. The office was now closing for the extra-long holiday weekend, and only a small staff would be manning it for the next week. Things should be returning to normal after the new year.

He doubted if he would be returning to normal. He didn't know what normal was anymore. Amber had turned his entire world upside down.

After returning from Amber's this morning he had poured himself into the work that needed to be done. Now that he didn't have that as an excuse any longer, he needed to get his head on straight.

He glanced around at the four-poster mahogany bed, antique highboy, and the comfortable chair and table in front of the windows. His home away from home for nearly the past month still looked warm and inviting. He had been more comfortable here at Olivia's than he would have been back at his apartment in Boston. The work and his laptop were neatly packed and lying on the table. His suitcase was open on the bed, but so far he couldn't bring himself to put so much as a pair of socks into it.

It would take him five minutes to finish packing, another five, tops, to load his car and settle up with Olivia. He could be heading out of Misty Harbor within fifteen minutes and at his parents' house before they even got ready for bed.

Amber had made it perfectly clear to him that she didn't want to see him again before he left town.

With one last look at his empty suitcase, he headed out the door and down the stairs.

He found Olivia in the kitchen arranging cheese and crackers on trays. He swiped a piece of cheese and popped it into his mouth. "You've been feeling better?" He reached for another piece of Swiss and added, "You sure do look better than the last time I saw you."

When he'd come back this morning he had spotted Olivia running for the powder room. The countertop in the kitchen had been loaded down with ingredients for breakfast, but nothing had been mixed. When the two couples that were also staying there came downstairs Olivia still hadn't made her reappearance. He had found some bacon and eggs and had made everyone breakfast.

Olivia handed him a piece of cheddar. "Don't remind me." She opened up a box of crackers and started to arrange them on another tray. "I didn't get a chance to thank you for cooking breakfast this morning." She leaned over and kissed his cheek. "Thank you."

"You're welcome." Olivia looked like a picture of health, all radiant and glowing. It was a total contrast from this morning when she had actually had a green tint to her pale face. "Pregnancy suits you." He couldn't help but wonder how pregnancy would suit Amber. Perfectly would be his guess. Amber would look beautiful growing big and round with his child.

"It didn't this morning." Olivia added a couple sprigs of parsley to the tray and then pressed her hands to her still-flat abdomen. "The Weidmans said you did a wonderful job filling in for me this morning."

"Anyone could fry bacon and scramble a couple of eggs." His stomach rumbled. He had missed lunch, and breakfast had been a long time ago. "Where's the nearest place to grab a sandwich?" He wasn't in the mood to go anywhere fancy. He knew where the pizza shop was in Sullivan, but that was about it.

"How's roast beef on wheat sound?" Olivia headed for the refrigerator.

"You don't have to feed me, Olivia." He didn't want to put her to any trouble, but a roast beef sandwich sounded mighty good right about now.

"Nonsense, I owe you a bunch of meals considering you've been missing a whole lot of breakfasts around here." Olivia started to pull ingredients from the refrigerator. "If you can hold out for another hour or so you can come over to our place and join Ethan and me for dinner."

"Thanks, but I don't think I'll be good company." He

started to make his own sandwich. "I think I'll just stick around here tonight."

"Do me a favor?" Olivia found a bag of chips and dumped some onto his plate. "Start the fire in the living room fireplace for me."

"No problem." He sliced his sandwich in half and started to put away all the ingredients. "Anything else?"

"Tell the Weidmans and the Moyers that the cheese and crackers is my way of making up for the lack of Belgian waffles this morning. Hopefully, tomorrow morning junior here will be more cooperative." She wiped the counter and straightened the trays. "There's also soda in the refrigerator and of course the coffeepot is there for anyone to use." Olivia glanced around the kitchen.

"Go on home to Ethan, Olivia." He had seen the speculative look in her gaze, but she didn't ask about Amber. He was thankful she hadn't voiced those questions, because he didn't know the answers.

"There's a tradition in this house. We always keep a bottle of brandy in the cabinet above the stove. It's there if you need it."

Olivia went home to her husband and he went to the living room to brood and eat his sandwich.

Six hours and two brandies later he was still sitting in Olivia's living room feeding logs to the fire and contemplating the lights on the Christmas tree. Amber's tree was prettier. The Weidmans and Moyers had retired to their rooms. He was alone with his thoughts and the remains of the cheese tray.

Why in the hell hadn't he ever questioned Amber's marriage before? Why in the hell had he listened to, and believed, James's version of the perfect marriage? He was old enough to know that every story had another side. Why hadn't he considered Amber's side?

He had known James well enough to know what he was really like. James had been a great guy, a good friend, and a hell of a business partner. James also liked to get his own way. He had never seen James throw a temper tantrum or even get angry. James got his own way by being the good guy. He knew how to manipulate people and to twist everything to his advantage. It was one of the reasons he had been such a great salesman. James was a smooth talker.

He never once thought what it would be like to be married to such a person. To be in love with such a person. To want to please such a person. Amber hadn't stood a chance.

James had been his business partner, and he hadn't stood a chance. Every time a major decision had to be made, the end results always had been the way James had wanted it. He had always given in to James. The amazing thing was, James had had excellent business sense. If it hadn't been for James, M & M Ad Agency would have still been a two-man, one-secretary operation out of a second office in a good, but not great, section in Boston. James had built the business to what it was today, an entire floor in a high-rise overlooking the Charles River.

What James had wanted in the business, James had gotten. Just like Amber had said about their marriage. Problem was, what James had made of the business, Ian didn't want. James had relished being the boss. Ian hated it. He had even gone so far as hiring some more employees, and promoting some to take the pressure off himself. To free up some time so he could do what he loved best, create. It hadn't helped; the darn business had grown, and there was now more pressure than before on him.

James had picked the perfect wife, and the perfect business partner. He and Amber had more in common than he'd first thought. They had both been pushovers when it came to James. At least Amber had grown that backbone and admitted their marriage might have been heading for problems. Maybe James would have agreed to Amber having those babies she wanted, or maybe he would have gone out and bought her matching diamond earrings.

He, on the other hand, had never admitted to not wanting the business any longer. It wasn't his dream; it had been James's.

Ian pulled himself from his musing to toss another log onto the fire. In another hour it would Christmas Eve day. He had over a five hour drive in the morning, he should be in bed, but he just didn't feel like climbing those steps and crawling into that lonely, cold bed.

Amber's tears this morning had ripped at his heart. All he wanted to do was pull her into his arms and tell her everything was going to be all right. It wasn't going to be all right. On top of the dresser upstairs was a black velvet jewelry box, Amber's Christmas present. He had driven to Bangor and picked it up the other day when she thought he was back here working. Nestled in that box was an emerald necklace. He had selected that particular necklace because the emerald had matched the color of her eyes.

Amber didn't wear a lot of jewelry, and she had a very good reason to despise necklaces in particular.

Ian polished off the last sip of brandy in his glass and realized he was furiously angry at James. Why in the hell hadn't James made Amber happy? Ian read between the lines of Amber's story. The Caribbean had been James's idea. James had promised Amber those babies, yet he hadn't delivered, and as far as he knew, never planned on delivering on that promise. He wasn't going to tell Amber about the sailboat James had been looking at the day before the accident.

James hadn't deserved Amber's love. What kind of man put his own pleasures before the wants and needs of his wife? A self-centered and selfish one, that was who.

All those years he had idolized James's marriage, and the whole time its foundation had huge cracks in it. Amber nad deserved better than that. Amber had deserved better than James.

Here it was thirty minutes till Christmas Eve day and he was about to drive away from the woman he loved. Why? Because the whole time he had been loving Amber, he never thought he had deserved her. He had been comparing himself to James and coming up on the short end of the stick.

He had been a fool.

He was better than James. He loved Amber and would always put her happiness before his own. She wanted a family. He wanted a family. She loved living here in Maine. In the short time he had been here, he had come to appreciate the small fishing village and its close-knit community. He could work anywhere, but it would be impossible for Amber to run the jam business from Boston. There was nothing holding him in Boston but a lonely apartment and a business he no longer wanted.

He had nothing to feel guilty about. He had never betrayed James while he was alive. He wasn't betraying James now, either.

Ian sat there watching the twinkling of the Christmas tree lights reflect on the windowpane and smiled. James's ghost had finally left him in peace. He closed his eyes and enjoyed the silence of a clear conscience.

A moment later he pulled his cell phone out of his pocket and dialed a number from memory. On the third ring someone picked up. "Hi, Mom. Sorry to wake you.

"No, everything is fine." He smiled at the sleepy concern in his mother's voice.

"I'm just calling to let you know I won't be there to-. morrow, and I'll be missing Christmas Day, too.

"No, I told you everything is fine." He watched the fire consume the last log and wondered if Amber had a fire going tonight.

"I'll be there the day after Christmas. If I'm real lucky, and someone forgives me for being an ass, I'll be bringing your future daughter-in-law with me." He pulled the phone away from his ear as his mother screamed something he didn't quite catch.

"Of course you know her." He chuckled. "Her name is Amber McAllister and I've been in love with her for years."

Chapter 17

Grace turned her hand one way, and then the other. It didn't matter which way her hand went, the diamond Abe had given her the other night sparkled like a firecracker. She half wanted to take the ring off this morning, once she saw Amber, but she had been afraid she would misplace it.

Her niece had looked like hell yesterday morning when she finally showed up for work two hours late. She didn't know how it was possible, but Amber looked even worse this morning. If she ever saw Ian McNeal again she would be shoving a size-eight, wide, boot, with fake Dalmatian trim, up his behind. The man should be horsewhipped.

Amber had looked so dejected straightening up the stockroom and sorting the paperwork that had been piled on her desk. Grace's heart had started to break for the poor kid. Listening to Elvis singing on the stereo system about having a blue Christmas without you had just been the last straw. She had immediately gone to the CD player and changed the disk. Alvin and the Chipmunks Christmas CD hadn't cheered Amber up. Grace was at a loss on how to get her niece to smile.

Her last-ditch idea was to call Gladys. A girl needed her mother at a time like this. But she hadn't worked up the courage to call her sister yet. Gladys was going to have a cow.

What Amber needed was to get her mind off of Ian. She had invited her niece to join Abe and her for the annual Festival of Lights tonight, but Amber had declined. She never thought Ian would be so heartless. So cruel. She would have betted her favorite pair of earrings that Ian had been in love with Amber.

She was reaching beneath the counter for the bag of candy, to replenish the dish for customers, when the bells above the shop door jangled. So far they only had two customers, but it was Christmas Eve morning. Most of Misty Harbor's residents weren't the last-minute shopper types.

She stood up and clenched her jaw at her third customer of the day. *Speak of the devil!* Ian McNeal walked into the shop as if he owned it. She glanced down, saw that she was wearing red cowgirl boots, with rhinestones down the sides, and figured they would have to do.

" 'Morning, Grace." Ian shook off a dusting of snow and gave her that charming smile that had fooled her once.

She glanced at her watch. It read four minutes after twelve. "It's afternoon." She folded her arms across her chest and stared him down.

Ian's smile slipped. "Awful cold today, isn't it?"

"Colder than Rudolph's hindquarters."

"Is Amber here?" Ian stepped to the side so he could glance into the workroom. "Her car's at the apartment, but she's not there."

"I sent her over to Krup's for some lunch." Grace refused to allow his look of disappointment to soften her heart. She could be a hard-hearted woman when she had to. "She's probably over there drowning her troubles with double chocolate milk shakes."

"Will it be all right if I wait for her here?"

"Maybe you should just be heading on back to Boston. Why break her heart twice."

Ian cringed. "I deserved that."

"You deserve my size eight up your wazoo."

"Grace," Ian said, "I'm not heading back to Boston. I'm staying here. Right in Misty Harbor."

"You'll be heading there eventually." She wasn't stupid. Ian owned that fancy ad agency back there. His business was in Boston. She had been hoping Amber would be going with him. She would have missed her niece dearly, and there was the business to consider, but what was a few blueberries when it was Amber's happiness at stake?

"I need to settle some business there, and then I'll be going back periodically to visit my family."

"Spit it out, Ian, what are you trying to tell me here?"

Ian smiled and shook his head. "If I tell you before Amber, she'll never forgive me." He winked. "Besides, you'll be on the phone with Amber's mom before Amber finishes that milk shake."

"So you really aren't leaving?" Grace considered the possibility for a moment. "You're staying here, with Amber?"

"If she'll have me."

Grace snorted. He took that as a good sign.

Ian knew he shouldn't be talking to Grace before he had everything settled with Amber. One look at Grace and he had been scared to death she had been ready to throw him out of the shop, and none too gently. If Amber refused to listen to him, he would be needing an ally on his side. He couldn't ask for a better ally than Amber's aunt. Grace, being newly engaged, was head over heels with the concept of being in love.

Grace would move mountains to see her niece in that same condition.

He glanced at the diamond on Grace's left hand.

Amber and he had celebrated with Grace and Abe the night after they had gotten engaged. Amber had cried tears of joy for her aunt. Abe looked like he had just won a million dollars, and Grace had been trying to decide what looked better with diamonds, black lace or red silk. Grace had been planning her trousseau.

"Grace, I know right about now you want to string me up, but I promise I'm going to make everything work out between Amber and me." He nodded to her ring. "Can I ask a personal question?"

"Depends." Grace was back to frowning, but she didn't look as angry as she had five minutes ago. He might just live to see Christmas dawning.

"What would Howard think of your upcoming wedding to Abraham?"

Grace seemed surprised by the question, but she didn't hesitate on the answer. "At first Howard might have some concerns about Abraham, but deep down in his heart he would know that Abe was a good man. Abe's got a good heart and Howard knows Abe's not taking his place within my heart. No one could ever take Howard's place."

"So he won't mind?"

"If Howard were here among us, he'd mind like hell." Grace laughed.

"What made you fall in love with Abe? What does he have, or what did he do, that all the other men in town that you dated didn't do?" He had met quite a few of Grace's dates during the past several weeks. He was curious as to what made Abe stand out.

"Abe makes me happy." Grace blushed. "It's as simple as that. Abe makes me happy."

He could make Amber happy, if she gave him the chance.

"Amber loved James." He wondered if Grace knew how much her niece had loved her husband.

"I know."

"James didn't make her happy."

Grace picked a candy out of the bowl, unwrapped it, and then popped it into her mouth. She gave a few good sucks. "Amber never complained."

"No, she never did." Ian couldn't argue that point. "I've been fighting James's ghost. I kept thinking my loving Amber was a betrayal to our friendship. To our partnership. Every time I turned around, fell asleep, or thought about a future with Amber, I felt James's jealous rage."

Grace shook her head and stared out the window toward the street. "If I had been the one to go first, I would want Howard to find happiness. To get on with his life. To find a new love. Ian, there is no jealousy in heaven."

Ian turned as the bells over the door jangled. He felt his stomach clench as Amber walked into the shop. Grace should have strung him up. Amber looked like hell. He'd never loved her as much as he loved her that very moment.

Amber glared at him. "Have a safe trip, Ian." She walked right around him and handed her aunt the small bag she was carrying. "It's the Thursday special, ham and Swiss on rye."

"Thank you, dear." Grace took the bag and glanced at him.

He guessed that was his clue to start winning the girl. "Amber, I'm not going anywhere."

She unzipped her coat, but didn't look at him. "I thought you were supposed to be at your parents' today."

"I called them and said I couldn't make it today. Can't make Christmas day, either. They were upset, but they understood."

"Understood what?" Amber finally turned and looked at him.

"Amber, love, have I made you happy the past several weeks? Honest answer only. Have I made you happy?"

She hesitated for a moment and the hard glint in her eyes softened. "Mostly."

He laughed and gave Grace a big wink before sweeping Amber up into his arms. "Looks like I'm going to have to work on that one, Grace."

Grace chuckled and fluttered her hand against her heart. "Oh, my. Whatever is in the town's drinking water, they better keep it there."

"Ian, put me down." Amber wasn't buying the romantic gesture or the polluted drinking water.

"Grace, my love, do you think you can handle the store for the rest of the day? Amber's going to be indisposed."

"Sure, we close early today anyway."

"Now wait just a minute," Amber cried.

Ian headed for the door with Amber swinging her purse against his chest. "Knock that off before you hurt yourself. You don't need for that to come open and spill everything out. It could take us the rest of the afternoon to find the key to your apartment." He stepped out onto the blustery street and started the short walk to Amber's home.

"Ian"—Amber's teeth were clenched—"put me down."

"No, you might run." He grinned down at her and kept walking. He was telling her the truth. He was scared she would run. Last night as he lay in his cold lonely bed he had visions of her running home to Providence and her mother. If she hid behind her mother, he would never see her again. Just hearing Gladys's voice on the answering machine he knew she was a formidable woman.

Thankfully, Amber wasn't the running home to momma type. It bode well for their marriage. He didn't want to spend his life running all over the northeastern part of the United States looking for his wife. During their life together there would be some disagreements, even a fight or two, but it would be a normal, healthy marriage. He was already looking forward to the making-up part.

"People are starting to stare." Amber buried her face against his coat. "This is embarrassing."

"Not half as embarrassing if I did what I want to do to you right this moment." He tossed her higher against his chest so her bottom would stop banging against a very sensitive, and highly aroused, part of his body. He was bound and determined to make it to her bed this time, but only after they had a nice long discussion about the future.

Gordon Hanley, the owner of the Pen and Ink bookstore stepped out onto the sidewalk and chuckled. "Lovely day for a stroll isn't it?"

Amber groaned against his chest. It was snowing and the wind was picking up. A storm was moving in. They were in for a very white Christmas.

"It's a beautiful day." Ian nodded to the bookstore owner as he walked past.

Amber shook in his arms. He couldn't tell if it was from anger, or from laughter. "You're going to pay for this, Ian."

He grinned as a truck went by honking its horn. A moment later he turned up Spruce Street. "I will gladly accept all responsibility for my actions."

He was starting to breathe hard when Grace's house came into view. "Put me down before you have a heart attack." Amber wiggled some more.

He gave her a quick squeeze. "Stop wiggling or I'm going to drop you." His romantic gesture had sounded great in theory, but he hadn't counted on the uphill climb on Spruce Street. He couldn't imagine what the steps to her apartment were going to do to him. Amber wasn't heavy, but a full-grown woman weighed a lot more than a couple of bags of groceries. He was pathetically out of shape.

By the time he reached the bottom of Amber's stairs

he was beginning to wonder if strokes ran in his family. His arms were beginning to feel funny.

"Ian, put me down. I can walk up the steps."

"No, I'm sweeping you off your feet, so let me sweep." He started up the steps.

Amber glanced around nervously and wrapped her arms around his neck and hung on tight. "If you drop me, we are both going to break our necks and I will never forgive you."

"Ye of little faith." With a last burst of energy he climbed the remaining five steps to the landing and leaned against the door. His breathing sounded like he had just run the Boston Marathon.

Amber reached around him and inserted her key into the lock. The door swung open, and they almost went tumbling into the foyer. Ian's quick stepping saved them.

"Warn a guy the next time." Ian lowered her to her feet before closing and locking the door behind them. He braced his hands on his knees and started sucking the much needed oxygen into his lungs.

Amber filled a glass with water and handed it to him. "Here, drink this." Amber no longer looked angry, she looked concerned for his health.

He gulped the water down in four huge swallows, then handed her the empty glass. So much for impressing the woman of his dreams with his physical prowess.

"More?"

"No, thanks." He wanted more, but he was trying to make a good impression. Giving Amber the impression she weighed too much wasn't it. Amber seemed obsessed with her hips and thighs, claiming they were way too big. He had told her they were perfect, but the fool woman wouldn't listen. He prayed she would listen now.

"How about we sit down? There's a lot I need to say." He glanced around the apartment. The bedroom was out, because they wouldn't be doing any talking in there. There was the couch or the floor, but considering all the non-talking activities they had been doing there, they weren't a good choice. That left the kitchen table. Her very small, safe-from-any-lecherous-activities, kitchen table.

He draped his coat on the back of a chair and sat. If he concentrated real hard, he could regulate his breathing to a near normal level. His rapidly pounding heart rate was a different matter.

Amber hung up her coat and took the chair across from him.

"Notice anything missing?" He wasn't sure how to start this conversation. A marriage proposal would have been a real eye-opener, but he needed to get a few things out of the way first.

"Like?" Amber glanced around the apartment.

"James's ghost." Ian watched the way her expression hardened at the mention of James. "He's gone, Amber."

"How did that happen? Last I heard he was rattling chains of guilt and betrayal."

"That saying about the truth will set you free is pretty accurate. All this time I've been comparing myself to James, and I always came up on the short end of that stick. I'm not James, nor will I ever be him."

"Who said you had to be?"

"I did. I had this set vision of you in my mind. The vision had been created by James over the years. You busted that vision the other morning and it threw me for a loop. I wasn't sure which end was up. You weren't the Amber of my vision."

"What Amber did you fall in love with? The me who was married to James, or the Amber living in Maine and running a jam business?"

"I'm in love with the Amber sitting in front of me." He watched the hope bloom in her gorgeous green eyes. The eyes that matched emeralds. "I was attracted to the college student. I was envious of a friend for having the perfect wife. Over the years I had a whole host of feelings for you, but they weren't love. I fell in love with the woman who rode a toboggan straight into a snowbank and came up laughing."

Tears filled her eyes. "That is the sweetest thing anyone has ever told me."

"I'm going to be telling you sweeter things than that in a minute."

"Like?" Amber brushed at her tears and gave him a watery smile.

"Where do you want to live?"

"With you."

"Since I refuse to live without you, that's a no-brainer, but I want a location. Pick a spot, any spot that will make you happy."

"Misty Harbor would make me happy, but I'll settle for living in Boston with you, and visiting here as often as we could." She gave him a confident and determined look. Amber was going in to this relationship speaking her mind. "We could buy a place up here and that way we can come whenever we want."

He knew Amber had the money to do that if she wanted to. Hell, he had the money to buy a nice little place here if he wanted to. "What about what would make me happy?"

"You live in Boston?" Amber looked confused.

"You didn't ask if I was happy there."

"Well, your business is there, and I will be there with you. Why wouldn't you be happy there?"

"The business was more James's than mine."

"How could that be? You were equal partners."

"James built the business, not me. James was the one who insisted we move from the small second-floor office we rented. James was the one to hire on more employees. James found the office space in the high-rise, and then dragged me along to go look at it and sign the papers. James pulled in more clients than I could handle, and then he went out and hired even more employees. James was the muscle behind M & M Ad Agency. I kept my nose to the drawing board and went along for the ride.

"When James died I was pulled away from my drawing board and was forced to accept the fact that I was now stuck with a huge business I didn't want. M & M was James's dream, not mine."

"Sort of like our marriage."

"He made excellent picks for a business partner and a wife."

Amber looked at Ian and wondered what it had cost him to realize the truth. She no longer had to worry about her marriage that had begun to shake, but Ian was still stuck with the company. The whole company. He had paid James's estate for her husband's half. Ian owned it all now. "What are you going to do?"

"I've already had offers from three separate individuals for James's share. One of the guys could buy half the business outright. The other two would find it a financial struggle, but both are extremely talented and will take the company far."

"So you're going into another partnership." She didn't know why that had disappointed her, but it did. Ian would still be stuck with half a business he didn't want.

"No. I contacted all three this morning with a counteroffer. Each could buy one third of the business. Those three would each get a third partnership, and they get to keep the established and well respected name, M & M Ad Agency. If they all accept, and two already did this morning, then I will be officially out of a job."

"What are you going to do?" She wasn't worried about money. She just wanted to hear Ian's plans.

"Start up my own ad agency. It will be a one-man operation with maybe a part-time clerical helper on the payroll. I'll need someone to handle the phones and the paperwork."

"That's great." She was really excited for him. Finally he would be getting what he wanted out of the business.

"You haven't heard the best part."

"What's the best part?" Ian looked so darn excited that she couldn't help but smile.

"It's the Berries Jam Company is going to be my first client."

She shook her head and felt like Scrooge. "You can't be doing that until I find someone to take my place. Grace is hopeless with computers and knowing Grace, she's going to spend the next several months planning her wedding."

"The other best part is I'm starting my business in Maine. I'm thinking right on the coast, maybe in a small little fishing village. Something quaint. Quaint's big right now. Maybe I'll use a lighthouse or a puffin on my letterhead."

She jumped out of her chair and ran around the table. "Really, we're staying here?" She sat on his lap and started kissing his laughing mouth. Was it possible to love this man more? "You'll do that for me?"

"No." His hand cupped her face and he put a halt to her playful kisses. "I'm doing it for us, Amber. You're happy here. I'm happy here. It's the logical solution."

She kissed the strong line of his jaw. "I love logic. I love you."

Ian wiggled his hand to the inside of his coat pocket. "There is one more thing we need to discuss before I lose what little control I have left and ravish you on this table."

She eyed the table. "I don't think it will hold both of us."

Ian shook his head and held up a small jewelry box. "The reason I didn't come pounding on your door late last night was because of this." He shifted his weight. "This morning I had to drive to Bangor and exchange the Christmas present I originally bought for you."

She knew it was a ring box he was holding in his hand. The imp inside her had to know. "What was the original present?"

"A necklace."

She frowned. She wasn't real keen on necklaces, but Ian hadn't known that till the other morning.

"It was an emerald necklace that matched your eyes perfectly." Ian cupped her chin and turned her head so she was looking at him, and not the tiny box. "I didn't know."

"It's okay."

"I'm going to be turning thirty next month, so any time you want to think about starting that family is fine by me. I'm not getting any younger." He kissed her. "I'll buy you an emerald necklace to match your eyes the day you start tossing up your breakfast like Olivia."

"If I get that sick all the time I might be tossing the necklace back at you." Her friend wasn't having an easy time being pregnant.

"No, you won't." He kissed her again, but this time he took his time doing it.

When she came up for air she was hot, bothered, and looking for love. Ian's shirt was unbuttoned and her fingers were working on the snap of his jeans.

"It will match this," Ian said as he flipped opened the ring box.

Her fingers stilled. There, cradled in black velvet, was the most gorgeous emerald ring she had ever seen. It sparkled and glistened and held a fiery depth that matched the love she felt for Ian.

"Will you marry me, Amber? Will you become my

wife and the mother to our future children? Will you
live with a man who loves to spend his days in front of a
drawing board and his nights in your bed? Will you love
me forever?"

"Yes." Her mouth skimmed his jaw. "Yes." Her mouth
feathered across his eyelashes. "Yes." Her lips teased his
chin. "Most definitely yes." Amber's mouth captured his
and poured her love into a kiss that scorched his soul
and had them tumbling from the chair onto the soft
carpet.

Ian grabbed her and twisted his body so he took the
blunt of the fall. She landed on top of him with her
knee dangerously close to the family jewels, and she
wasn't thinking about the ring box. Her chin connected with his chest with a resounding snap. "Gawd,
you're hard." She wasn't talking about the landing. She
rubbed her chin.

Ian grinned wickedly. "It's a condition I find myself
in constantly around you." He moved his legs and positioned her so her knee wasn't in danger of putting a
quick end to that wonderful gleam in his eyes. He maneuvered himself between her thighs.

She wiggled her hips and felt the solid hardness of
his desire. "You really do have a thing for floors, don't
you?"

"Hey, you're the one who fell off the chair. I just
came along for the ride."

"I'll give you a ride." She nibbled on his lower lip.
"Just as soon as I try on my Christmas present."

Ian's hands were busy unbuttoning her blouse.
"You're my Christmas present, and I can't wait any
longer to unwrap you and try you on." He was trying to
pull the blouse off her shoulder and suckle her breast
at the same time.

She looked around for the ring box. It was lying a
good three feet away from them. Light, thinking she

was an extra from the *Lion King* movie, was stalking the black box. "Oh, no you don't."

Amber grabbed for the box and her future happiness just as Light pounced.

ABOUT THE AUTHOR

Marcia Evanick lives with her family in Pennsylvania. She is currently working on her next contemporary romance set in Misty Harbor. Look for HARBOR NIGHTS in July 2005! Marcia loves to hear from readers and you may write to her c/o Zebra Books. Please include a self-addressed stamped envelope if you wish a response.